Fairyland

NOVELS BY SUMNER LOCKE ELLIOTT

Waiting for Childhood
About Tilly Beamis
Signs of Life
Water Under the Bridge
Going
The Man Who Got Away
Edens Lost
Some Doves and Pythons
Careful, He Might Hear You

Fairyland

A NOVEL BY

Sumner Locke Elliott

1817
HARPER & ROW, PUBLISHERS, New York
Grand Rapids, Philadelphia, St. Louis, San Francisco
London, Singapore, Sydney, Tokyo, Toronto

This is a work of fiction. Names, characters, places, and incidents are either the product of the author's imagination or are used fictitiously. Any resemblance to actual persons, events, or locales is entirely coincidental.

FIRST EDITION

Designed by Alma Orenstein

Library of Congress Cataloging-in-Publication Data

Elliott, Sumner Locke.
  Fairyland: a novel / Sumner Locke Elliott.—1st ed.
    p. cm.
  ISBN 0-06-016221-X
  I. Title.
PR9619.3.E44F3   1990
813'.54—dc20   89-45649

---

90 91 92 93 94 CC/HC 10 9 8 7 6 5 4 3 2 1

For
Frances Lindley
with love

PART ONE

WHEN THEY GOT OUT of the limousine at the Library (the invitation asked the honorees and their guests to please use the Forty-second Street entrance rather than the Fifth Avenue steps between the lions), the first thing that Seaton noticed was that Gin was standing halfway up the steps under a streetlight. "Did you know she was coming?" he asked Tony, but Tony's look only suggested that not even his God nor anyone under the heavens or in the waters beneath questioned what Gin might or might not do. There was something disconcerting about her standing there. "She can't be invited inside, it's a sit-down dinner," Seaton said. He was being honored with Alfred K. Rouse, Gerald Weston, Laura Z. Hobson, Eric Sevareid, and twenty-five others, all of whom, the invitation read ambiguously, might bring a guest "of either sex."

"Hello, Gin," Seaton said. "What a surprise." He made a movement, as he always did, to kiss her, but she took a quick step backward, facing him with that ancient innocent air she had (with the old-fashioned buns she still wore over her ears, her hair parted at the middle of her forehead, as neat as pins, she could have just stepped outside the Ocean Avenue flat she had lived in twenty-odd years ago, she had so hardly changed) and said in a matter-of-fact way, "There'll be no more of your harmful love, Seaton."

One of her apostrophizing remarks. But then he saw what she was taking out of her large handbag and thought how curious it was that Gin had always made everything adjustable to reason, even a gun. It was logical. But he also saw that she had misapprehended his entire life for this moment of truth. In this moment of her correctness she was the one in the wrong, he thought, and turned away from her to go on up the steps when the explosion cracked open the sky, deafening him, and feeling nothing but mild surprise, he saw the depth open under his feet. At first it was only a black dot within a dazzling penumbra, but it gradually widened and became an all-encompassing brilliant light, expanding to fill the universe with the glare of a thousand galaxies, and in the glare he saw that he almost understood his life and his reason for being, as if he were on the verge of finding a simple answer to the equation he had been searching for, and in trying to hold on to it so that he could touch infinity, he stretched out one hand just before he fell sideways into nothing.

What'll you give me if I tell you?

THE LITTLE GIRLS AND BOYS who went to Miss Peel's classes at the Prince Albert Day School were superior—not in manner but intrinsically. There was no question about their superiority. It was as manifest as their uniforms: the little girls in pleated tartan skirts of a gray, black, and tan design and white blouses that tied in neat bows, the little boys in gray flannel short pants and blue blazers with an embroidered gold lion and unicorn (for the Empire) on the pockets.

The little boys and girls all came from the big houses along Wentworth Avenue, Point Piper, and from Wunulla and Wyuna roads, Rose Bay, and some of them sported double-barreled names such as Fowler-Jones and Duff-Lyons, indicating the union of old family money with other old family money. They were all staunchly Church of England with the exception of Maureen O'Connell and the Levy girls (who pronounced their name *Levvie*), and their fashionable mothers often lunched together at the select Queens Club and then played auction bridge or mah-jongg. Their fathers were very seldom seen. As they grew older, the boys would gravitate to the Edgecliffe Preparatory School and then to Cranbrook or to Scot's College and the girls to Ascham or SCEGGS (Sydney Church of England Girls Grammar School) as their parents had done before them. They lived in happy insulation from brutal facts. Their arcadian country was a long way removed from the rest of the world and had a consoling climate where the worst-of-winter July weather was seldom colder than fifty degrees and, except for that worldwide conflagration that had happily ended war forever, there had been no trouble nor fear of the future whatever in the safe, prosperous land where they lived and breathed and had their being (and if those little squinty-eyed Japs ever attempted anything, why the British Navy stationed in Singapore would rush immediately to the rescue) and where change was so delicate it was hardly noticed, except in an election year in which, God forbid, the Labor Party might win. Thus, under no obligations whatever, they inspired in one another a genial satisfaction in the trumpery.

Miss Peel's classes were held in a large sunny room in the Prince Albert Yacht Club, whose generous lawns ran right to the edge of the lapping water and whose windows offered panoramic vistas of Sydney Harbor with its hubbub of boats and in the distance the sight of the Manly ferry coming to and fro (which later inspired Seaton to remark to a collector of oxymorons, "Well, and what about Manly fairies?"). Miss Peel was an ageless virgin of perhaps fifty who wore an astonishing amount of very white face powder that ended at the chin, leaving her neck the dark color of a spoiled pear and who assumed knowledge she didn't have and persuaded parents to invest money in the school under an acquiescence of noblesse oblige. She smelled faintly of what the Lifebuoy soap ads called B.O. Winter and summer she wore a black velvet beret pierced by a silver arrow, which she was never seen to take off, even for a moment to comb her skimpy hair. With visiting mothers she was obsequious to a degree of oiliness.

Miss Peel was a born categorist and knew in a second just where to place little Seaton Daly. "Now, Seaton dear, you will sit here for the time being," she said on his first day at school, and isolated him at a table with John Lawson, who was the best-looking boy in the school and who had the lowest intelligence. And everyone knew that the Lawsons' money came from the recent acquisition of a factory that made lavatory seats and other bathroom appliances. The little girls sniggered and whispered to one another because Seaton was the cousin of old rich Miss Dalgarno's *maid*. In the garden during the playtime recess (the whole curriculum was almost playtime anyway, with no strict rules governing periods, children coming and going as they pleased during the morning "work") the children automatically divided into little partisanships, and it was quickly evident that Seaton belonged in none of them and he was left to eat his chocolate biscuits and apple under a wattle tree alone.

The choicest group during playtime was the one that gathered around Rhoda St. Neots, who was the oldest girl and in her last term at Miss Peel's. She was also the most heartily disliked and the most kowtowed to. She came from a vast house resembling a Scottish castle, which would become in the fifties a Roman Catholic seminary (horrors). Her parents owned three cars, a Bentley, a Packard, and a Morris Minor, and it was boasted that Rhoda had never been on a tram or bus in her life. She was named a prefect, which emboldened her to boss everyone around. She gathered the children from their houses in the morning and, rounding them up like a sheepdog, herded them to the yacht club. Half a head taller than the others, she paraded them along with a sharp staccato gunfire of little reminders that she was in charge of them as the laughing, chattering group moved down the Macquarie steps under the dappling sun and shadow of giant elms. Before class she handed around sharpened pencils and pink rubber erasers and at playtime the sycophants gathered around her to be given the intriguing backstairs gossip Rhoda was heir to at the parties and dinners she was allowed to stay up late to attend. Having whetted appetites with provocative whispers and hints on the walks to school, Rhoda would narrow her eyes and say, "What'll you give me if I tell you something I know?" Thus she would collect tin badges, pretty beach shells, peppermints, and half-used bottles of eau de cologne in exchange for dubious information about people's butlers and maids, possible divorces, and imminent childbearing. It was Rhoda's hoarse whisper (loud enough to be calculated) that had alerted Seaton to his fate.

"Don't ask *him* to come," he heard Rhoda rasp to Meg Fowler-Jones. "He's only a cousin to Miss Dalgarno's *maid.*"

It was true of course.

His blue blazer and gray flannel pants had been bought for him at Farmer's boys' department by Miss Dalgarno herself (who called him in lighthearted moments "my thrippenny-bit" or "Mister Tuppence"). And Essie, dear Essie was Miss Dalgarno's loving servant. Essie, his cousin on his father's side, cooked, cleaned, washed, ironed, baked, stewed, peeled, polished, got up at six in the morning and often wasn't in her bed until after eleven. At times Essie looked fagged out and so pale that she might not have seen sunlight in months, which was not far from the truth. Once in a great while Miss Dalgarno awarded her a day off, and she and Seaton went to the pictures at the Crystal Palace or Hoyts in Double Bay. Not that Miss Dalgarno was draconian—it was merely that nothing occurred to her until there was a dramatic confrontation. Not until you fainted across the vacuum cleaner did it occur to her that you might be over-worked. Then she was all solicitation and kindness, urging you to take a week off at her expense in some mountain resort or go to her doctor in Macquarie Street. Once when Essie had had a fit of crying over a fallen soufflé (because literally she was dazed with fatigue) Miss Dalgarno had pressed a moonstone bracelet on her. Because of Miss Dalgarno's monstrous nonchalance, the fact of Seaton's illiteracy was brought home to her with a thunderous amazement, and she said at once that the little darling must go to Miss Peel's starting on Monday, why on earth didn't you tell me, Essie, that the little dear can hardly read? Miss Dalgarno was so exercised that she telephoned and made arrangements that very morning that Seaton was to be accepted at once, and when Miss Peel murmured something about her children being from the "preferred" families, Miss Dalgarno cut her short ruthlessly to say that little Seaton's father had been given the Victoria Cross in the war, the most distinguished medal in the Empire and that his little mum had written the words to Australia's most sacred patriotic song, "Just a Little Soldier Woman," still played to this day during the march on Armistice Day. Miss Dalgarno's tone implied that Miss Peel had better not forget that a hefty check came to the school from her once a year.

So Seaton was enrolled but not accepted. He was not hoodwinked by the patronizing smiles and the mechanical gusto with which especially the girls greeted him. "And how are *you* this morning?" they chirruped and immediately walked ahead quickly so as to leave him behind. He ate his chocolate biscuits alone under the tree and accepted ostracism as one must accept one's fate.

"Can I sit down with you?"

She was usually way over on the other side of the schoolroom under the map of the Empire. She was Hilary somebody. He nodded and she sat down on a smooth rock near him and began to open her play lunch.

"I'm Hilary."

"I know."

"What's your other name, Seaton?"

"Daly."

"Are you the Dalys in the big white house in Beresford Road?"

"No," he said and waited a bit, "we live with Miss Dalgarno." He waited a bit more and then said, "My cousin's the maid."

"I see," Hilary said. Her big brown eyes looked deeply at him and without a trace of bogus tolerance.

"That's nice," Hilary said. "Could I try one of your chocky biscuits?" And when he handed over his box, she took one neatly and said, "Thank you very much and won't you have one of my butterfly cakes?"

He was so unused to conciliation that he dropped the little cake upside down on the lawn.

"Oh, never mind, have the other one," Hilary said. "Do you have any brothers and sisters?"

"No," he said, "every one else is—" he looked away a moment and then said it very quickly—"dead."

"I see," Hilary said and didn't bother him with the usual tut-tutting and pitying, like grown-ups frequently did, patting his head and saying awful stuff like what a brave little soldier he was and so forth. "Have another chocolate bick," he said and held his box out to her.

"Thank you very much, I will," Hilary said, and it already seemed as though they had known each other for days and days, maybe weeks even. But not knowing what to say he let Hilary take the lead.

"What lessons do you like best?" she asked and wiped a crumb from her mouth, which was very red and prettily shaped. She was altogether a pretty little girl with her glossy dark brown hair cut short and combed on the side into a little barrette.

"Um," he said and didn't really know, hadn't thought about it. "I like it when she reads to us." On Fridays Miss Peel read aloud from *David Copperfield* and sometimes she recited poems like "The Highwayman."

"Yes," Hilary said, "I just detest sums." She talked in a grown-up manner, he thought, using words like "detest."

"I've got an older brother," Hilary said. "He's quite a bit older than me, he goes to Cranbrook." She leaned toward him and asked in a softer tone, "Are your mother and father dead, too?"

"Oh yes," he said. "Everyone's dead."

"Well," Hilary said, getting up and straightening her pleated skirt, "there's the bell, we'd better go along. Do you want to walk home with me one day?"

"Yes," he said. "That'll be all right."

"All right, then." She smiled at him. She had very pretty straight teeth. "Ta-ta for now, Seaton." He noticed she didn't rush ahead and whisper and giggle with the other girls.

"What did you do today, darl?" Essie asked him that evening, and after a thought about it, he said, "I met a girl called Hil'ry."

"Oh reely?"

The following morning Hilary was already under the wattle

tree when he came outside for playtime. Today she had beautiful coconut ice and bread and butter covered with the delicious little "hundreds and thousands," which was like eating sweetened birdseed. "How many did you get right in the geography questions?" she asked. "Four," he said. "I got eleven," Hilary said, but without boasting. "Do you like to go swimming, Seaton?" Then to his joy, "P'raps one day you'll come and swim with Mummie and me, then, would you? We go to Watson's Bay usually, there's better waves there because of the currents or something."

Whenever that would be he didn't know, but he felt the thrill of cold green water and saw Hilary in a bathing cap. Perhaps they would build a castle together. He wondered if her mum was as nice as she.

Sometimes in the classroom, he would look across to where Hilary sat under the map of the world and catch her eye and then he would wriggle his fingers at her in a half-concealed wave and Hilary would give him her grave smile in the same calm manner she did everything. She never seemed rushed or overanxious, never bored or petulant. She existed purely as a color exists; she seemed to imply that there was no need to be anything further than just herself and in the implication was a lovely tranquillity. He would remember her in years to come somewhat like a river.

And her odd questions asked in quiet sincerity: "Do you like the look of trees at night?" Then the next moment, "Are you fond of ham? *I* am." "Will you walk home with me, today?" she would say as they were getting their coats and hats after classes.

"Hilary Deane and Seaton Daly," snapped Rhoda St. Neots, rounding up her charges to march them to their gates. Rhoda was the only girl to turn her Panama hat up at the back to show her superiority.

"We're coming," Hilary called and then said to him, "Let's straggle behind." They did, coming out from the yacht club into early heat, the day pulsating around them in warm waves and the trillion locusts croaking in the trees. They were embalmed in the Australian smell, eucalyptus and salty sunlight. They walked along straggling slightly behind the others, holding their schoolbag in one hand and swinging the other so that occasionally they touched. At the steps that led down to Wunulla Road, Hilary parted from the other children, but when Rhoda caught Seaton going off too, she was onto him like a wasp. "That's not your way home."

"I'm walking home with Hilary today," he told her.

"Suit yourself," said Rhoda, and he and Hilary went down the old worn steps between the flowering shrubs to where Rose Bay hung underneath them, nestling its painted boats all pointing in agreement with the tide.

"Don't you love boats? *I* do."

"Do you have a boat?" he asked.

"No. Daddy hasn't got time," she said. It was the first time she had ever referred to her father. "I think boats are like people a lot, different. I like some of these better than others, just like people." They leaned on the wooden fence that overhung a large boat yard where several launches and dinghies were pulled up on mossy slips.

"I like *you* very much, Seaton," Hilary said in her grave manner. He wished he could say something nice back, but he was tongue-tied with the pleasure of it and the featheriness on his skin. But in his silence, in the locust uproar in the hot air, something strange and unfamiliar touched him that might have been only just beyond his credibility and as near as a moth whirring in his face. It was the fetus of love in him, the very first pulse in his life of something he did not yet understand, but the power of it almost took away his breath and without hesitation he put his arm around Hilary, and so they stayed there gazing down at the blue water and the little boats nibbling on it just as though they were very old people.

"What a nice gentleman you are, to walk Hilary home," her mother said as they stood at the front door.

Home looked inviting from the view into the hall. An Indian rug on the polished floor and a bowl of fresh yellow roses on a hall table and a nice cat insinuating itself down the stairs,

rubbing against the banisters. Somewhere in the distance someone was singing.

"This is my friend, Seaton," Hilary said.

"How do you do, Seaton?" said Mrs. Deane. She was altogether such an older edition of Hilary with her dark glossy hair
cut into a shingle that they could almost have been sisters.

"Won't you come in and have a glass of lemonade?" Mrs.
Deane asked, and he hesitated on the brink of such amiability but
faltered, knowing the worry it would cause Essie.

"No, I have to go home," he said.

"Well then, you come and have afternoon tea with us some
time very soon. Hilary will see to it, won't you?" As he went
down the neat garden path, Hilary called out good-bye and,
turning, he saw her wave to him.

My friend, she had said. The momentousness of it was almost choking. He closed the Deanes' gate reverentially.

Then the following Monday morning Hilary was not at
school. Nor was she on Tuesday. Whatever kept her out must
have been considered trifling since nobody said anything. Besides, children were often absent for a day or so when their
parents took them on short trips such as to the polo in Cobbity
or even to the Melbourne Cup. Perhaps Hilary had a summer
cold.

Then all of a sudden, as mysterious as a cold gust of wind
in this hot weather, a word was being blown around like a leaf.
The children stood in little groups with their heads together, and
Rhoda St. Neots was bumptious with information and impor-
tance. Something prodigious had made Rhoda's little piggy eyes
glitter. She was seething with her own prominence this morning
as at playtime she went from group to group and finally Seaton,
enisled under his wattle tree, heard her say to Meg Fowler-Jones,
"No, let *me* tell him."

Rhoda flounced across the lawn and flung herself down on
the grass, hugging her legs and rocking to and fro with the
delight of her superior knowledge. Her little eyes shone with her
greedy enjoyment of it.

"What'll you give me if I tell you something?"

Did he have to? He was silent.

"Come on, what'll you give me?"

"I don't have anything much," he said. But Rhoda could see what one most liked even in the dark.

"What's *that?*" She pointed to his pocket, where the top of his treasured colored pencil showed. It was an imitation silver pencil that wrote in red, green, or blue when you pushed down whichever lever.

"That's just my color pencil," he said.

"Show me."

Reluctantly he handed it over, and Rhoda looked at it with contempt and then sighed and clipped it onto her blouse and said, "Oh well, I'll tell you anyway. Hilary Deane died the night before last." Nothing happened, there was only the air and the warm sun. In the silence though, he could feel his heartbeat.

"Don't you want to know how?"

So he had to say it.

"How?"

"She had a burst appendix and it turned into peritonitis."

"Oh," he said and then, "I see."

She was waiting to see what he was going to do, so he wasn't going to let her know. He looked away at the harbor and the boats, then he looked down at the grass for quite a long time. Then he wrapped up his half-eaten banana and put it back in his lunch box, and all this time he said nothing until finally Rhoda had to speak to get herself off her own hook.

"We're all putting in to send a wreath to the funeral, so will you ask your moth— whoever you ask, to give you three shillings to bring to school tomorrow. Don't forget now."

Rhoda was let down. She had hoped for tears, with luck more, even hysteria. She got up sulkily and walked away.

But it was just as if someone had put an invisible lead weight on his shoulders suddenly and when he stood up, his feet were in iron boots so that he could scarcely lift them to walk over to the classroom when Miss Peel rang the bell.

Inside, he continued his copying lesson. He wrote "Tom sat on a rug and ate a fig." "Do not lag, Sam," he copied neatly. Just before school broke up, Miss Peel made an announcement. She said, "Now, children, you've all heard by now the sad news. I have to tell you that I have spoken to Mrs. Deane, and she has asked everyone to understand that the—the arrangements are going to be private, attended only by the family. But on Thursday morning at about the same time, we will all stand up and observe a minute's silence." At which Rhoda, to get her own back perhaps or through some malign gift of perfect timing, broke into noisy weeping and was consoled on all sides with pats and hugs and offers of scented handkerchiefs.

So then (he was bewildered), it seemed that it was like this when somebody died; everything went on as usual, as if it had never happened. On Thursday morning at half-past eleven there was a great deal of pushing of chairs back and coughing when Miss Peel said, "And now we'll all stand for a minute and think about Hilary." They stood for a minute that seemed like half an hour, and then Miss Peel tinkled her desk bell and they all sat down again. She rapped on the world map with her pointer and said briskly, "Now, today we are going to learn something about the longest river in the world, which is the Nile, and which is here, in Africa." So it was either everything as usual (and the Nile) as though there never had been any Hilary (already a new little girl, June somebody, was sitting in Hilary's place, and it wasn't even a week yet) or else it was bunk from Essie, who had cuddled him and said, "Darl, you're not to cry too much." (He had not wept a tear, only felt extraordinarily cold and sore inside.) "She is in heaven with the angels," Essie said. Like his mum was supposed to be. Dead people were supposed to be wildly happy or so it seemed. He didn't imagine poor Mrs. Deane was wildly happy.

And then in accordance with everything being just as usual, an invitation to Molly Lawson's birthday party came in the post for him, although, coming at such a late date, it had provoked in Seaton the suspicion that he was a last-minute replacement for some child who had had to bow out.

A little tin toy stove with pots and a kettle was bought for Molly Lawson and he was brushed and combed. Essie, wearing her good outdoors dress of lettuce green linen with white bows and white shoes to match and looking nothing like the other smart mothers in their casual tailored clothes, looked too dressed up for words. It was a long walk from the tram in the hot sun, and they arrived at the Lawson house like penitents. They might just as well have been arriving at Sandringham for the grouse shooting. It was so formal, being greeted by Mrs. Lawson in the great hallway. Mrs. Lawson took one look at Essie's hat and said, "Would you come back for him about five?" Whereas other mothers had been invited for tea and sherry, Essie, poor Essie, knowing at once that she was mutton dressed up as lamb, in spite of her matching green gloves covering her workaday red hands, said yes, righty-oh, smiling and showing her shining dentures, and went off obediently down the stone front steps. Seaton was led by a maid into the lower garden, where the children were joylessly playing croquet in the deep shadows cast by a giant Moreton Bay fig tree.

Presented with a mallet and sketchily told the rules, he went along, partnered with Meg Fowler-Jones, knocking balls at random, hopelessly hitting hoops and getting redder and redder in the face until he was rescued by an announcement that there was now to be the treasure hunt. This time he was partner to a strange little girl who said huffily that her name was Audrey and that she'd rather have been Brian's partner. Together they read the difficult clues found tied to twigs or under stones and, utterly baffled, they strayed too far or not far enough from the next clue until (naturally) Rhoda St. Neots crowed from the water lily pond that she and Keith Stevens had found the bag of milk chocolate doubloons wrapped in gold paper.

Next "Oranges and Lemons" was played on the upper lawn, and it seemed suddenly to revive their flagging spirits. Little tremors of excitement at the thought of playful murder seemed to run through their fingertips as Mrs. Lawson, a cigarette in one hand and with a grim, beleaguered mouth, assembled them into a line, eleven facing one way, eleven facing the other way, with the two tallest girls, Sheila Duff-Fuller and Angela Macrae, facing each other and lifting their arms with hands touching to form the arch that would come crashing down and chop off the head of the last child to dance through it.

Delighted with mayhem, the innocent voices began piping the old nursery rhyme:

> "Oranges and lemons,
> Say the bells of St. Clement's.
> You owe me five farthings,
> Say the bells of St. Martins.
> When will you pay me?
> Say the bells of Old Bailey.
> When I get rich,
> Say the bells of Shoreditch.
> When will that be?
> Say the bells of Step*ney*.
> I don't know,
> Says the big bell of Bow."

and here the stepping through the upraised arms quickened and the piping voices grew louder and childishly lustful:

> "Here comes a candle to light you to bed,
> Here comes a chopper to chop off your *head*,
> Chop, chop, chop chop."

And with every chop the eager arms came down on the unfortunate one caught going through, and he or she was "Dead" and so the round continued. "Oranges and Lemons, the Bells of—" starting in a singsong, treacherous chant and gradually building to the climax of shrill hoots and uncontainable laughter as their ingenuous malice frothed out of them.

At the fourth time around, Seaton reached the archway just before "Here is the chopper" and instinctively stopped in his tracks until the child behind pushed him forward aggressively, saying, "Go *on.*" Then the four arms came down on his neck and shoulders with what seemed to be an enjoyment of brutality, fat Bruce McGregor and skinny Joy Blackwood were flaying him with their arms and continued to flay, and when he turned his head, he saw the little bubbles of saliva at the corners of their mouths and the heads of the children behind them were nodding in feverish delight and "chop, chop, chop, chop" the children chanted, quicker and quicker as he struggled against the barricade of arms and legs and pinkish knees and skirts and pants until Mrs. Lawson interrupted and said, "That's enough chopping, children, now *really.*" Somehow he got through the maelstrom, almost fell on the lawn beyond in relief, and saw John Lawson standing near a red salvia bush.

"Are you dead?" John asked.

"I suppose so," Seaton said.

"I am too."

Then to his surprise John Lawson said, "Do you want to see my rabbit?"

He supposed so, what else was there to do? And they went through a gate toward the back of the house and there in a wooden hutch was a white rabbit twitching its pink nose at some wilted lettuce and a carrot.

"Oh," Seaton said. "What do you feed him?"

"Lettuce and things," John said, seeming totally uninterested. It was the first time they had ever spoken to each other, although they sat next to each other in class where John was certainly the best-looking boy with his golden hair and wide blue eyes, but he was also the dumbest; left-handed, he wrote, or rather printed, laboriously in a peculiar upside-down method with his hand curled around the pencil, pointing at himself, and with his head lowered almost to the paper and his mouth open. He was two years older than Seaton and due to start at Edgecliffe Prep next year if he could pass what was said to be a difficult entrance exam. Never once had Seaton seen John laugh or smile—he seemed to be preoccupied with distance—and now here they were alone together, gazing at a rabbit hutch and the

distance seemed stratospherical and the silence profound, holding some kind of secret.

"What's its name?" Seaton asked, to break it.

"Rabbit," John said.

"I see."

He had begun to have a fancy about John and it was rather
pleasant and very personal; he would tell no one. John would
rescue him from danger. Not from silly fairy-tale sort of danger,
the Red Riding Hood kind, but from very real and present
danger, fire perhaps, or being waylaid by thugs (whatever *they*
were) and John, stepping out from behind trees in the lurid
half-dark of the imagination, would put them to rout and then—
this was the nicest part—would walk home with Seaton and just
to further shield him from harm would put his arm around
Seaton's shoulder and thus, close together, in step they would
walk in this warm charitableness through the fast-falling eventide
(as the hymn put it).

Now they were rescued from the immensity of silence and
profundity by a distant gong. "That's for tea," John said and led
the way back to the lawn.

But Seaton was entranced, walking behind him, with the
suddenness of this vision, the conception of an idol, and surprised
that it had not occurred to him before that he felt something
special about John Lawson, something fanciful and unique and
it was as comforting as warm water lapping around one's naked
body. It was enchantment and it stayed with him through the
whole birthday tea, through the fuss of paper hats and the procession of meringues, lamingtons, coconut ice, hundreds and thousands, licorice babies, and finally the splendid candled cake, and
although John was far across at the other end of the table, he
fancied John occasionally looked toward him and in those moments of gushing delight he turned and spoke animatedly to
Maisie Kittlewell who was actually a prune and not worth a word
of conversation.

Then at last, each with a little bag of tin whistles and chocolate bunnies, they were all lined up to shake hands with Molly

and Mrs. Lawson and to thank them for the lovely party, and Essie, in her terrible white hat with the green plume, nudged him and said, "Say good-bye now to Molly and Mrs. Lawson and thank them nicely," and he felt this sudden desperate need to substantiate his feeling of immense newfound tenderness; he pushed past Molly and Mrs. Lawson to where John was standing and, without a word, put his arms closely around John and kissed him on the cheek. There was quite a stillness for a second and then Rhoda St. Neots laughed a quite objectionable hacking laugh as if something were caught in her throat and then, as if hideously delighted, crowing, she shrieked, "OOO*er* you kissed a boy!"

And given their cue, the other children began to laugh, the hallway rocked with their assurance, but John Lawson merely looked away into some exorbitant distance.

Outside, Essie, dear Essie, said comfortingly, "That was very sweet, Beanie."

She meant polite, of course. But it wasn't polite, he knew, it was thrilling, like stealing.

Just a little soldier woman

*F*IRST THERE WAS HER.

At the very first She was mainly a blur, picking him up and setting him down. She was the warm rubber nipple of the bottle. She made noises like a dove cooing to him. Whazzuzz, She said, and budda budda budda. She was hands and warm water, soft towels and little pillow cases, lavender smell and the soft snow of talcum.

But slowly She came into focus and he saw her nose and eyes, very dark and brown under the strong eyebrows, and the front teeth rather large and then She dangled bright colored things, rattles, balls, a little pink teddy bear, and a monkey. "Here's Teddy," She said, "and Nanyang." There was someone celluloid named Peggy Knott who sometimes sharply got under him in sleep and had to be pulled free. All the world was lap, smell, and the feeding, the changing after he watered and sat on what She called "potty," the world was rocking back to sleep and waking up for bottle and in between, great darkness in the warm of cot not unlike the previous warm darkness in the liquid of heartbeat before the great tide had swept him out into the first morning of life, amazed.

Everything now became faster and in no time (two days, two minutes? what was time?) he could see cup, spoon, tell red from blue, see the lamp lit in the night after he had wakened and cried and She came to him, to rock and soothe away the spiders of dreams and soon he was in a high chair beating "spoony" on its little tray ornamented by green frogs dancing and he was told to "hit the google," which later translated into hitting the boiled egg with a spoon to break the shell. Then in no time at all, it was steps, drunken and wobbling over onto the linoleum but getting steadier and resisting helping hands; he staggered, tottered, grew to resist things. "No," he said and angry, threw the mug, the bib, the bonnet onto the floor. "Want," he said and "milk" and was rewarded. What a goooood boy!

But still later there was the awkward thing between them when She would nestle him on her lap and take out the big picture album and turn to the photograph of the man and point to him, saying "Dad," and they were supposed to look at it for some reason, this man standing up in a strange sort of suit and a big hat turned up at the side, which much later he learned was the war uniform that all the men had worn. And She would sit and stare at it over his shoulder and he felt her breathing on his neck and the silence was precipitous. She went on staring as if eventually the picture would move or speak to her; it was embarrassing. Unable to squirm off her lap, looking at the picture, on and on and on in thick silence and they were strangers, She and him, but never more so than when She had him close to her, when She had her arms around him and he didn't dare push her away.

Then there was Sam, the big man, who came clumping into the cottage in his heavy boots and who was jolly and smelled of tobacco and beer. Who called him "nipper" and her "lovey" and who carried him about on his shoulders piggyback at a great height and sometimes threw him up and down, pretending almost to drop him but never doing so and causing him to giggle. She would stop whatever She was always doing at her desk and cook stews for Sam, or even a baked rabbit, and after dinner ("tea" they called it) Sam would sit on, smoking his pipe while She did the washing up and from his little bedroom he would hear their voices droning on up and down, occasionally laughing together (the only time that he had ever heard her laugh was with Sam) until much later She would see Sam out the front door. Until *that* night. That night he was awakened by their voices raised in disagreement. Anger and then silence and then anger again. Her saying, "Don't you ever bring it up again," then silence, then him saying, "Lovey, I only want the best for you and the nipper," then silence, then her saying wildly, "Don't you understand there never could be anyone else, can't you see that all of me, my *heart* is buried with him, for God's sake, Sam, leave me alone." "Too right I will, cobber," Sam said in a dreadful voice and then the front door shut heavily and they never saw Sam again. "Where's Sam?" he asked and She said, "Gone away, darling." He always flinched when She called him darling—it sounded so forced.

And then, several birthdays later (he was five, he found out later) Essie came.

And everything changed; he was loved. Essie came nearer and nearer to him and She faded further and further away until She and he hardly even spoke except to say, "Excuse me, sorry, is it raining out?"

Essie, it turned out, was his daddy's country niece. She smelled strongly of carbolic soap and had skin like a Granny Smith apple, silkily green, and pale thin yellow hair she pulled back into a bun, pale eyelashes, and great red hands. Essie had come to Sydney to attend night school to learn shorthand and typing so that she could get a job and stay and no longer have to get up at five in the morning to milk twenty cows and feed fifteen farmhands during the harvest. She had written to Her asking if she could be put up in exchange for some housework and looking after the little boy, and She had accepted gladly and said Essie could have what used to be a spare bedroom.

Right from the start Essie had been astounded by the state of things. Right off she got on hands and knees and scrubbed the dirty kitchen floor. She emptied the meat safe of all kinds of provisions that had gone or were about to go bad. She rescued the living room sofa from a mountain of old newspapers and

magazines and even weeded the front garden, which had become
a jungle of paspalum and shivery grass. She got at the brown ring
around the bathtub and she did all this with an energetic gusto,
getting around Her by saying things like "You don't really need
this dirty old straw mat any longer, do you? Will I just throw
it out?" or "Are we all out of witch hazel?" More and more She
kept to her room with the mystery of what She was doing and
left simplification to Essie.

The mystery had to do with her being a WAIF. She had
organized the WAIFS—the Widows of the Australian Infantry
Forces—and every Armistice Day, November 11, She marched
at their head in the Armistice Day Procession in the city and
every time the band played the song for which She had written
the words, "Just a Little Soldier Woman, Marching On, Marching On," to the tune that had been composed by her friend Katha
Dunks who was not a WAIF, not even a widow, but who had
a way with a tune. The song had caught on and She and Katha
had sold it to a music publisher who had got the better of them
for only a penny a copy and sold sheet music in the thousands
so that all over the country, misty-eyed women were standing to
attention and singing:

> "There's a sacred kind of duty
> In a trench of kitchen smell,
> She knows nothing about shrapnel
> She knows something about hell
> She's a Little Soldier Woman,
> Marching On."

And the widows wrote to Her from all over the country. "Dear
Hope" they wrote (for that was Her name and it looked appropriate on the sheet music, "Words by Hope *Daly*") and they sent
a shilling to cover the cost of a small piece of purple ribbon which
She would send them to wear on their bosom on November
eleventh, in memory of the bravery of the dead boys who had
been given a Victoria Cross like Her own courageous love who

had given his life for a little bronze cross attached to the purple and which now was framed by flags on the dusty sideboard of the house in Clovelly.

Then, at last, on a smoldering brazen day in November, Essie took him to see the procession ("He's old enough now, Hopie, to understand, don't you think?") and to see Her marching in it, and they went into town and stood in the crowd in the red, white, and blue thickets of flags on Pitt Street and watched the silver blazing bands march by and the Returned Soldiers, some of whom limped or had lost an arm, the light cavalry on their polished horses, the buglers, the generals seated in open cars, saluting, and then faintly in the distance came the sound he knew of as the Tune. Somehow he had heard the Tune somewhere before, perhaps on a fuzzy gramaphone record sung by a wheezing soprano to the accompaniment of what sounded like elves and now here it was coming nearer, "—Woman, Marching On," and getting louder and more defiant and the crowd leaned forward expectantly and several women got out handkerchiefs in the expectancy of tears and the sound came from about fifty women marching to a brass band, "—Little Soldier Woman, Marching On." And then, appalled, he saw Her marching in front of them at the salute, Her hand to Her soldier's khaki hat turned up at one side. She was wearing a long skirt of dark blue and a blouse cut from the Australian flag, the Southern Cross at Her breast. All around them, the women were waving flags frantically and weeping as She turned, saluting, from one side to the other, and the Tune was deafening now. "She knows something about hell," the women sang, the widows, the young widows marching instead of the brave husbands and by now there was not a dry face in the crowd. "Wave your flag, darling," Essie urged, but he turned away in disgrace at the sight of Her, draped in a flag with that soldier hat on and the weeping women, waving their Union Jacks and cheering Her, his *mum*.

But strangely, Essie must have felt the same because when the last bands had marched out of sight and the police began to clear away the barricades and the procession was over, Essie took his hand to lead him away and said, but more or less to herself, "Poor thing, the war's over," and he knew she was referring to Her. Was it a pity then, that the war was over? He supposed so and when She arrived home late that afternoon, She stopped him in the hall still dressed in Her Australian flag and wearing the digger hat and asked, "Well, darling, did you enjoy seeing the procession?" "Oh, I s'pose," he said high-handedly and then with deliberate cruelty just stared out the window and said nothing about Her, nothing of praise whatever, until having waited long enough, She sighed and went into Her room and shut the door.

Not until he was a grown man and it became necessary for him to go through Her papers before he left the country forever, did he discover what it was that She was composing behind that shut door as blank as her face; when he discovered the dozens of patriotic stories and poems She had written for long-ago defunct magazines with names like *Digger* and *Battalion Bulletin*. Reading them he was flushed with outraged pity for Her and shame for his priggish parsimoniousness toward Her. They were, patently, all about herself and they had titles like "The Little Subaltern" and "Doing Her Duty" and the heroines were always slips of girls standing bravely up to Cruel Huns behind the lines and rescued by big gentle lieutenants who took their tiny hands into their great strong paws and gazed into their liquid eyes. He now was able to see Her against the background of Armageddon that She had created for herself after his father was killed and that for Her the war which had brutally taken from Her the source and reason for Her living had been adjusted or rather She had rearranged it into a singular compassionate glory. It had provided Her with the partial escape from the utter hell She was in and it was because of this, the glory and purple ribbons, the Tune of Her song, that She fought so relentlessly against the war's gradual recession into a melancholy past that most people wanted to forget, and it was with these affronted eyes that She saw the diminishing crowds at the Armistice Day Procession and that the dear songs about roses in Picardy and about keeping the home fires burning were beginning to fall on deaf ears. And so, disillusioned and outraged, She died.

Not overtly. Drenched to the skin through a frail cotton dress in a furious rain that had fallen with what seemed to be a dark purpose on the WAIFs' rally for membership in Moore Park, She sat all the way home on the crowded tram and then walked the rest of the way in a bitter July wind, Her thin shoes squelching. She came in at the door like a wet otter, shivering. Even with Essie's ministerings of hot buttered rum and a hot water bottle and "into bed with you this minute," there seemed to be a premonition in the determined way that She coughed and in the furious haste by which She was taken first into bronchitis, then pleurisy, and finally pneumonia. She seemed to be persuading the virus to abet Her escape because when Doctor Crabtree told Essie that the sooner She go into Clovelly General the better, She struggled to sit up in bed, fighting Essie with Her thin arms against being taken out of it into an ambulance and hoarsed, "over my dead body," then began to laugh at Her own joke in long hawking guffaws that ended in a gasping for breath while Essie comforted Her, laying Her down again on the pillows and saying, "All right, darl, nobody's going to make you, I'll see to it." But by the next morning She had wandered into delusions and when he was taken in to see Her, She was scarcely recognizable; this dead-eyed creature turned a strange yellow color looked at him across some immense void and muttered something. He sat there by the bed for as long as he was told and listened to the stertorous breathing and hoarse whispered things She uttered. "I'm on the dark side," She said once, and later, "We'll be in Como." (Como, Essie told him in later years, was the little lake where his mum and dad had honeymooned just before he went off to France.) At nine o'clock that night, She simply stopped breathing and after five minutes of the deathly silence Essie said quietly, "She's gone, pet." Kissing him and putting him down into bed, she said, "Now there's only us. Don't be sad, darl." She said at the door, "She's with *him* now," and he knew Essie didn't mean God.

Little notice was paid by the papers (he still had the yellowed clipping in a du Maurier cigarette tin along with his father's medal). The *Evening Sun,* under the heading "Little Soldier Woman Dies," briefly stated, "Hope Seaton Daly, author and poet who had written the immortal words to the song and other poems and who was organizer of the 'WAIFs' has died at her home in Muriel Street, Clovelly over the weekend. She was the widow of Captain Orton Daly VC. . . ."

There was only thirty-seven pounds, eighteen shillings, and ninepence in her bank account (all the rest, the royalties and such other income that she had had been gradually attenuated by expenses for the WAIFs, gone in purple ribbon, mailings, and the renting of halls for meetings), not enough even to pay for the funeral, and so Essie had had to telephone to her mother and dad all the way to Bally Brook in Victoria for urgent help, which was grudgingly given because her dad's younger brother, Uncle Orton, had been the family favorite and a VC, don't forget. ("More likely VD," Essie's brother had muttered and had been soundly shushed.) Possibly a hundred or so WAIFs turned up at the service in the Chapel of Heavenly Rest at Rookwood, but they had mainly come to enjoy a good cry and a nice sing-along at the end with the organ to "Little Soldier Woman, Marching On."

He refused to weep a tear and Essie looked at him from time to time, it seemed, in admonishment.

When they got home from the cemetery and were having anchovy paste on toast, Essie said, "We're in a bit of a hole now, darl." She looked very pinched around the nose and she had eaten off all her lipstick, making her aghast. "But we'll pull out of it somehow. I'll get a job scrubbing or ironing, don't you worry." He hadn't thought about worry up to now.

Because such things are sometimes but not frequently assigned by the gods, by some spectral source, the fourteenth ad in the help wanted column of the *Herald* read, "Live in Cook-Housekeeper, light laundry and cleaning, all meals. L. Dalgarno, 27 Wentworth Rd. Point Piper. Apply mornings only."

It occasioned two long tram rides and a fair walk uphill where the big houses rose around her like cliffs and, rounding a corner, she came into a quiet street of clipped hedges and bursting gardens where only the luxury of locusts disturbed the tranquillity of affluence and where the graceful iron gates had polished brass handles. In one driveway a chauffeur wearing rubber boots was hosing down a limousine.

Miss Dalgarno was tall and dressed in expensive but dated style. She might have just come from lunch aboard the *Titanic*. She wore her hair in great scoops over what had been known as "rats" and which women had abandoned even before the war.

"Do sit down," she said. "You're the first one this morning to wait until she was asked. Can you *imagine*? A servant sitting down to be interviewed before being told she might?"

Essie noticed that Miss Dalgarno's stockings were ornamented with clocks and her long feet encased in thin pointed shoes with marquisette buckles. Miss Dalgarno's large brown eyes seemed to embellish a poignancy, perhaps a sadness that no man had ever wantonly crushed her body to his and so as a form of consolation she had dealt kindly with other single women.

"Miss, is it?" she asked Essie, then wrote with a steel pen on a pad of creamy paper, "Esther Daly."

"Essie."

"That's nice. You see, Essie, my Irish girl I've had for two years has suddenly decided that she wants to be a nun. *You* aren't a Catholic, are you?"

"No."

"I prefer someone who is going to stay. I had Mrs. Greer for twenty-two years until she could no longer manage the stairs."

Then, creeping up, came the duties:

"There is light laundry as well, and ironing."

But Essie was already appraising the mahogany.

"I'm a good ironer."

"And can you do a little mending and darning when wanted?" And so on. Finally the salary was mentioned laconically. It was clear that Miss Dalgarno had been getting away with mayhem.

"But I dine out every Thursday evening at the Cosmopolitan Club in town and also on Christmas Eve, so you would have those days off, as well as one Sunday a month and any Sunday morning you desire to attend church service. You will find I am not demanding except that I expect excellence. I'm seldom up after ten at night. Now, does it suit you?"

Sitting on the edge of the tapestry chair and the horns of her dilemma, Essie had to bring up finally the rift within the lute.

"There's a little boy, my cousin, an orphan."

"Oh dear."

"He's no trouble."

"Would he be a noisy child?"

"He hardly says a word."

"He sounds approvable."

And as Essie was being ushered out, Miss D said in a sudden gush of confidence, "I've grown fond of you already."

They had a big room to themselves at the back of the house, which got the morning sun and looked out on a blaze of morning glories haunted by dragonflies. He learned quickly that, except for salary, Miss Dalgarno was something of a pushover. She was easily moved to tears. "Mister Tuppence" she called him. She gave Essie her finished-with gloves and plenty of advice: "Don't wear cream, you're pale and you vanish into it."

There was a semblance of kindred between them all. Nevertheless, the only time Essie had all day to rest her feet was after the lunch washing-up until half-past three when she must change into her stiff black uniform with the starched apron and cap and prepare and serve the sumptuous afternoon tea for Miss D and the dim ladies who came carrying silver-handled canes and wearing pince-nez.

Morning until late at night, Essie was on the run from the kitchen to the pantry to the larder, from the cellar to the attic. Her eyes burning with fatigue, her back aching, she only left off work to carry out chores. Let her sit for a moment to darn Miss

D's voluminous underclothing known as "combinations," and she would be routed up to search in the spare-room wardrobe for a lost blue feather boa. Kicking off her shoes at night for a moment's "lay down," she would be summoned to fetch hot milk and whiskey which might help Miss D sleep. Only after eleven-thirty could she be sure that it would be safe to get out of her uniform and into her nightdress.

On Thursdays, her day off, she was too tired to do anything but make a pretense of meals and to sleep, and the child was left to wander alone through the vast garden and to gaze through the iron gate down the silent cultivated street where no dogs barked.

But they ate.

There was a roof over their heads, they were warm on winter nights, and, best of all, he was permitted to attend Miss Peel's school along with the children of the privileged, thanks to the generosity of Miss D. Except that the long summer school holidays became the doldrums because it would never have oc-curred to Miss D that anyone might have expected a two-week vacation on salary and so Essie simply drudged on and on regard-less of the season. Every Christmas Miss D gave Essie a large bottle of expensive pink bath salts. They stood on the bathroom shelf, unopened, until there were six of them.

By now Seaton was given two pennies to go on the tram one way and back all the way to Double Bay to attend the state primary school where the boys were not as pristine as those at Miss Peel's but still very combed and brushed and judging by their hoity-toity accents came from "naice" homes.

And so it continued, seemingly ad infinitum, no bend in their road being visible to them until the utterly shocking day when Miss D, perhaps with an effort to suppress melodrama, said calmly, "Essie, I am selling the house. I am going to live for a year or two with an old school chum in England, in Weald, Kent."

So the earth opened up to swallow them without warning. Essie had had to sit down without permission to take in the shock.

"Now, Essie, will you and Mister Tuppence be all *right?* It breaks my heart to break up my little family, but the years are not being kind to me and if I am ever to go to Gladys, my chum, it must be now or never. But I would like to know that you are settled before I board ship."

Essie's nails were bitten down to the quick and she was given permission to use the phone, but neither Mrs. St. Neots nor Mrs. Fowler-Jones nor Miss Toft-Monks needed a live-in maid, not even part-time help. She must look further afield.

But it was not hopeless. She could, she found out through other working girls who met at the Maidenhair Tea Shoppe in Edgecliffe, earn easily as much money as Miss D's parched salary by cleaning, washing, and ironing three or four days a week. But rents within the environs of where they now lived were out of the question and there were no rented rooms, there were only mansions and garage flats used by the chauffeurs. Now, if she had only intrigued some nice young chauffeur—! Poor Essie, with her pale eyelashes and a sullen mole beside her left eyebrow, all hope gone of becoming the shorthand/typist of her dreams, hadn't the hope of Buckley (whoever *he* was) of snaring a chauffeur-husband.

There were only two weeks left before Miss D sailed on the *Oronsay* when "Small villa, reasonable rent, garden, view Botany Bay" appeared in the "to let" column in the morning *Herald*.

Well, Arncliffe.

Arncliffe, on the Illawarra Line, might as well have been Timbuktu to them and it was, they knew, an unenviable workingman's suburb reached by a chuffing steam train that ran through Redfern, Tempe, Banksia, and other suburbs with picturesque names and dirty reputations, and the wooden cottage leaned slightly to one side as if soporific but home it had to be, at least for the time being. The aboriginal name, "Camberwarra," tacked onto the blistered wooden gate meant "water, water far away," but not as far away as hope. The view of Botany Bay was in between two immense gasometers, the garden was pigweed and rusting soup tins.

The "lav" was outside.

They tramped through the empty rooms while they waited for the moving van bringing the pieces of leftover furniture Miss Dalgarno had bequeathed them from her attic. "You reely want to move this stuff?" the head moving man had asked, looking with scorn at the moribund bits and pieces declaring themselves charity in the sping-spang of broken springs, as did the neighbors on Waratah Street at the poor chairs missing splats and the spongy old velvet sofa. Essie snubbed the movers haughtily: "Just put that over there." "Careful with that glass door."

They ate their first meal in their own house out of tinned salmon.

"Could be worse, Beanie," Essie said. "We're not down to Surry Hills *yet.*"

Surry Hills, of course, was unmentionable, slums, not safe even to walk down the streets in broad daylight. But Arncliffe was not Point Piper. They were unused to the coarseness of voices calling over fences in the twilight, "You come inter your tea now, Eunice, or I'll dong you." Dinner here was "tea" for some reason. Sometimes there were screams. "Who let the bloody dog out? You catch that mong, Ernie, or you'll get skinned alive."

But there was also an overall camaraderie. Mr. Lovett of the Ham & Beef rested hairy arms on the counter and greeted you. "Hello, lovey, got some nice brawn today." Brawn made you shudder at the sight of quivering greasy aspic. And the butcher, Mr. Maddox, would smile a dentured smile at you. "Got lovely liver today, got nice brains, tripe, cut you orf a piece er lamb tender as a mother's parting words, ha ha. Throw in a nice piece er mutton fat."

It wasn't that the neighbors weren't pleasant, only that they didn't feel they belonged. Perhaps unwittingly they had become snobs.

There was only one barefaced word for Arncliffe—common. It was the common denominator. It was the omnipresent Monday morning washing on every clothesline in every similar backyard, the unadventurousness of hydrangea and cosmos and lantana, the pretentiousness of plaster storks holding up bird-baths. It was the waxed fruit on the dining room table and the wedding photographs arranged on the piano and peoples' never-used hand-embroidered guest towels as pious as their teetotalism. It was the dull nasal voices expecting nothing new, the men all wearing collarless shirts but showing the collar stud at the adam's apple, the women in curlers and carpet slippers wet-mopping the veranda tiles "of a Saturday morning," the plaintive twangy voices of the children. It was hearing for better or worse the steely pianolas playing "Tip Toe Through the Tulips" and knowing that the Sunday roast with two vegetables was as certain as birth, marriage, and death and that there was nothing else to look forward to and, worse, their unheeding of their dreadfulness of not caring. It was the common bond of their commonplace assurances that held them together, and although at twelve years of age he was not yet able to digest the significance of this, he had become quietly aware, perhaps ashamed, of his knowledge of growing secret antlers, possibly wings. That among these people he was a changeling.

But not even to Essie, not even in a whisper or a dream, did he ever voice it. "I am different."

What are you boys doing?

T HE NOISE COMING from the playground of Bexley High could be heard streets away and sounded like the screaming of the damned burning in hell but was only a hundred or so boys, some barefoot, kicking a ball around and wrestling or merely being larksome at high pitch. "Larrikins," Essie said and, catching hold of one, asked where they could find the headmaster. "In the yeller buildin'," the snotty-nosed child said, pointing.

Mr. Elston did not remove his hat in deference to Essie but kept it on while he asked Seaton a few easy mental arithmetic questions and an unanswerable one on algebra and of what was Suva the capital. He then declared Seaton passable for First Year Class 1A and told him to report the following Monday and to bring with him his own pen and ruler, compass, four plain exercise books, and one with graph paper. Ink was provided, Mr. Elston said, removing his hat for the first time and mopping his warm bald head with a handkerchief. No doubt, the school had an aura of decay, the wooden floors were silken with the years of trampling boots (the way the boys hurtled into class was more a stampede than orderly) and the classroom walls were a dirty peach. On some of the cracked maps one might still have located Prussia.

On cold mornings, the smell of thirty-four warm young pubescent bodies permeated the old room with its maleness.

Perhaps because of their awareness of a male presumption, something as yet unexplainable and mysterious, they were wary of the least manifestation of any tenderness. Displays of friendship were the sudden rushing forward and locking of heads in half-nelsons and headlocks accompanied by punchings. A popular caress between especially close friends would be the sudden wrenching of the friend's arm backward, forcing the hand upward until the excruciating pain gradually bent the person to his knees, accompanied by oaths and guffaws. "Yer stupid fuggin ape." Then, peaceably, on an even keel:

"Whadder youse have for English homework?"

"Fuggin 'Idylls of the King.' Whadder youse?"

"Fuggin Enoch Arden."

"Youse goin' ter the pictures Sat'dy night?"

"Shit yes."

"Our class is bein' let off Wensdy to go into the city to see the school Shakespeare matiny half-price. Twelfth Fuckin' Night."

"Shit on that."

Not yet men and yet begun. Not informed of anything in this suburban puritanism, they were like unwatered plants growing stubborn tendrils in the dark; they sensed an onus, that whatever was coming was shockingly, perhaps thrillingly, inevitable and fed on scraps of hearsay passed in hot breathy whispers. They thrived on the often misinformation they passed to one another in the privacy of the playground "dunny" where the older boys in Third Year knew that onanism was rife.

Geoff Rollins sat across the aisle from Seaton. He had a naughty elfin face sprinkled with sandy freckles and a rabbity nose that twitched discernibly when the thought of larkiness occurred to him, which was often. He seemed to be bursting out of his body ahead of time with muscular development, and although he was only thirteen his voice was changing and when the afternoon sun caught him bent over his desk there were already suggestions of golden hairs on his calves above the rudely pushed-down woolen socks. He pitched in to the afterschool soccer with the third-year boys; he was an excellent swimmer and in between larks and inattention he was a bright student. In his senior year he would be expelled for being caught waving a "french letter" over the fence to the girls in the next-door playground. His father being the local chemist, he was privy to various means of safer seduction.

Reaching for adulthood impatiently, he was bold and a braggart, he even knew two or three older girls who sometimes addressed him in cool haughty tones. Yet he was still child enough to use his rubber catapult while the teacher was occupied at the blackboard and hit someone in the face with a sharp paper wad or a wet spitball. Somewhat grandiosely he would allow Seaton (hopeless at all mathematics) slyly to copy his answers to impossibly difficult algebra posers. Once when Miss Crawford in First Year French bent over to glance at his translation and caught him prying into her flat chest, she reared back and spat at him, "Did you get a good look?"

After any lark like that he was all puckish innocence. Like the afternoon he asked Seaton, as they were buckling on their schoolbags, "Whadder you doing now? Like to come over to our place?"

Seaton should have noticed that Geoff's stub nose twitched slightly. But what harm could there have been? Most days now, Essie went off to work on the eight o'clock train in the morning for the day's cleaning or washing or whatever it was, sometimes across the harbor on the ferry to Mosman or up the North Shore Line, whoever wanted her, and as she was often not home until after six, the afterschool hours yawned ahead vacantly.

"OK," he said, thinking it was nice of Geoff, who was looked up to as a sort of leader of the class.

On the dusty walk to Geoff's place, which was over past the bottling works and across a drab football field, they mumbled school talk about how crumby old Elston was and of how Squizzy Taylor, the science teacher, had frequently been heard to fart, when to Seaton's shocked admiration, Geoff took a squashed cigarette butt from his trouser pocket and lit up, taking long puffs with the aplomb of a man of the world or maybe that chappie Adolphe Menjou in Hollywood pictures.

The Rollinses lived in a large house of dirty white stucco with a stone swan on each side of the front steps. Mrs. Rollins was a small pouter pigeon–chested lady with tight little blond curls around her face, which was a facsimile of Geoff's. "How nice," she said when Seaton was grudgingly introduced. "Haven't I seen you in Sunday school? I teach the baby class at St. Thomas's. I'll have some lemonade for you in a little bit."

All of a sudden it was different, being with Geoff alone; he was kingly and remote, he seemed suddenly to have grown taller, his socks were pushed way down on his muscular legs, and he strode ahead of Seaton with a sense of his own priority. "Want to see my turtles? Want to see my bike?"

Then, bending down through a small open doorway, they went into some sort of storeroom under the house to see where Geoff was making his model airplanes on a workbench where there were pieces of balsa wood and bottles of glue, and here in the half-light and the warm stale air Seaton noticed that he had begun to sweat and that it was not so much from the lack of ventilation as from the conviction that something new and dangerous was about to happen and because Geoff was looking at him in a strange way and his rabbity nose was twitching and the whole atmosphere seemed drenched in naughtiness.

And then all conversation stopped and he could hear Geoff breathing hard next to him, holding a wing part of balsa wood in a grubby hand, and then little electric specks seemed to be passing between them as Geoff asked him in a strange glottal voice had he ever got spunk? He didn't know, of course, what was it? Sperm, Geoff said glottaly and, gulping, said, "Want me to show you?"

Then it was the fullness of Geoff's stiff naughtiness in his hand, the thrilling silkenness of it and of his own sudden molten acquiescence in Geoff's and them standing together face to face in the gentle pulling of, strutting, legs-apart glorious boldness when, without warning, came the sound of glass tumblers clink-ing and a shadow blocked the low doorway. And Mrs. Rollins was saying, "I've brought you some lemona—. What are you boys DOING?"

Crash went the tray onto the floor, glasses and bottle spinning in lemonade froth as Mrs. Rollins beat Geoff over the head, around his ears, savagely, and she was panting like a dog, her little stub nose white with rage, her golden curls shaking but so like Geoff that he might have been being beaten by himself.

"Filth," Mrs. Rollins cried. "Dirtiness, *obscene* little boy, you disgusting boy, doing *that* unmentionable thing. Don't you *know*—do you know what happens if you go on doing *that?* That piece of you will *fall off* and you will go blind. Do you know what they used to do in the Bible to people who did *that?* They put them away with the *lepers!* That's what you deserve and if I ever, if I ever catch you again—"

She stopped cuffing him and drew back against the workbench, silent with outrage, her small eyes burning him and as Geoff had attained that look of perfect purity, she took one step and slapped his face so hard that it reddened startlingly. "Filthiness," she said. "And involving a friend you brought home on purpose to *do* it. Filth." She turned now to Seaton. "And I'm surprised at you *letting* him. You, a nice little Sunday school boy. And aren't you the boy whose father was a VC in the war?" He nodded numbly. "Then aren't you doubly ashamed? Pick that up, Geoffrey," she added, pointing to the wrecked tray and broken glasses, "and bring it into the house and Sefton, is it? You had better run along home. I hope you have both learned a lesson. You ought to thank your lucky stars, Sefton, that I don't tell your mother."

"I don't have a mother, it's my cousin."

"Never mind who she is, it doesn't alter the blame."

She indicated the doorway, implied an exit. The boys glanced at each other.

"So long, Geoff," he said. "Abassinia."

"Abassinia Samoa," Geoff said as usual.

At any rate, shock receding, letting himself out the front

gate, he now had a secret. At any rate, he now knew not only what spunk was, what sperm meant, but something important had happened between him and someone else for the first time and oddly enough in spite of all the shame and confusion of their being caught (red-*hand*ed as it were, almost funny) it seemed to him to be, in spite of its naughtiness, sacred. It seemed to him to have been provoked by some fate or power away beyond what he had ever imagined and there was something intentional in its significance that could not be denied. He felt the movement of great wings as if a giant bird had lifted him and was carrying him off to a strange and thrilling country where under green palm leaves, Geoff would be waiting for him with his—.

But not to call it by the crude name everyone chalked on fences because that was what made it obscene, dirty. Because now what he knew about it had something to do with secret trust, and more importantly (only he would never tell this to *anyone*) it had to do with love.

Shamefacedly he glanced in the bathroom mirror to see if there might possibly be some noticeable change in him and he thought there was a semblance of strength in the jawbone that had not been there before, as yet not fully realized, but this may only have been because the mirror was fraudulent and if you bent down your forehead contracted into your hairline.

Even though Geoff showed no sign whatever of anything having happened, ignored him completely the next day, shot marbles all playtime, there was still a tacit significance that stretched between them across the aisle as thin and silvery as a spider web. Even though no word passed beyond "gidday" and "hooroo" between them and he noticed that Geoff was more chary about letting him see the answers in algebra, covering his work by leaning on an arm, even though nothing was said, the distance between them had altered, narrowed, and he knew that Geoff knew it, too, and it was because of this knowledge that he had grown unconvincingly aloof. It was once too often that he almost caught Geoff glancing at him.

But he had almost succeeded in putting it out of his mind

when, once, taking the shorter cut through the leafy back lane to Oakley Street, he was grabbed suddenly from behind and Geoff said huskily in his unpracticed grown voice, "Come on." "Where?" he asked. "There's a boska place behind this shed, quick now."

This time there was no interruption, no dire biblical warnings of the peril they were risking. They were secreted from the world by giant vines sprouting lewd-looking chokos from the tin roof of what had once been a henhouse.

And all Geoff said was, "Whaddid yer answer in the history question?"

"Governor Macquarie."

"Same here."

Alone, uninterrupted, they grew more bawdy, they stood astride worlds like ancient warriors brandishing their swords. Afterward, deflated, they walked away, prim as deacons. An arrangement had been effected, it could be detected by the twitching of Geoff's nose or a glint in the eye, even by the manner in which he jostled Seaton as they were getting into their overcoats on colder afternoons, and "see you" meant exactly that.

Although he was not aware of any proprietorship in their understanding, Seaton had begun to accept the fact that it was their exclusive privilege and so it was a shock to come upon Geoff in the abandoned henhouse with Alex Bottsford, and it was made the more embarrassing by them behaving as though Seaton wasn't there and continuing their mechanical lustiness with a cool casualness that exacerbated his sudden feeling of hurt and betrayal.

"Excuse *me*," he said, haughtily as possible.

"See you," Geoff sang out. He was taking puffs on a cigarette butt. Alex Bottsford said nothing. Neither of them had even had the decency to turn away.

Then, as if it were an ironic trick played on them by some mischievous Pan, Seaton and Geoff were chosen to play a middle-aged married couple in the school play, but more likely they were picked out by the myopic Mr. Westmacott because they both sat near the front of the class. They were to portray a Mr. and Mrs. White in *The Monkey's Paw* on play night before school broke up for the long Christmas summer holidays.

Geoff, being the taller, was to play the husband. Informed that they were a middle-aged forty, they doddered, trembling with ague and spoke their lines in quavering falsetto. However, at rehearsal when Mr. White was required to caress tenderly and console his wife on the accidental death of their twenty-year-old son (to make the situation more bizarre, their son was being played by Alex Bottsford), Mr. White was often rendered speechless with laughter.

But when on the great night the curtains of the Mechanics' Institute Hall swept back to reveal them seated side by side in their canvas-and-cardboard living room, blinking dazedly in the sudden glare of white lights, disguised by crepe hair (a mustache for Geoff, a gray wig for Seaton that looked like the back end of a sheep and two pairs of socks masquerading as bosoms under a housedress of Essie's), the hall burst into war whoops and whistles and cries of "Good onya Geoff" and "Kiss him, Seaton" and the feet stamping was such that they had to wait several minutes before they could speak their first lines. Calm restored, they entered upon their marriage with solemnity and as Mr. White tenderly embraced his wife there was thunderous applause, and at the end of the melodramatic play, they were called back again and again to bow, and Mrs. White was so overwhelmed at the ovation that she made a faltering curtsy and had to be helped back onto her arthritic legs by her amused husband. Oh, you were marvelous, tip-top everyone said, even the headmaster, Mr. Elston, said they were a jolly good pair, a real married couple, as they stood together fumbling with wig and mustache and smiling.

Essie said, making them a cup of cocoa to calm them down before going to bed, "Well, you were so lifelike, Beanie, both of youse, you and Geoff, like. I mean, youse never broke up or anything, you were like a real married couple, reely *real.*"

Well, he thought, laughing silently, in essence, although it might only amount to a parody, he and Geoff had been having a connubial arrangement for two years now.

"Lord Westminster's horses are at the portcullis"

T WO UNRELATED THINGS happened the following year in December; Seaton passed his Intermediate Certificate Exam, graduating from Bexley High, and Grandfather Daly died in Bally Brook, and the property being sold, all the grandchildren, including him and Essie, received the bounty of 362 pounds each. In the midst of the Great Depression this amounted to the fortunes of Croesus. They celebrated the two events by going into the city one Saturday evening to have dinner at the posh Cahills in Castlereagh Street and then going top price in the loge to the Prince Edward to see the lovely Marlene in *Shanghai Express*. Something else of a darker color obtruded. Essie put down a fork and said out of a startling blue, "There's something you're old enough now to be told, something's been on my mind for some time now, dear."

She sat down heavily into a kitchen chair and fretted with her ringless hands as she did when she was exercised by any thought other than chores.

"Now, you won't be upset, will you, promise?"

"Why?"

"Because."

"Of what?"

"Because, Beanie"— a long sigh—"your dad didn't die in the Great War, love. The truth is, your poor dad got killed in a

44

fight in a pub in London on Armistice night, that's why. Now, don't be upset, dearest, but it's better you know. It's been on my mind."

Then what? He wasn't the son of the Great War hero, the boy born of the winner of the Victoria Cross? Then what about the Little Soldier Woman and the WAIFs and all that? All that was a sham, too?

"You mean he didn't get the VC, then? Do those things?"

"Oh *yes,* he got the VC all right, he was brave all right, brave as a lion. He went out alone across a minefield and took a whole nest of Huns with a grenade to save his men. Oh, he was a hero, all right, otherwise the King wouldn't of given the VC to him, but, you see, at the end of the war, that November, he was on leave in London and, dear, he loved a pot or two of beer and everyone was getting blotto that night, the end of the war, see, and somehow or other he got into some argument with some other blokes in this pub in Putney and—"

And somehow, some bloke or other (he was hardly listening) took exception and one thing led to another and he got hit over the head with a bottle and so—

He automatically glanced at the photograph in the tarnished frame on the sideboard, the photo of The Idol beside which She had placed a red rose every Armistice Day and on his birthday in April. The soldier stood to attention, wearing the VC and the digger hat turned up on one side, and it seemed now as though the stalwart figure lurched sideways drunkenly.

Every Saturday night at the Hoyts' Acme in Rockdale before the newsreel, the colored picture of the King came on the screen, in a naval uniform with the Union Jack flying behind him as the crowd stood for "God Save the King," and now, as though he were seeing it, King George winked and the national anthem sounded speeded up in a falsetto of little tin instruments played by rabbits.

He couldn't, of course, smile in front of Essie or reveal the crescendo of relief he was feeling. Because he was free at last of the bondage of being the son of the VC, the intrepid, the holy warrior.

It had been, in a sense, a fairy tale, and his mother had sustained it, her dutiful heart had managed to evoke the glory of the single-handed bravery in minefields and to march to the drums of that glory rather than to the tin horns of drunken brawls involving beer bottles.

But rather than admit an elation, he shocked Essie another way.

"What're we having for din?"

But Essie only got up from her chair heavily and answered him in kind.

"Brains."

It may have been at this exact point of time that a subtle transformation took place and that because of the drunken father, he need no longer be the beloved orphan child, no longer even a child. A renounced orphan, he was released from Essie's loving arms into his concept of himself.

It was not yet in proportion. Like his fledgling body, his suddenly protuberant nose over the still childish mouth, the hair-line startled into waves, the faint down on the cheeks not yet shaved, the youthful personality was not yet formed, shy of exposure into the unknown, awkward and coltish in the new long trousers, the heavy brogues bought on sale at Gowing's, still fresh to starched collars and to studs, dimly startled by being charged the full price at the picture theaters and on trams. But still thankful to be out of childhood.

First thing, Essie said when they got news of the bounty Grandfather had left them, was for him to use a little of his inheritance to further his studies. Like what? he asked, surprised. Well, for instance, to learn typing and shorthand, it might be an additional asset (and because of her own frustrated stenographic career, she perhaps saw her restitution in his becoming a good typist), and what about a course in journalism? Might he not one day want to get a good job on some newspaper? His dad (mentioned in asides as always, as though the ghost might be listening) had had a bit of a journalistic career, working on the *Bendigo Gazette*, didn't you know?

At the Pluto School of Typewriting, up near Central Railway in an old building that smelled of pink lavatory disinfectant, he was the only male in a roomful of burgeoning female secretaries all pounding away on stalwart Royal Standards, declaring that the time had come for all good men and the lazy dog and the brown fox into the bargain. At recess he said nothing to the girls and they said nothing to him. Miss Renquist moved like a slow frigate up and down the aisles to make sure that nobody was cheating by glancing under the metal sheet that secreted the keyboard. The speed tests were a little electrifying when Miss Renquist blew a whistle and they all had exactly two minutes to complete a difficult paragraph land-mined with words like *incommunicado*. But Seaton only lost out on the top mark for having had three *z*'s in the word *quizzical*.

At Handrum and Myers School of Journalism, things were humdrum. One was inducted into multiple ways of avoiding the preposition at the end of a sentence. One was induced to write a mock news item describing an accident as graphically as one could without the use of adjectives. Mr. Haggett oversaw his juvenile efforts in a small glass-enclosed room. Mr. Haggett was red-eyed from reading too many scholarly papers in the poor light from the frosted glass walls. Occasionally when Mr. Haggett sat next to Seaton to go over his journalistic forays, he felt Mr. Haggett's leg pressing against his.

Toward the end of the year and after his sixteenth birthday and now having certificates, signed floridly in ornate scrolls, in both typewriting and journalism, the putting-off could no longer be tolerated. He and Essie both faced it grimly: he had to have a job.

The search for nothing eventually possessed one, Seaton found, the hopelessness imbued one with a passion, an overwhelming determination, shaking the fruitless tree, goaded by its very uselessness. Seeing the long line of men and boys stretching two blocks or more down the street, nevertheless, shamefaced, one joined it. "The job's filled," someone would call, coming out; even so the crowd broke up reluctantly, ashamed of its defeat. Once in a hundred times or so one might even attain the goal of speaking with the interviewer. Sometimes one would hear, "Keep you in mind. Phone number?" "I don't have a phone." Shrugs dismissed one.

Every weekday morning he took the seven-fifteen train into the city with ads in the day's papers ringed with red pencil in order to be in whatever line there was before nine o'clock and always to find himself blocks behind those who had got there at six in the morning. Sometimes the job was already filled before he got to the address; a dirty envelope thumbtacked to the door dismissed him. Sometimes he had gone through the list of possibilities from one end of town to the other and yet it was still only ten in the morning.

Filling in the rest of the day became the weary treadmill of walking nowhere, and from time to time he transgressed and substituted a late-morning movie for the meat pie and cup of tea for one and sixpence at Sargent's. In too many of these films, it seemed to him, rich people rose and left a voluminous meal in a tiny huff or on the skimpiest excuse. Sometimes Kay Francis in silver lamé consoled him until he came out into the dreary daylight and was forced to step over a scarecrow in rags holding out a greasy cap for pennies.

Tucked away between Pitt and George streets was Rowe Street, a lane of pleasant little shops like Margaret Jaye's Objets and a small coffee place called rhapsodically *Rue de la Paix,* which had only six small tables covered with pretty blue-and-white-check tablecloths and with a baby pot of geraniums on each one. On the clean white walls were prints by Mondrian and Chirico. For ninepence you could have a cup of excellent coffee and two sweet biscuits, and if you were lucky you could get the corner table right in the front window and watch people go by on less purposeful missions, and if you dawdled over your coffee, it could fill in a good half hour or even more, and quite often, surreptitiously, he would eat a sugar cube or two out of the bowl for energy. Once one of the two amiable ladies who ran the shop came over and asked lightly, "More coffee?" "No thanks," he said. She ahem'd behind a hand and said, "I'm sorry, but you must either order another cup of coffee or free the table. We have *other* clients."

Then one magical morning, halfway but slowly through his coffee, two young girls came in, prancing like thoroughbred horses on their high heels, and expensively attired to imply discretion even in their modulated alto voices, but quite obviously still only sixteen or so and impersonating their mothers' gestures of unhurried suavity. Almost at once Seaton recognized the taller girl as Meg Fowler-Jones from the long-ago Miss Peel's classes through the disguise of grown-up lipstick and under the bird's-nest hat with tiny veil. So, for no reason, he paused on his way out.

"Aren't you Meg Fowler-Jones?"

"Yes." Her hand, holding a powder puff, arrested, cautious.

"I'm Seaton Daly."

"Oh, Seaton, fancy, yes of course. How you've grown, you used to be the littlest boy in the school." She was all imitation nicety and sham warmth. "And this is Betty Jollivet," she added. But Betty Jollivet was all light, if she were touched it might cause electric shock. He and Betty Jollivet said hello.

"And what are you doing now?" Meg Fowler-Jones asked.

"Oh this and that," he said, couldn't say.

"And where are you living these days?"

"Arncliffe," he had to say.

Meg Fowler-Jones tried to reach Arncliffe and couldn't make the distance, but Betty Jollivet did.

"Isn't that up near Botany Bay?"

"Not far."

"That must be nice."

There was a light in her, she burned with an incandescence that had nothing to do with looks; but was all joy in her. She was wearing white shantung and it reflected her, beamed with that radiance only seen in the very privileged. She said, "Won't you sit down and have coffee with us? We're just resting our poor old legs."

"I was just leaving," he said. It sounded pompous.

"Oh, do sit down and have a coffee," Meg said.

He had already had his; this would make it eighteen pence and all he had was two shillings and his return train ticket. Oh well. They had imitation conversation. Do you ever see the Lawsons? No, they went to live in Malaya, didn't you know? How's Maureen? *God* knows. He wasn't practiced in brittleness and failed Meg time and again, but every few minutes he turned to see Betty Jollivet.

She was delight. Her hat was a horseshoe of straw corn-flowers, the blue of her eyes, and her smile was remote and seemed to be preoccupied with some immense pleasure. She turned the sugar bowl around and around in her hands as though it delighted her. "*Superb*" she kept saying to whatever drivel was coming from Meg Fowler-Jones; "superb" she would repeat entrancingly. She seemed not able fully to express her complete satisfaction in Meg, in the tablecloth, the sugar bowl, and when her eyes rested for a moment on Seaton, in him.

Extraordinarily he had begun to think what it would be like to ask her to dance. Absurdly (he had never danced with a girl in his life), he pictured them stepping together onto the dance floor where an immense orchestra was already playing some enrapturing thing by Jerome Kern or Irving Berlin, and all the time Meg Fowler-Jones was going on about how she and Betty had recently joined the something-or-other club. "What was it again?" he asked apologetically. "The Drury Lane Players," Meg said, "sort of fun." "Superb," said Miss Jollivet. "We're getting tired of the endless charity thingeroos," Meg said. "We thought we might be actresses for a change." The club was run by Miss Ivy Streeter and they put on plays at the St. James Hall. The girls hoped that they might soon be court ladies in some historical thing about Richard the Second. All of this passed overhead like air whilst he and Betty Jollivet waltzed and tangoed in their dream shapes (which arm does one put around the girl?), and he came to when the orchestra stopped dead as the girls started fumbling in their handbags to pay the bill. So he forked up his two-bob piece.

"Oh let's shout *you,* Seaton, it's been so long," Meg Fowler-Jones said generously. So it was going to be her treat.

"Jolly kind of you," he said like a blithering idiot trying to be Pommy, talking that English accent sort of lofty stuff.

Outside there was nothing left to say except ta-ta. "Well, Meg, ta-*ta,*" he said, jocular as hell, and then to Betty Jollivet, "hope we'll run into each other some time again."

"Sup*erb,*" Betty Jollivet said and looked deeply into him a second as though she might have been considering kissing him. The girls teetered off up George Street in their high heels and he was left with the rest of the day.

The rest of his life. He was, of course, hyperbolizing, but the casual meeting had had the effect of bringing not a past but a future into focus where no future apparently existed; the remote possibility of a life that was not circumscribed by pounds, shillings, and pence wherein the luxury of not having to fret and worry over every sixpence released you into a configuration of endlessly entertaining situations.

But the reality was the three-twenty train to Arncliffe through gritty Redfern, Flat Mortdale, and then the long walk uphill home past the same as ever dreary fences.

He wondered what fee Miss Ivy Streeter charged to join her band of players. Well, either way, no hope. No job, no hope. The only thing to look forward to was Saturday off to rest from doing nothing. But like Enoch Arden in Second Year English his lonely doom was to come suddenly to an end.

Bumbling through what appeared to be a forgotten street near Circular Quay, he had stopped to look in the window of a small shop that seemed to have been left behind when everything else moved away and which referred to itself grandiosely as LA BIBLIOTHÈQUE and explained redundantly that it was BOOK SHOP AND LIBRARY. L. LEMOYNE. And among dusty-looking novels and some old prints of Paris streets was a card on which was printed as though shrinking from the very idea, BOY WANTED.

The slightly hunchbacked lady dusting shelves was dressed also as if she had been left behind from another era. She removed pince-nez on a black ribbon and pointed to a curtained archway. "See the manager, Mr. Lemoyne," she said.

Behind the curtain Mr. Lemoyne was in the midst of rolling a cigarette between nicotine-stained fingers with dirty nails. He wore a green celluloid shade that cast his pointed features into palish apple. His faded green velvet jacket was so old that it had turned to moss around the armpits, but when he spoke it was in the high-fluting tones of a duchess floundering to rise above an Australian-ese lower class.

"Kaindly tike a chair, won't you?" Mr. Lemoyne said, lighting his cigarette with a flourish. "You are innerested in the sitooation?"

"Yes, I am."

"May I arsk, are you acquainted with books, then?"

"Well, I read a lot."

"Might I arsk what type of lidridture?"

"Well," he said, swallowing and lying somewhat, "Dickens, Thackeray, you know, and, and—a bit of Thoreau, Katherine Mansfield."

Mr. Lemoyne nodded.

Seaton gripped the arms of the chair and, swallowing the shame he had in resorting to her, added, "My mother was a writer."

"Indeed, what name?"

"Hope Seaton."

No, Mr. Lemoyne had not heard of her, perhaps, his manner assumed, she had slipped by unnoticed, so Seaton said, "She wrote a lot of short stories and poetry, mostly during the war."

"Ah," Mr. Lemoyne brightened. "You see, during the war I was managing an estaminet in Épernay near to Verdun, sonny. I was in la belle France the whole time." Mr. Lemoyne brushed ash off his jacket disdainfully and said that, well, the job mainly was concerned with repairing books in the libr'ry and taking care of "Books that come in sometimes in a shameful condition. The way some people handle books is tray deeoboleek, vous connay." But Mr. Lemoyne thought that Seaton might fill the bill; he had "took a liking to him already, son." The pay was fifteen bob a week and it was nine to six weekdays and get orf at twelve Sat'dys.

"Can you start tomorrow, à der*mann,* as we say?"

He walked out employed. Whatever other tortures Mr. Lemoyne might display besides abominable French paled beside the fact that it was a job at last.

"At *last,*" Essie said. "Hooray, Beanie darling, hallelujah."

The smell of the basement where he was to work was earthy and mixed with something fetid, which turned out to be bottles of foul-smelling glue. A naked electric light bulb spread merciless glare on a workbench where there were piles of books in various stages of disintegration and rolls of equally unpleasant-smelling green oilcloth.

His job was to cover the books and then to print the title and author in white ink on the front and spine. But the oilcloth was difficult to cut with the large shears and once pasted with glue more likely to stick to him than to the books and, moreover, to create ripples on the books so that the whole cover had to be pried loose and thrown away and started again. The fetid smell of the glue was nauseating and the constant glare of the electric light bothered his eyes, but none of these annoyances was as wearying as the visits of Mr. Lemoyne, who would lean on a pile of books, rolling his cigarettes, and then embark with imitation gaiety upon anecdotes of unparalleled dullness.

"The wife and I orfen tarry with a bottle of Tintara white port to go with the haddock," Mr. Lemoyne would start, holding out one finger fastidiously as if pouring from the decanter and then lick his cigarette paper fastidiously. "Sometimes we prefer a dry chablis pert etterer or even a surprising hock, but I orfen say to our teetotaller chums, 'You don't know what you're missing if you don't have the je ner say quaw of a nice wine avec le pwosson.'" Sometimes, Mr. Lemoyne lamented, the chauvinism

of his countrymen gave him a pain, but then not all of them were
as lucky as he was to go orf in the war and live in la belle France
where you get uster the finer things of life, compree?

At times a sadness came over Mr. Lemoyne's Arabic face,
but it was more the sadness of a mule unable to reach over a fence
for a weed. Sometimes Seaton caught Mr. Lemoyne looking at
him covertly under wiry eyebrows as if he might be expecting
some word of approval for his innate fastidiousness. A quality
with which Mr. Lemoyne also credited Seaton. He had become
fond of coupling them together in some despairingly sought
upper strata and was fond of saying that only *they* could appreciate the finer, subtler points of living. "I feel, Seaton, in this short
time we've been together that we have developed what you
might call a nice ontont cordeeyal," Mr. Lemoyne said gravely,
elevating them above the hoi polloi. "But alas, you and I are
voices crying in the wilderness." Without encouragement, Mr.
Lemoyne hoisted Seaton up under a mossy armpit so that they
might view the wilderness together. It was like being stranded
with Mr. Lemoyne in a small airless elevator. Silently Seaton
pasted green oilcloth.

Then one afternoon, as if on a stealthy mission, Mr. Lemoyne descended the stairs, carrying a large wine-colored
leather-bound volume and placed it on the workbench with a
significant nicotined finger to the lips.

"Say nothing, Seaton," Mr. Lemoyne said with breathy ad-
monition. "One of a few precious volumes from the salon pree-
vay, you might say, over which I thought you might care to
linger, like I."

The volume, distributed only to the "connossewers" of such
enlightenment, had been published in Athens in 1892, Mr. Lemoyne said and proceeded to open the large book, which had
come his way by a matter of chance "through a thoughtful but
now deceased chum who was elevated above the humdrum like
yourself, dear lad."

Large photographs, yellowed now and dim, of naked boys
on some Greek island. Hot and incensed at the presumption,

Seaton could only stand sweating while Mr. Lemoyne turned the pages. Not outward obscenity, no out-and-out sexual calisthenics had been recorded, but the implication was worse; the artificiality of love had been implied in the groupings of the naked boys, some with garlands of flowers in their hair, their hands reaching toward each other in beseeching attitudes of lust and the requitement of it, standing beside ponds or in front of waterfalls, seated on rocks in twos and threes, their pubescent genitals translucent as white grapes. Becalmed by concupiscence, they gazed at each other with subdued melancholy; some held lyres in their hands, some offered fruit. They all looked like accomplished frauds.

"Pure *art*, " breathed Mr. Lemoyne heavily, and to Seaton's horror, he put an arm on his shoulder, enticing him into the Grecian isles. "Not all would agree but fortunately mercy is above their sceptered sway, wouldn't you say, dear Seaton? These are the young Apollos in their virginal prime, caught in the instant they awoke to the music of the bacchanal perhaps, anyway to some music heard only by a few, as you and I are only too well aware. If you will allow me to quote the tragically ill-famed Oscar who was sent to prison for it, it is the love that dare not speak its name."

Mr. Lemoyne turned, breathing heavily, and little beads of sweat for the urgency of being understood appeared on his upper lip. His small eyes were starry with the secret he was imparting, trusting to Seaton with appalling gratuity.

Possibly it was only the smell of the glue. "Excuse me," Seaton gasped and ran, pulling open the door to the lavatory only just in time.

When he came back, Mr. Lemoyne and the book of the young Apollos had vanished. From that day on there was no word from Mr. Lemoyne apart from an abrupt "bong jour" or "bong swar." Wages were handed out in aggrieved silence.

That was all downstairs to drudgery.

Upstairs was all delight. Upstairs at 10 King Street, up above the Mary Elizabeth Tea Room and Gypsy Palm Readings, was the floor occupied by Miss Ivy Streeter and the Drury Lane

Players. The loft was painted apple green and around the walls were hung bright posters of the previous productions of the amateur company. Miss Schiller had accepted his hard-earned guinea membership fee and intimated that one day he might even meet or speak to or (miracles abounding) be spoken to by Miss Streeter herself. Glanced at from a distance, Miss Streeter was as wide as a sofa and looked as though she should be hung around with cushions. She had ebony black painted hair drawn back into a bun and wore large earrings and she seemed to be continuously occupied behind screens teaching young girls Juliet's potion speech or Portia's plea for mercy. It was surprising to learn that Miss Streeter had a husband named Moynahan and three children out in Campsie.

Luncheon (as Miss Schiller termed it) of sandwiches and tea was provided for members for one and sixpence, but in Seaton's case only sixpence was charged for a cup of tea when he brought his own sandwich from the Ham & Beef nearby, and it became a habit for him to break from the nauseous glue and oilcloth for an hour and take refuge at "the clubroom."

The clubroom was Paris, London, the golden city of Samarkand. It smelled of cigarette smoke and excitement, and the lunchers were all stars. They scarcely noticed him, and because of only paying for his tea, he never pulled up a chair directly into the group. Most days in the group the stars were John Wycliffe, Molly Coote, Rita Royce, a Gertrude Somebody, Miss Heart, and Mr. Byron Hall. There was also Mimi Ostral from time to time, an even bigger star by her extravagant gestures and her hoarse laugh.

There was no sign of Meg Fowler-Jones or the lovely Betty Jollivet, who had first mentioned the club to him.

The stars kept up a thrilling mercurial conversation about the theater during lunch. Although none of them had in actuality been further than suburban Manly beach in their lives, they seemed to be in as close personal contact with goings-on in the West End of London's theatrical district as if they had just dropped in from Shaftesbury Avenue. With a kind of professional languor they discussed the latest convolutions among Noel and Binkie and Gertie and Bea and quoted the bon mots of Ivor and Emlyn. They knew what CB had said to Boo and that Sir Gerald's play was a flop. The fact was that they subscribed to *Theatre World*, which they read avidly, and they bought paperback copies of the new plays at Andrades Shop to see what roles might properly suit them were Miss Streeter to do the play. They often assured each other (through direct contact with a lucky friend returned from London) that their own Rita Royce had been better in that Priestley play than the original girl in London.

The stars not married and handicapped by children all had plans eventually to get to the West End where they knew they were destined to be instantaneous successes; they even had the names of some actors' agents. "I'm probably going to be handled by Miriam Warner," one would tell another. "I'll start off in a good rep, probably Birmingham," another would say. In between these rosy predictions they nibbled tomato sandwiches and gazed out at flat King Street.

For all their prognostication they all went home on the Double Bay tram or Chatswood train and not one of their names was fated ever to be seen on any poster nor in the lobby of any London theater. Of the stars, one in particular was accorded noticeable deference and that was Byron Hall. Known to the favored few of them as "Buck," he sat always at the head of the luncheon table and it was to Buck that most of the pronouncements on plays or performances would be offered and it was his yea or nay that decided the issue. "I wouldn't exactly say *rare*," he might opine and before Jack Robinson could be out of the box they were all agreeing, "No, absolutely *not* rare."

Byron Hall was only just short of being handsome in the manner of pen-and-ink drawings of Victorian poets. He had a fine profile which he turned from side to side when speaking, a thin aquiline nose with a tiny red dot at the end, which gave it a mark of insouciance, and he had fine light brown hair, which fell softly over his forehead and which he was apt to toss back as an exclamation point. When his eyes rested on you even momen-

tarily, they seemed to burn dimly with latent sorrow for you or
to flicker with a fatigued impatience at everyone's shortcomings.
So great was his popularity and so effusive were the means to get
his attention that Seaton was almost deranged with pleasure and
embarrassment when one day Byron Hall leaned over toward
him and, casting him a smile of infinite kindness, said, "Why are
you sitting way over there? Come in and join the group."

The other stars smiled at him with fake benevolence and
possible generosity toward his truly preposterous imitation wor-
sted suit. From time to time Miss Schiller allowed him to usher
at the St. James Hall, thus allowing him to see the shows from
the back row for free, and so it was he was able to enjoy Molly
Coote, John Wycliffe, and Mimi Ostral thrillingly unlock closets
of skeletons in *Dangerous Corner* with an ease that could only
come from long experience and to perceive that they took their
curtain calls with the assurance of players from the real Drury
Lane, offhanded but mildly gratified. But it was nothing compared to the histrionics of Byron Hall and Mimi Ostral in and
around and up and down a staircase in *Jealousy,* a display of
hatred and revenge so exhausting that Byron had practically to
assist Mimi to the footlights at the curtain. When Byron came
into the clubroom for lunch the following Monday, Seaton, taking courage in both hands, edged toward him and said that he had
seen the show. "And you were simply—simply outstanding, Mr.
Hall." Byron looked deeply at him with his softest expression
and said, "I'm Buck." So rewarded, Seaton carried the words
back with him to his pasting and gluing to recur like a gentle
phrase of music.

Sometimes it is the little half-concealed paths that lead to
glory.

"You can be a page in *Rose and Thorn* if you like," Miss Ivy
Streeter said to him in passing, baptizing him. *Rose and Thorn,*
he learned, was a huge hit at the Haymarket in London and was
a play about Richard the Second couched in modern vernacular
so that people of the royal court said things like "Good God,
Buckingham, you can't be serious, my dear fellow" or "The king

seems a teeny bit hungover this morning, that Flemish sack goes to the head like buckshot." "More likely that the Flemish princess kept him from sleeping, my dear."

Seaton's entire role was on one page of typewritten "sides" and read as follows;

(cue)—food was most peculiar.

A fair page enters and kneels.

PAGE: Lord Westminster's horses are at the portcullis, your Grace.

BUCKINGHAM: How agreeable of them. Send ostlers to attend his Lordship.

PAGE: Yes, your Grace.

Page exits.

At night three bright lights hung from the loft ceiling under green glass shades and cast great pools on the floor so that the actors moved from brilliance to shadow, which heightened the effectiveness dramatically. The coincidence of the Duke of Buckingham being played by "Buck" Hall added to the nervousness Seaton felt by having to wait well into the second act to make his one entrance, but when he did, it was over in seconds and no one, not even Ivy, commented in any way nor even seemed to notice. He seemed to kneel professionally enough and to rise gracefully. Toward the middle of the second week, Buck Hall, who had begun to address him as "fair page," said, "Fair page, say your line more forcefully if you can. Make the horses very urgently at the gate so as to feed me the laugh."

So it was that on the opening night that the house roared when Buckingham paused beautifully and said drily, "How agreeable of them!" In the meantime, scenery had been brought up into the loft and was being painted into turrets and dungeons and behind a flat, sitting on a box in her own glow, was Betty Jollivet.

There she was. It was like sudden good news.

"I'm Seaton Daly," he said.

"Of course you are," she said.

"I met you with Meg Fowler-Jones in the Rue de la Paix coffee shop."

"Of course you did."

"Are you in the play?"

"I'm a hussy in the tavern scene and then later I'm the second lady-in-waiting to Queen Anne and I get to say 'My, lady, you have a burning fever, shall we fetch the king?' and then 'Look there, my lady has fainted' and I go off."

There was an appealing gravity to everything she said, even humorously, never smiling, but also in the sparkling way she looked directly at him and made little pronouncements: "superb" when pleased or "horror" when displeased.

One evening while they were watching the scene where Buckingham is seduced by the queen, Buck Hall and Mimi Ostral circling each other with slyly lascivious movements in a sexual exchange of clever barbs, he roistering and she concupiscent, Betty said laconically, "They're lovers."

"She's trying to woo him to back the king in the war with France."

"No, I mean *really.*"

"How do you know?"

"You can tell. I can always tell."

She really was quietly extraordinary.

And then when they moved to the St. James Hall into costumes and scenery and lights, they were metamorphosed into a living tapestry of color at the dress rehearsal, which due to delays in changing the scenery and because two of the light dimmers were not working, went on until after two in the morning. Seaton was half-drowsing in the darkness of backstage when Buck and Mimi made a noisy exit and, coming into the offstage dimness, he took her suddenly into reality with a fervent embrace to which she responded with a consummate eagerness. Structurally, Byron was most satisfying in tights and he knew it, he had splendid legs, firm as young trees, and Mimi's full breasts were packed to overflowing in her low-cut costume. They merged together in the crepuscular light like the practiced lovers Betty Jollivet had perceived them to be and then they laughed low chuckling laughs full of intimate knowledge of each other.

(Some time during the war Seaton was to read in the evening paper that Mimi Ostral had died by gassing herself in her Potts Point flat, that she had come from the amateur theater to being a leading lady on the professional stage and had parts in several local films. Her real name had been Miriam Pinckus and her father had owned a corset factory over which she had been born in Leichardt. This may have accounted for the hoarse scornful laugh with which Mimi had excoriated her ordinary past, her life, everything, even Byron.)

But now everything was concentrated on the opening night, the sets, the gay clothes of Chinese silk and fake velveteen, craftily painted with Richard the Second's heraldic lions and unicorns. Quickly everyone was silenced into nervous intakes of breath and whispers of "good luck" or "merde"; the curtains swung back, two other pages knelt, shooting dice, the king swung on all in blue and white. "What? Dice in the corridor? You'll awaken the owls in the east tower. Up, varlets, light the king to his supper, on with you, boys." Music. Tabs parted on the large supper room, laughter.

Almost two hours later, his scene over, Seaton was watching through a crack when he was seized from behind and clasped to warmth, velvet and a smell of spirit gum, strong arms circled him and he saw the powdered hands glinting with fake jewelry and felt the kiss on the back of his neck. "Hello, Fair Page," said the Duke of Buckingham and snickered, then quickly let him go as jailers approached with lanterns for the last scene.

Nobody said anything to him about the first-night party at the clubrooms so he went home on the train, wondering about Buck Hall. But no sign of intimacy was even hinted at for the next two Saturday nights of the seven-week Saturday-night run of the play. Buck appeared to be preoccupied mostly with his false beard and with shoals of people who came backstage afterward, cooing and toadying to him. On the third Saturday, as he was leaving the dressing room provided for the small-part people, Seaton was confronted on the stairs by the Duke, stripped to the waist and covered with a makeup towel. "Rushing off? Want a coffee at Cahills?"

He botched it. "If I miss the eleven-thirty, there's no train until quarter to one and my cousin worries."

"Rush home then."

Damn.

But rescue came the following Saturday. "Listen," Buck was theatrically casual, "what're you doing tomorrow arvo, like to take a Sunday walk?" Oh *yes*, he said, all too eager, all sparkle. Elizabeth Bay then, did he know it? Down by the boatshed in the little park by the harbor. About four-ish?

He dressed shakily with disgraceful care, best shirt and tie and the application of a great deal of greasy stuff named Pomade de Soir without which no Arncliffe boy would be seen dead socially even though the girls protested in horror at the gooey stuff and kept their hands from wandering to the boys' necks. Sheepish, he lied to Essie, saying his date was "one of the girls in the show" and regretting his biggish nose in the mirror, recombed his hair for the fifth time, wetting down a dog's hind leg. The pitiful disguise for all this primping and readying himself only exacerbated an involuntary disgust at his willingness, this headlong rush to be seduced by possibilities that had the weight of probability and more than a whiff of the counterfeit about them. All the way into town on the train he was assaulted with a conviction that the ultimate was meant to come about.

The awe in which he found himself, not sacred and yet not wholly profane, merely voluptuous, thickened his tongue from the moment Buck emerged from behind the boathouse wearing a weathered Harris tweed jacket in smoky colors and they began what seemed a purposeless walk. Yes, he murmured, he had seen this and that film, no he had not yet been to enjoy the delightful Alice Delysia at the Grand Opera

House. Fancy, he said to everything as they trudged disinterestedly by the big white Californian-Spanish mansion of the Albert family built, Buck informed, from the millions earned by sheet music and "Boomerang" mouth organs.

Heartsick as the day waned, he began to accept the appalling possibility that this was all it was intended to be, a *walk.* He had become predisposed to a foregone conclusion, surrendered, and now it was corrupted with anticlimax. Now they trudged on joylessly through Billyard Avenue past buildings of uninteresting flats and with flatter conversation. How would it end? and was Byron Hall so bored or else so unbelievably obtuse that he didn't know how to end it?

But then quite apocalyptically rain began, quite heavily, and Buck said, "Turn up your collar and we'll run, I'm only a few blocks up the hill from here," and they ran up Elizabeth Bay Road and turned a corner and came up panting in front of a severe-looking old brick building of flats with "Ashburn Court" in frosted glass over the entrance of dirty white marble steps that led into a dim lobby of unused cracked leather furniture and steel engravings. Buck lived in the ground floor apartment, which had been converted into "roomette" flats consisting of one large room and a corner into which a sink and tiny gas range had been inserted; the bathroom and lavatory were down the hall.

"Take off your wet jacket," Buck said and took off his. There was nothing in the least presupposed in the way things happened—Buck's knee just happened to graze Seaton's and the next moment they were in a tight embrace, not entirely realistic. There was no affectionate talk, no murmuring of sweet words as they were somehow precipitated onto the large bed under the window and into undressing in an agreement of pretended surprise. Buck even laughed once or twice, deprecatingly. He was as skin smooth undressed as he was in conversation and assured as a general in battle. But they ventured then into a serious silent agreement during which their eyes never left each other, as though only through their eyes could they maintain a feasibility to the fable in which they'd become involved and some time later (time passing slowly and silently) they achieved it, they arrived together at a supreme junction within seconds of each other and they were marvelously released and, loosening their hold on each other, they sighed and, drooping, they relaxed onto the pillows in a state of astounded joy.

Only then, at long last, did Buck lean over and quickly, light as a moth wing, kiss him on the mouth, but in the glancing touch Seaton felt more emotion and gratification than in the whole orgasmic eruption and then, glancing sideways, saw that Buck had sat up and was absorbed in something across the room, saw that he was looking into the mirror facing the bed and that he was stroking his fallen hair back into place.

Then shortly it became extraordinarily formal, covering their former excesses with towels and finding each other's socks and shoes, the getting into underwear in a prissy precise manner as though they had been at a gymnastic class or had had a medical examination. "Borrow a comb?" he asked. "It's stopped raining," Buck said at the window and then as Seaton combed his hair said kindly, "Don't put that greasy stuff on your hair, it spoils the nice wave you have, and it's common-looking. Let your hair stay dry and soft."

Which he was to do for the rest of his life. And remember this late wet afternoon.

"The Tudor Inn," Buck said, "for a bite of dinner. What say?" Just up around the corner and expensive, Seaton knew, but it would postpone the inevitable conclusion.

Even though it was the mildest June evening, the antipodean early winter was being observed in the Tudor Inn by a crackling log fire, cheerful flames reflected in hanging copper pans and bedwarmers on the walls. They were immediately given priority seats in the best banquette by the fireplace, Buck obviously being known here, and the Elizabethan-dressed waitresses, whom you were expected to summon by crying "wench," bobbing to him. They were handed large menus of parchment scrolls upon which were handwritten in flowing Shakespearean script the list of entrées at hair-raising prices (the sirloin of beef with Yorkshire pudding was seven shillings and sixpence, half of Seaton's weekly wages) and, assuming nonchalance, he ordered the inexpensive tripe and onions.

"Don't be silly," Buck said teasingly, "have the half of roast chicken, you silly goose, it's *my* treat this evening." You minx, Buck added teasingly as the serving wench departed. "Minx," he said again. He seemed to be enjoying his role of *patron*. He squeezed Seaton's hand under the table and said what a shame that in this puritan "wowser"-ridden country the serving of alcoholic drinks was forbidden after six o'clock, otherwise they could have toasted each other. It wouldn't be the same in dear old England or anywhere else on earth that had a smidgen of intelligence about good living. He added that he intended to shake off the dust of Oz forever just the minute he had the fare, never to return.

But of course. He meant that he would become a star, there was no doubt of it.

His deeply pure eyes seem to swim with affection; it was as heady as any amount of drinking just being with him.

And exciting, debilitating to the appetite. Seaton barely picked at the delicious roast chicken, said no to a parfait. Outside, now dark and under the streetlight, they parted eventually.

"You know, don't you?" Buck asked. They were shaking hands like business acquaintances.

"What?"

"What I'm thinking about you. Do you?"

"I think I do, Buck."

"Minx. Good night, minx. Sleep then. Good night, sweet prince."

Rocking, all the way back to the tram, then train, then walking. Rocking with a new inner sense of secret knowledge and a profound new anxiety. How long would it last? Would it be snatched away from him or might it go on, might they be long-lasting mates? A dreadful word but all they had to describe each other in public. One would never be permitted to say "this is my lover, my love."

But the following Sunday there was no artful pretense about taking walks and Buck opened the door in a dressing gown and seemed to be in a hurry, almost irritable, anxious for them not to waste a precious minute on small talk or polite chitchat even though, foolishly, Seaton had been saving up tidbits all week of comic interludes at work, overheard inanities. They were swept by tidal influences onto the rumpled bed, unmade from the night before. This time, more leisurely, it seemed to Seaton astonishingly, that love with Buck had begun to be an extension of Buck's need for admiration and the act to become the physical exercise of self-praise. Again it was performed in churchlike silence and this time there was no afterward kiss, no hand touching. Buck leapt up and into his Chinese green robe and said startlingly, "I wonder would you hear me my lines, old son." He had been cast as the king in Shaw's *The Apple Cart* and it contained one uninterrupted speech of nearly six pages. Thus they sat in the pretend world of Shavian witticism in the fading light, after which Buck took a shower but didn't offer the bathroom. Again they went to the Tudor Inn where the wenches bowed them in, but tonight there was no fire either in the fireplace or in their hearts, it seemed. Buck laughed a lot at very little and occasionally glanced at his watch and this time, the treat patently not being his, did nothing to restrain Seaton from the tripe. "Good night, old son," Buck said under the streetlight and walked quickly away, running into two actressy-looking friends and greeting and laughing with them boisterously.

The third and last Sunday (there was only one more Saturday then left of the run of *Rose and Thorn*) the intermingling became even more perfunctory and this time Buck said abruptly as though lovemaking had already delayed important business, "I have exam papers to correct" (he taught first-year French three mornings a week at a girls' private school at Pymble) "so if you don't mind, kid, we won't dine this evening." He was already holding open the door to the hall and while Seaton was getting into his overcoat, there were creases of slight impatience around Buck's mouth.

It couldn't—

At the door, helpless but impelled from behind by a wave, Seaton leaned over to kiss Buck and kissed air as their heads bumped in a slapstick evocation of what really was going on. "Silly billy," Buck said, laughing, and "seeyuh." The door to the flat shut Seaton out.

It couldn't—

It couldn't be that this was the end, could it? That it was all a flash in a pan? Was it only the hunt that aroused Byron Hall? Was it a fact that once the stag had been struck with the arrow there was no further interest?

During the following wondering days, Seaton permitted Buck endless extenuating circumstances. "Look," he said aloud to the mirror, "he has a difficult job and a huge new role to learn, you know." "You know," he told himself, "men don't appreciate too much tenderness, you were an idiot to want him to kiss you good-bye."

"Talking to yourself, darl?" asked innocent Essie at the door of the bathroom. He was spending Sundays with that same girl, she had been told. Perhaps one Sunday he'd bring her home for tea in the evening, she'd cook a nice roast of lamb, pet.

There was no manifestation of the slightest interest on the last night of the play, no being seized from behind and held and kissed, no reaching for his hand in the dark as they waited for their curtain calls, but Seaton had stuffed a saved ten shilling note into his shirt pocket in the forlorn hope that he might confront Buck and invite him to last-night supper, but it seemed from voices calling up and down the dressing room hall that bloody awful Mimi Ostral was giving a party at her flat for all the principals and that three taxis were coming to transport them.

As Seaton dressed and hung despairingly near the stage exit in the last lost hope that the loved, the adored might at the last moment—

Might even come to say so long, bye-bye, Fair Page. When Betty Jollivet appeared, carrying her makeup case, he grabbed her and said, "Where are you going? Have supper with me?"

"Aren't you going to Mimi's party?"

"Wasn't asked."

"Then I won't go either."

She took his arm firmly. It was positive just walking with her. They went into Cahills where a haughty hostess crammed them into an outside hall table, possibly because they were so young.

"But there are tables in the big room," Betty protested.

"Reserved."

"Not after nine P.M. Says on the menu."

The hostess sighed and led them into the big room. Threw down menus.

"Have a cheese dream," Seaton said. If you assessed somebody's value by the prices on a menu, then Betty Jollivet was worth a cheese dream. She was looking at him through her cigarette smoke with a mixture of curiosity and perhaps slight *noblesse oblige* because of his callowness. She was aged about thirty-two in her sensibility about things and at other moments, sixteen in her enthusiasms. "Super duper," she said as they brought the platter of melted cheese in a forest of asparagus. "This is so nice, Seaton," she said and patted his hand. She might never have been asked to supper before and yet had probably danced with all the most eligible young rich men in Sydney. Seaton had not yet danced a step in his life, would not have known how to hold the girl.

First, he was amazed at his own boldness in asking her out and, second, even more astonished to find now that they were like long-acquainted people at ease with each other. Part of the miracle of Betty Jollivet was the accomplished ease with which she managed to balance a relationship between politeness and close intimacy. As the Cahills after-theater crowd diminished, they grew more and more loquacious, at times interrupting each other and "Sorry, no, *you* go on," they said. "Superb," she said and "marvelous," encouraging him with her frank open looks and smiles until he was racing ahead with opinions on this and that, opinions he had had no idea he held, almost as though he were the ventriloquist dummy on the knee of a worldly, highly intelligent grown man of vast experience. Until he struck a rock.

"I would like to be more like Byron Hall" came out of his mouth for some reason.

"Why?"

"Because he knows exactly what he wants all the time and goes after it."

She was silent, seemed dubious, her chin was poignant with doubt. "Byron Hall," she said, wonderingly, trying perhaps to conjure him up. Was he tall? Supreme in any sense?

"Oh," Betty said, "but he isn't *real*. I'd want to be like someone much realer than Byron Hall."

"Sorry, but we're closing now," said the glacial hostess, descending on them with the bill. They were left with so much to say that they had not noticed they were the last people in the restaurant.

I'll see you into the tram, he had said when she mentioned Darling Point Road, and when the tram trundled up he said, "Let me see you home," and got on with her. Because it was chilly they sat inside. Few people were on this late-night tram. Because they were so young and so agreeably captivated by one another they were assumed to be lovers by an amiable drunk.

"G'night, sweet-art, til we meet tomorrer," sang the drunk. Perhaps in an effort to achieve jauntiness he had clipped a little blue tin butterfly to his tie. "The saddest butterfly I ever saw," Betty said.

"Are you sweet-arts?" the drunk inquired. "Are you? Are you?" In the alcoholic inquisitiveness that knows no quenching, "You sweet-arts, darlings?"

"Say yes," Betty said, "or he'll just keep on and on."

"Yes," they said together.

"You sweet darlings, what a darling pair." The drunk was straphanging directly over them although there were seats in abundance. Rose Bay matrons looked fixedly at their skirts in distress. "Live together, do you, darlings? Go to bed together, do you?"

"Yes," Seaton said eventually.

"Listen," the drunk said, swaying all over them, "don't let the barstards stop you, they'll stop you if they can, the barstards that run this friggin' world, they took away my sweetie and turned her into an ox. I'm married to a flaming ox now, biggest arse you ever saw. Give us a kiss would you, darlings?" Sidestepping the gasoline fumes of alcohol, they slithered past him at Darling Point Road and got off the tram, but the tearful voice followed them across the road.

"Keep on keepin' on, darlings, you sweet little doves, you got the whole fuckin' world, darlings, but it won't last, nothing lasts in this bloody world."

When they reached Betty's gate, there were steps leading down to lawns seemingly clustered with moonlit black-and-white bushes of great rhododendron. Lights could be seen in the big house and Betty said would he like to come in and meet the family. "Because in all probability they're still up listening to the test cricket from Lords in England on the shortwave."

No thanks, he said and then, assisted by the emotion of night and trees, blanched silver flowers, moonlit water, and with the small wavering oval of her face lifted to him in the provocative way she had, all purity but intended to provoke, he leaned down and kissed her on the mouth and, having gone beyond all imaginings, held her closely to him and moved his face up against the sweet softness of her hair and suspended for moments in this fallacy, possessing her only perfunctorily, but momentarily deluded by the similarity to conquest, he continued holding her closely until she moved away and spoke in a voice of quiet certainty.

"Now don't *you* be unreal."

She unlatched the gate.

"Good night, Seaton dearest."

So she shook him out of the falsehood. So she knew. She knew about him in the way she had known about Byron and Mimi Ostral being lovers. She knew the way of him and that it was as ancient as sin and as irredeemable. She knew and yet she wisely and lovingly cared. Seaton dearest.

Good night, he said, committed now to loving her for the rest of his life.

Drawn like the murderer back to the scene, drawn in exquisite misery, unable to resist the damnable urge, he hopped on a tram after work up to Kings Cross and walked down to Elizabeth Bay Road and to Ashburn Court for no other reason than to stare uselessly up at Buck's lighted window (the blind was pulled down, perhaps he was marking exam papers, listening to the evening news on the wireless or maybe just sitting disconsolately) and all because—Because, he had told himself aloud for the thirtieth time, he remembered Buck saying it was a nuisance his not being reachable by phone. "Suppose I suddenly have great need of you. Couldn't you arrange for me to leave a message somewhere in code, like it's your dentist phoning to remind you of your appointment with him this evening?"

All the time drawing imaginary rings around Seaton's navel. "Why would I be going out with my dentist in the evening?" "Perhaps you have a thing going with him." The boisterous laugh.

Or Buck might even come out of the flat and throw his arms around him and exclaim "oh happy day," or something of the sort. Say he was feeling blue and lonely, perhaps, how dear of you to turn up just when I needed you.

As the day darkened the streetlights came on. Occasionally a shadow passed across the window blind. How long was he going to stand here rooted to the spot and perhaps attracting curiosity? He walked slowly to the end of the block and slowly back and again took his stand under the window, deriding himself for being such a fool and yet unable to break off from the faint excitement of being physically adjacent to where sweetness was and became so inured to the somber musings it provoked that he was completely unaware of time passing or of lights being put out in windows until he heard, or seemed to hear, his name spoken matter-of-factly and, turning, felt the onrush of a deep red flush through him at being caught, heart beating suddenly with excitement and shame, and Buck said, "I thought it was you."

Buck, wearing an ugly tan raincoat, was looking at him sharply, the red dot on his nose seemed larger, and he was with, of all people, Merle Mayhew, the assistant stage manager and "props" at the Drury Lane. She was a small, pale, tired-looking girl with dull hair, always vanishing into ecru voile dresses, who had little to say and to whom no one said anything much except "Do you have my sword?" She had thin lips that met almost in a crack and at her best, whatever that was, she was far from personable. Yet this evening she was transformed into sulphurous lightness. She might as well have had on a placard reading WE HAVE BEEN DOING IT; her little mouth was drawn back into a smirk of triumph as she stood with her arm through Buck's, radiant with the joy of being well and truly ravished, hanging on to her handbag as if it were the coronation orb of England. "Hello, Seaton," Merle said and grinned as Seaton flusteringly mumbled some blather about having been delivering a book from where he worked which was urgently—

The three stood there in the full knowledge of one another's fraudulence until Buck said, "We're taking a cab down into town. Can we drop you?"

"No thanks," Seaton said, backing away and in further foolishness, waving at them.

"Good night, so long."

He had been dropped already, thank you.

And according to Betty Jollivet by someone who wasn't real.

How can you treat a poor maiden so?

C AMILLA LAYE DICK was Brobdingnagian in two ways. In her high heels, which she seemed to wear in scorn of nature, she was nearly six feet tall, and she was the biggest wheel in the burgeoning advertising agency business in the country. She wore her heavy blondined hair in a thick pageboy bob and she had exceptionally large nostrils that gave her the look of an aristocratic horse. She dressed mostly in white, in expensive linens and sharkskin, which burnished her beach-tanned skin, and her severe unadorned dresses were slyly cut to embolden her already emphatic breasts. Her office at B. H. Lowe's Advertising was all white with splashes of passionate orange, and she was the first woman in the country to have a white telephone. She was ahead in everything; her walls were ornamented with unfamiliar Braques and Klees. She had had the first copy from America of the novel *Gone with the Wind*.

Seaton first saw her from afar in both distance and stature. While sitting in the B. H. Lowe agency waiting room, he glimpsed her at her desk far down a white carpeted hall where she seemed to be never unattached to the telephone. The moment she put it down it rang again. Sometimes he heard her say abruptly to someone out of sight, "Get that, would you, Brenda?" Once she came out to the receptionist and said, "Find out if we can borrow a freighter, would you, Gwenda?" Another

73

time she rose from her desk and, waving a sheaf of copy, came down the hall and stood in the doorway of someone's office and was heard to say, "This is putrid, get someone else on to it." "Who?" a voice asked. "Hemingway," she said and went off again. People meeting her in the hallway tended to step aside to let her pass, so grandiose was her demeanor. She was omnipotent.

So much so that when she paused in flight near the reception desk and her imperious glance seemed to fall on him, he quailed.

"Who are you waiting for?" she demanded rather than asked.

"Mrs. Dick," he said.

"I'm Mrs. Dick. What's it about?"

"I was to see her about the Cream of Oats ad?"

"How old are you?"

"I'll be twenty in October."

"Hmm, bit on the old side. Still—" Her nostrils widened when she smiled. "What's your name?"

"Seaton Daly."

"Who's your agent?"

"Nobody, I heard about it from a friend, Dick Goodall."

The nostrils deflated.

"Him! He's not with us anymore. Well then—come and we'll take a photograph. Come along then, you sweet thing."

He was taken into a photographic studio where Mrs. Dick gave orders he was to be put into a striped sports shirt. "Rumple his hair up," she said. "I'll be back in five minutes."

He was seated on a box; lights were arranged around him. A minion brought a red-and-white striped shirt which others helped him put on. Somebody rumpled his hair and he was left sitting there for twenty minutes. Mrs. Dick, someone relayed the information, was on the long-distance phone to Melbourne. Mrs. Dick could keep anyone waiting as long as she liked. It was Mrs. Dick who had fashioned one of the most effective commercials on radio. At certain hours of the evening, usually toward bedtime, the plaintive, birdlike, virginal voice of a young girl was heard singing an infectiously sweet English folk tune:

Oh, don't deceive me,
Oh, never leave me.
How can you treat a poor mai-den so.

Then a coaxing male voice, guttural with subdued passion, urged, "Then treat her to a soft Sleepwell mattress pliant with inviting kapok and yet resilient with supplicating springs that will give her the night of her dreams."

Pause.

"—with her knight in armor."

So popular was the song that it had been for some time now a regular feature of the Community Singing every Thursday at the Town Hall.

Now Mrs. Dick, strutting in on stilt heels, said to him, "Now, darling, cup your mouth as if you're calling out to the whole mob 'Coo-ee, Mum's made Cream of Oats.'"

"Come on," Mrs. Dick encouraged, "call out to me, darling, come on, coo-ee, coo-ee." Several photographs were taken, his position was changed, then several more. Then lights were put out and he was told he could get dressed again.

In her office, Mrs. Dick was on the phone, but she motioned him to stay by thrusting out her hand and taking hold of his, which she continued to hold, possessively. Finally, hanging up, she said, "We'll look at the pictures and see. Phone number?"

"I don't have a phone."

"Don't have a phone and want modeling jobs?"

"I'm sorry."

"Come in next Monday then, Seaton." The horse nostrils widened in a somewhat disturbing manner; there was in it the suggestion of privacy as if she were experiencing some deep orgasmic pleasure.

"You sweet thing," she said to him. She almost neighed. But the following Monday Mrs. Dick was totally businesslike in burnt orange jersey. "You're too old, darling, you're not for Cream of Oats, in the proofs you look your twenty." She put down her pen and put on heavy black horn-rimmed glasses.

"Why do you want to do this anyway? I mean, where's it going to get you?" Betty Jollivet had asked the same thing a week or so ago but more gently.

"Oh well, something for the time being."

"You ought to be thinking about the future, Seaton. Posing for ads is for queers and milksops and their careers are over in ten minutes, *I* know. I hire and fire them. What do you want to *do?*"

"Well," he hated to tell this, "I'd like to write."

"What, write what?"

"Plays, perhaps."

She took off her glasses and sucked at the frames.

"Do you think you could write advertising copy?"

There was an opening at B. H. Lowe's for a junior copy writer. She would try him out; she would start him off on Monday as assistant to Miss Frewn; she had rescued him from the dead sea of inertia. She now took him by the hand to Miss Frewn. "This darling boy will work with you, Blanche, on the Parler d'Amour account and whatever else you think he might be useful in. You *can* type, can't you?" The salary was three pounds fifteen a week; he could scarcely believe it was happening. Not yet enough to enable him and Essie to move away from the humiliation of Arncliffe but a first step.

For nearly eighteen months, ever since Mr. Lemoyne had reluctantly closed up shop when the library had reached a rock-bottom membership of eleven, he had drifted, perpetually postponing any real decision until, he hoped vainly, it would materialize and activate him. By nature he was indeterminate in a contrived rebellion against his mother who had marched at the head of her widows and who had been a born *provocateuse,* the little soldier woman who had unintentionally created in him a mild dispensation to stay neutral. He had been a night waiter at the Grantham flats, where luncheon and dinner were provided on skimpy menus to mostly elderly widows who actually donned evening dress and were torn nightly over the choice of oxtail or mulligatawny soup, who addressed him as "dear." He had picked up a little coin by appearing as an extra in two local films out at the Cinesound Studios in Bondi and in the second one had opened a taxi door for the American actress Helen Twelvetrees who, encountering a dullish patch in Hollywood, had consented reluctantly to do a "quickie" in Sydney. He and Essie had been to see the film eight times. He had sold magazine subscriptions to a periodical about artesian wells but that had petered out. Patently none of this was leading anywhere and worse, he seemed not to have the energy to dispel the doldrums. He needed a catalyst and in Camilla Dick he had struck oil.

"Too flowery," Camilla said about his first try at copy for the perfume Parler d'Amour. "We gave up April and spring rain years ago. And too many words. Do you know what the classic advertising slogan was? 'It's moments like these you need Minties.' "

She frowned, the nostrils diminished.

"Say one word that denotes perfume to you."

He thought.

"Dab."

"Not bad. 'A dab of Parler d'Amour and you will be drenched in romance.' It won't do but keep on. Smile, sweet one, you look so dour."

He smiled directly at her.

"That's my boy."

Sometimes he didn't see Camilla for days on end; at times she went to Melbourne or Brisbane for talks with clients. She would stop him in the hall by gripping his hand and then, holding on to it, would ask him one or two questions about work. After he had been at the agency three weeks she cornered him one evening as he was leaving and said, "What are you doing Thursday, are you free for dinner?"

Word had reached him that invitations from Mrs. Dick were command performances.

"I'd love—"

"My house. Seven. Not dress. Brenda will give you the address."

Rose Bay. Ultrastylish, newly built in what was then called "moderne," adamant orange brick with rounded corners and identified only as "51" intertwined in verdigris copper. The lobby and stairs were carpeted in the new fashionable rust. A card under lit glass read "Flat 2; Milton Dick."

The gentleman who opened the door was a shock. Seaton had fully anticipated a handsome husband as tall and wide as Camilla herself, probably square-jawed, with teeth gripping a pipe, athletic shoulders moving under glen plaid, abundant dark wavy hair—the man in the Stonewall Tobacco ads. This short apologetic-mannered little man's pinkish baby hair, almost gone, receded from his baby face in shame, and his anxious-to-please eyes swam over a rosebud mouth. He was wearing, astonishingly, a frilly pink apron over shirt and trousers and had on beautifully embroidered velvet slippers. "I'm Mill," he said, "and of course you're Seaton, and I know you, not because you're the last but because you're so *you.*"

There was absolutely no denying the implication.

Beyond, in the open circular drawing room, all white and chrome, surf splashed up against a picture window as four people turned to see who had arrived, then resumed conversation as Camilla rode toward him like one of the Valkyries, soaring in a clinging cream housegown that left no doubt there was nothing under it, so enticing were the rounded folds and so spectacular was the cleavage. She seemed burnished.

"Sweet one," she said and took him firmly by the arm. It was rather like being arrested, she was so compulsory. He was introduced to Theda, Rat, and Grenville. The men rose and shook hands; they were both carefully groomed and dressed as though to emphasize an eccentricity. Rat Ratcliffe was thin and tall and wore gold-rimmed glasses, giving him the look of a peeled banana with spectacles. He was, Camilla interpolated, fashion photographer for *Vogue* and *Woman,* who had made famous beauties out of Margaret Vyner and Jean Black. He was so smooth-skinned and adolescent-looking that he might still have been twenty-eight but was probably nearly forty. He gripped Seaton's hand in a vise. Grenville Baker was fat and iridescent with a permanently infuriated red face. There was no mistaking the gender or lack of it in both the men. Theda Rasmusson was introduced as an Icelandic communist recently back from the Soviet Union but curiously, hung as she was with bogus jewelry, great blobs of colored glass, and metal flowers that covered her front, she looked like a deposed czarina. Her fiercely dyed red hair was coiled into a crown above her little simian face. She had been in the midst of expounding on the "inside" reasons for the abdication of King Edward of England. The dubious Mrs. Simpson, it appeared, had been corraled by Prime Minister Stanley Baldwin in order to lure the doltish king from the throne because of secret knowledge of his incapability to produce an heir, his being sterile. It had even been hinted, Theda was saying, that the now Duke of Windsor might have been duped by an extremely clever female impersonator and was now either too ashamed or too beguiled to reveal it.

"My dear," Rat Ratcliffe said, "I danced with the boy who had danced with the boy who had danced with the Prince of Wales," and everyone, including Camilla, laughed.

Seaton was handed a drink by Mill called Dead Man's Chest, a rum concoction mixed with God knew what exotic herbs, possibly an aphrodisiac. The first swallow caused tears to brim in his eyes and was so peppery that he gasped for breath but amazingly in a second or two this was assuaged by a sense of warm rapture, an enlargement of the psyche and a sense of hyperbole; everyone was larger and hugely compatible, especially Camilla in her cream robe, handing out Angels on Horseback, creamy mushrooms and sharp pepperoni. He made a pretense of room for her when she sat down next to him on an ottoman not large enough for two.

"Thanks for coming, dear one," she said.

"Cheers," he said and winked daringly at her.

"Dinner," Mill said from the door.

They sat down to an impeccable table of crystal and silver where banks of sweet peas lay between white candles in glass bells and where Mill served them exquisite whitebait nestled in parsley on white dishes as thin as membranes. Seated on Camilla's right, Seaton was privy to her sharp little remonstrances to her husband in asides like "butter knives" or "carver" while he said sorry, darling, right away, dear, frisked in and out. The chef, he did not join them for dinner. Duck was served orgiastically and sweet yams in some ambrosial sauce. "Wine," Camilla hissed and a dark burgundy was poured into the glasses. "To us," Camilla said to the table but looked sideways directly at Seaton.

But was Camilla an outright fool or merely desperate that she had chosen these ersatz men as husband and friends with her eyes wide open? So what did it mean? She was too intelligent to be duped.

"My dear," Rat Ratcliffe was saying to her, "Yousekevitch is to dance with the de Basil when they come. Aren't you gooseflesh?" Camilla admitted graciously that she was gooseflesh and that she had seats. Once or twice Seaton could almost have thought that Camilla's knee pressing against his was not accidental.

Mill served them pears in a brandy sauce, then aquavit. After which, being chef, his duties over, he vanished for the remainder of the evening as though he'd been put into a velvet-lined drawer with the rest of the silver. Camilla served them courvoisier and they played a game that they called Botticelli in which you had to guess the identity of a famous person in twenty questions and at which Camilla was extraordinarily sly and quick to guess people who ranged from Nietzsche to Betty Grable and the novelist Susan Ertz. Some of the famous people Seaton had never heard of and he limped along behind the others partly in ignorance and partly because the booze had taken over and he realized his thickened tongue could hardly get around the words and that, inanely, he could scarcely keep from smiling vacantly. He clung to the arms of a tubular chair and nursed his glass of courvoisier, nodding and smirking and from time to time letting out a stifled agreement. "Zright." "Assobolutely."

The light seemed to be dazzling and the center of the light

was Camilla, all white, and she seemed to come and go in and out of his eccentric vision and once she focused for a moment and apparently asked, "Are you all right?" "Puffectly," he replied, smiling, and reached out for her hand and missed and nearly toppled from the chair. But later, clouded, but in one of those instants when the alcohol seemed to clear away for some seconds and he heard Rat Ratcliffe say in his opinion that tonight Camilla was a poem, Seaton with a dreadful dignity was able to rise from the chair and, raising his glass, he said involuntarily and without slurring, "But she could only have been written with a golden pen."

And so Camilla, sitting next to him, grabbed his hand and in the enormous strength of her need, pressed it until he all but cried out in pain that she had surely crushed one or two small bones. Shortly (or perhaps a long time after, there was no time) the evening ended and he saw that he was being put into a cab and that nice Rat Ratcliffe was seeing him all the way home and that he was protesting that he was all right and that no one must come all the way to Arncliffe in the middle of the night, but when he was called upon to find Waratah Street in the dark he could not comply and they drove around aimlessly nearly all the way to Kogarah before he eventually saw them pass the Acme picture theater. Fortunately Essie had gone to bed because the little brick house was turning around and around and he sat down suddenly on the hall floor and could not stop laughing.

The following day he said that the food had been unusually rich and had caused him a slight bilious attack and that that was the reason for his drawn look and the purple circles under his eyes. He tapped on Camilla's office door and tried to apologize but she was on the phone and merely waved.

"Nobody noticed," was all she said later, brushing past his excuses in the hall.

But a month passed before the significant invitation. She said, light as a feather, "Care to come with me to Spindles for a weekend?" Spindles was the hotel symbolized on posters by a gigantic girl in a red bathing suit raising a glass and enticing eyes to a gigantic boy and jutting her breasts over the legend which read, "Life begins at Spindles, where the mountains begin." The fact was the Blue Mountains actually *did* begin just beyond Emu Plains, but the heavy-going jocularity and tiresome *double entendres* Spindles always evoked centered on the fact that one got off the train at Rooty Hill and the irony of it was that the crude joke passed over the heads of the very people who had not had "a good root" for ages, if ever. Funnily enough, his spinster cousin knew about Spindles. Essie sat down by him at the kitchen table, wiping and wiping a pan, always a sign of agitation. Wipe, wipe.

"You know, I worry a bit about you going to that hotel, Spindles. Do you know it has a certain reputation of being—" she hesitated—"fast. Fast people go there. Not always married and so forth."

"Oh, I know, only it's business for Camilla. The agency handles their advertising."

Wiping and wiping.

"Is this lady's husband going too?"

He hadn't asked. Just consented. He supposed Mill was going.

"Of course. I expect so."

"I hope so. You know, don't you, you've grown into quite a handsome boy."

"Oh now—"

"You have, Beanie, and some of these middle-aged ladies have no shame when it comes to nice-looking boys, whether they're married or not."

His answer to that was balls! No, not in any way physically could he remotely be called good-looking, it was one of his problems, his wretched big nose and his too babyish red mouth. His hair tended to be kinky moreover, even though, thanks to Byron, he no longer used pomade.

"Well, anyway, it's only for two nights," he said.

Surprising himself, he splurged and bought a sports jacket on sale at Gowings Men's Store. It was a Scotch plaid, or so they told him, black, green, and pale yellow tartan; the clan was unknown but he looked and felt opulent in it. The material was coarse and it had hard boxy shoulders that lent him a muscularity.

But was he buying it to please Camilla or himself? A vague feeling of apprehension was beginning to gnaw at him and it increased when on Saturday morning he found Mill Dick loading suitcases into a little blue roadster parked in front of the flat with its hood rolled down. Mill, in his velvet slippers and wearing a cotton housecoat, was certainly not dressed for the road.

"Here you are, my dear," Mill said and took his battered suitcase and put it in the backseat with Camilla's luggage just as she came out of the house carrying an attaché case and dressed in stunning tailored white slacks and a loose pink shirt. So they were going alone, just as Essie had prognosticated. Camilla was giving Mill orders about remembering if her secretary phoned to remind her about the florist and if Brisbane phoned to say that she was in a Saturday conference that would likely go on all Sunday but she would be back in the office on Monday at noon.

"Toodeloo," Mill said as they got into the narrow front seat together. He waved to them as Camilla drove rapidly up onto the footpath and then nearly into a privet hedge while turning the car around in the small square.

She drove as though they were escaping from a besieged town and scarcely even glanced at Seaton. In the glaring sun and with her heavy almost white hair, bent over the wheel, she looked like the figurehead of some proud sailing ship. She drove very fast and, like everything she did, with extreme competence, never saying a word. But when they were slowed down by Saturday morning traffic near Strathfield, she took hold of his hand in her titan grip and said, "Well, here you are," as though she had been surprised at his turning up. Her nostrils widened perceptibly. Suburbs of endless brick villas flew by until, thinning out, they became paddocks and gum trees and they rushed through the small town of Penrith and just beyond Emu Plains the mountains appeared momentously and the air seemed suddenly fresh in their faces as they began the gradual ascent and came to a billboard on which a huge pink hand with a phallic finger pointing upward read HAPPINESS IS JUST AHEAD AT SPINDLES. Turning corkscrew bends onward and upward, they came to stone gates and over the tops of pines Spindles appeared in pink stucco ramparts.

Green canvas blinds hooding front windows and balconies gave the hotel a slightly leering look of half-closed eyes. In the lobby, a first glimpse of Camilla sent the desk clerks into a bobbing dance of delight and displays of servitude: the manager came forward to take her hand, bell boys were sent scurrying for the luggage. Camilla took it all as merely her due; she was coolly gracious and knew everyone by their first name. Hello Arthur, hello there Gordon, she said, smiling. Somewhat to Seaton's relief their rooms were a long corridor apart, the hotel being extremely heavily booked this weekend. "But," the manager was saying with the suggestion, Seaton thought, of a smirk, "I'm sure you will be able to manage."

If loose carryings-on were the staple of Spindles, one wouldn't have guessed so by the looks of the people who passed by them going up the stairs and in the corridors. They seemed banal or else were cunningly disguised in golf clothes and walking shoes or by carrying tennis rackets.

At her bedroom door, Camilla stopped and began to unzip a briefcase and said to him in a hurried offhand manner, "Look, can you entertain yourself for a while? I have a complete new presentation to do for the Ipana people by Monday and it's going to take me most of the day. I'll see you in the bar about a quarter to six." She made a kissing moue at him and closed the door.

He lunched alone in the immense dining room and was stared at condescendingly by the guests who had been here over a week and knew the names of all the waitresses. After lunch he strolled around the seemingly endless paths that led nowhere in particular but had inviting benches along the way half-concealed by shrubbery and which must, after dark, provide trysting nooks. He lay on his bed and read, or tried to concentrate on a lifeless novel. The afternoon wore on in eternity. From outside came the whack of a ball from the tennis courts. He dozed a while and awoke to find it still was not yet four o'clock. At five o'clock he took a lukewarm bath and shaved and dressed carefully, putting on the new sports jacket. In daylight the tartan could almost be heard; he had been duped by the poor light in the store because the shrieking black-and-yellow plaid was right off the back of a vaudeville slapstick comic. But he winced at the thought of dining with Camilla ("the ladies *dress* Saturday nights, as you know," the manager had said) in his old navy blue blazer, which was shiny in the back with age and slightly raveled around the sleeves. He decided he would brave it out and walked brazen-faced and blazing in the coat of many colors into the bar where upon showing your room key and declaring that you had driven for more than thirty miles, you would be allowed alcohol after six o'clock under the strict blue laws of New South Wales.

Camilla's dress was a song of dark passion-fruit-and-green chiffon, so subtly blended into dreamlike flowers and ferns that she looked as though she were emerging naked from under leaves like the Primavera. She had moved the part in her yellow hair from the middle to the side and had pinned it back with a black ribbon and she had tinted her eyelids a greenish mauve. Her nostrils were exalted. When he stood up to greet her, she was an inch and a half taller in her stilt heels.

They had two gin slings each and she preceded him into the dining room. Camilla didn't just lead, she left behind her a wake on an ocean. She appeared to be unaware of being followed and yet the organization of her procedure was as apparent as if she had been leading a white horse. Heads turned in the dining room at the approach of this Brunhilde and the tinselly dressed little girlfriends (if such were the case) of the businessmen betrayed their anxiety by clutching at menus because there was no surpassing Camilla Dick.

He had begun to notice that outside of B. H. Lowe and work there was perilously little to talk about with Camilla. Either she appeared bored by any topic he raised or else she had never read anything in a newspaper other than the advertising. At times she seemed almost blissful in ignorance; it was as though she might not yet have heard of Adolf Hitler.

She seemed preoccupied, perhaps with the exploitation of toothpaste, which was predominant in her mind as they ambled through the five-course dinner, smiling a quick thoughtless smile at him from time to time as though she could not quite remember who he was. But just as they were finishing their savory of burned cheese on toast the sound of music from the distant ballroom seemed to revive her. "Oh, let's dance," she said.

Acres, it seemed, of burnished wood stretched ahead of them under orange-colored fake crystal chandeliers. No one had yet got up to dance and the floor was a terrifying vacancy, looked on by what seemed to be hundreds of contemptuous critics seated in the little pink-and-gold chairs around the walls as the "Mountain Jazz Cats," a small band, pounded out late hits.

He hadn't revealed to her the fact that he had never danced. As they stood up, he put the wrong arm around her but she calmly corrected him and immediately took the lead. As in everything she did, she led with an utter confidence and precision that made it seem as though he were leading her, ludicrous as they must somehow look, Seaton in his shrieking jacket (all she had said about him was "You certainly look startling, darling") and Camilla a good inch and a half taller. But she insinuated otherwise and cleverly turned him this way and that, gazing down at him with a wholly devoted look of complete surrender while holding him in an iron grip of possession, and it occurred to him that she probably would control the sexual act in the same manner, ravishing the man but appearing utterly submissive in doing so, and as gradually their bodies merged in the rhythm under her direction so did they appear to be in a physical rapture, and then to his embarrassment she began to croon softly in his ear, in a little-girl voice. "I'm a dreamer, aren't we all?" she confessed to him lovingly and that she didn't want to walk without him, baby, and that she wanted him to stay the way he looked tonight. Her hand gripped his so fiercely that it hurt and from time to time in his anguish he was forced to smile happily at passing couples (the floor, thank God, was now bustling with couples all intent on their own transposition of sex to inoffensiveness) and to applaud the band between numbers. In the little breaks he glanced hopefully at the chairs around the walls, but Camilla stood impatiently and tapped her foot, waiting for the band to begin again and immediately took him again into her embrace. On and on they danced, around and around the dance floor, his aching back, his hands and feet wet with exertion, they circled and circled. Ceaselessly she crooned; she must have learned the lyric of every song ever written in America and the little voice had a plaintive note in it, a nuance of weeping that didn't go with her momentous self-will. It was almost midnight before, to his exultant ears and mutilated feet, the band stomped away at "God Save the King" and the orange lights dimmed.

At the door of her room, Camilla bent slightly and, caressing him with one arm, said, "Just give me five minutes and then tap on the door. I've got some Johnnie Walker scotch."

Now then.

Well, it had to be faced, there was no escaping into any fantasy he may have clung to that nothing more was expected of him than companionship. But for what was she preparing that would only take five minutes? The thought of terrifying (to him) unknown precautionary measures? The memory of reading in some novel that the heroine had anointed her breasts prior to the lovemaking with some fragrant unguent. Is that what she might be doing? A vision of Camilla's orgiastic breasts arose in Technicolor and he sat down on his bed, actually quaking. There could not be the slightest doubt in Camilla's mind of his virginity, but neither was there any doubt that she could handle the situation with her inevitable command and with the teacher's rod in hand (an unfortunate simile at which he almost had the courage to smile). But in actuality, what would happen? What would *she* do while he undressed? Watch? Read a magazine? Would she comment perhaps with joy, perhaps with disappointment, on the dimensions of his precious part? Who would get into bed first? Would he be chided if he put out the light, thus curtailing her enjoyment of watching the performance? What if? What if he were totally unable to perform? He knew that women could and sometimes did falsify the joy of consummation, pretending the climax (it looked to him like white flowers bursting open), but God pity the poor male member unable to rise to the occasion.

He sat for five, ten, fifteen minutes and then, taking off the loud jacket and his tie, prepared for the execution, walked in dragging steps along the corridor to the electric chair and knocked more softly than his heart was beating.

She was in a snow white negligee and barefoot and held open the door. On the dressing table was scotch, glasses, and a siphon; sandwiches lay under a discreet napkin.

Impossibility blacked out the room, screened her out.

"Look—" he said, gulping. "I'm suddenly all in, just beat. Look, I'm awfully sorry, Camilla, but I can hardly keep my eyes open so if you'll excu—"

"I *see*," she said.

The slam of the door must have shaken the whole corridor and been heard in every room; the violence of it nearly knocked him over. Certainly the middle-aged man and blonde who might be posing as his daughter glanced curiously at him in passing. But without shame he fell into a deep dreamless sleep the moment he got into bed.

Jittery nevertheless in the morning, he faced the prospect of breakfast with her either in icy silence or taut with mountainous hurt feelings. Passing through the lobby on his way to the dining room, he was summoned to the desk where he was handed a small package addressed simply to "Mr. S. Daly."

Wrapped in tissue paper was a golden fountain pen from Proud's Jewelers. What on earth? Then he remembered. His drunken exaltation at her dinner party. "But she could only have been written with a golden pen." On the crushed plain white card she had written in her bold executive handwriting, "From a fool who thought you loved her."

He held the pen in his hand for a long time, then turned to the desk and inquired. Was she already down to breakfast, then? Mrs. Dick had checked out at seven that morning. The clerks were busy, could hardly spend time commiserating with this twitchy-faced boy. What? Yes, she took her car. Anything they could do? He stood there stunned for a moment or two and then, realizing his plight, asked at what time he could get a train. Being Sunday, he was told, there was no train to Sydney until four-thirty-five in the afternoon. The courtesy charabanc would take him down to the Rooty Hill Railway station.

"What about the bill?" he asked. Had he been left with it? There was no bill; Mrs. Dick and companions were guests of the management, *always*, he was told with some coolness.

The never-ending Sunday limped by. The little smoky train stopped at every tinpot station between Rooty Hill and Central. Essie, who never bothered with tablecloths when eating alone, was at the bare kitchen table having some loathsome "brawn" trembling on lettuce.

"You're home *early*, Beanie. What happened?"

Her innocence of him was paralyzing when he thought about it. There was nowhere to begin; he would have had to explain everything to her in absolutes—just what he was—she might never have heard of such a thing; it would have taxed her credibility.

"Mr. and Mrs. Dick had to leave earlier than expected," he lied.

"Was it a nice place? Did you have a good time? Did you wear your lovely new jacket?"

He might as well have said that there was something about him she didn't know; he was partly merman. Had a fish tail.

On Monday morning at B. H. Lowe's, jittery, he sat at his desk until Blanche Frewn (who was known behind her back as Bruce; she wore a shirt and tie and had been caught in the ladies' room passionately kissing Miss Lynch, the telephone operator) said to him, "Camilla wants to see you at half-past ten, Seaton."

Her demeanor indicated it boded no good.

When he tapped on Camilla's open door, she said to the secretary, "Brenda, stay outside for a few minutes and tell Eileen I'm not taking any phone calls."

"Sit down, Seaton," she said. She was all in battleship gray silk this morning, subdued. There was no light in her. She took up a paper from her desk and read it in silence for a long time and then glanced at him without any expression.

"What do you have to say to me?" she finally asked.

"Just—I'm awfully sorry, Camilla. I truly am."

He placed the gold fountain pen on the desk.

"I can't take this," he said. "I don't deserve it."

"Oh, I think that you do, *thoroughly* deserve it. Use it to write your excuses to gullible women."

So they stared at each other. Was she taking part of the blame for her own gullibility?

"What *I* find hard to excuse are your flimsy, piffling excuses. 'I'm suddenly so tired, all in.' " She pulled faces, imitating him. "You insult me with lies like that. Cowardly queers make me sick. If you had an iota of pride you would have said, 'I don't go to bed with women.' "

She was breathing heavily now.

"I made a mistake with you, I admit it. You haven't the dignity to admit yours." She picked up the steel letter opener and stabbed at the blotting paper. "Another thing. I've noticed the way you look at my husband. I've seen the little contemptuous way you look at Milly."

"I have never—knowingly—"

"Contemptuous, and I very much resent it and your superficial judgment of a fine person. My husband is one of the finest human beings it has ever been my pride to know. Just because he may have somewhat of a little epicene manner you take for granted he's one of your fellow travelers, just because he happens to call people 'my dear.' Because he's the cook and runs my house for me, you have the affrontery to look at him scornfully when *you* are the one who ought to be ashamed—"

"Camilla, I swear to you—"

"My husband is, as it happens, ten times the man you are. What do you know about it? How dare you assume? Do you happen to know about a time in my life once when I was very young, when I was so down and out and persecuted by certain things that had occurred that I was ready to kill myself? When I was waiting tables in a filthy little fish restaurant on a side street in Bondi where the chaps used to try to slip their hands up my dress and where they'd be waiting for me in the lane outside to *expose* themselves to me and call out loathesome invitations to me, night after night? You know who came and stuck by me and gave me hope and some dignity? Milly Dick. And who dragged me out of there and changed my name and gave me a new personality and some hope for the future and got me with help from *men friends* started in advertising—"

She stabbed at the blotting paper, threw down the dagger. "Why go on, it isn't worth losing my temper over." Her nostrils were dark holes now with enjoyment.

"Yes, why go on? Your work here has been unsatisfactory. I'm letting you go as of Friday. You'll be paid two weeks salary in lieu of notice. That's all, Seaton."

"I *see*," she had said when she slammed the door at the hotel.

"I *see*," he said, slamming his door on her now for her incompetence to deal with the situation in any other but this conventional manner. It was a lowering of her; he had expected a subtler, darker outrage. There was something about her reproach that implied dishonesty, not so much the facts but the manner in which she presented them; it was facile and it occurred to him that this speech of hers about Mill had been made before, possibly several times, and that her husband had often been made a victim for her to defend against someone who had angered her, almost as if he were kept in a clothes closet for this purpose. In order to maintain a semblance of his ruined self-esteem Seaton had left the gold fountain pen on her desk.

To his relief, Camilla had taken off for Melbourne the following day and was still away when on Friday he collected his two weeks' salary and formal notice of dismissal. Surprisingly, Blanche "Bruce" Frewn handed him a slip of paper as he was cleaning out his desk and said, "Here, Seaton. You might try these folks about a job in radio."

It was the address of something called Jobjoy Productions at Station 2XY. "Job and Joy Parry," Blanche explained. "Do you listen to them much? They're the heart and soul of the radio trashland nightly."

"Oh, thank you very much, Blanche."

"It wasn't I who thought of it."

"Oh, who then?"

"I was merely handed this address and told to tell you. I'm sorry to see you go, Seaton." Blanche sighed and ran a thin hand through her boy-cut hair. "But I'm getting accustomed to the firings around here."

He wondered how many others had been given a gold pen in exchange for their dismissal by Mrs. Dick.

On the following Monday he rode up to Station 2XY in a gilt cage and was shown across yards of strawberry carpeting to a door gilded with the title JOBJOY PRODUCTIONS. Miss Maxwell, in charge of a long room of typists banging away at deafening Standard Royals, asked him what it was in connection with? As he was beginning to explain, a woman in black satin with screeching hennaed hair came out of an office holding scripts. She wore several diamond rings the size of wrens' eggs and as she went past there was a gust of strong perfume as if from an exhaust pipe.

And what name? Miss Maxwell asked.

He said his name and the redheaded woman turned around and said, "Oh, I've been expecting *you*, come on into my office."

She was, it turned out, the Joy of Jobjoy and the star of "Breakfast with Job and Joy" each morning at nine o'clock. She riffled through papers on her desk and found a note. "I'm an old pal of Camilla Dick's," she said. "She's written to me about you. She says you're a most promising writer. We can do with a couple of promising writers."

He took the note she was holding out, but it was blurred with his sudden blinding incomprehension. Was this the final merciless kindness of Camilla? So that was it! Her retaliation was to kill him with forgiveness. Mrs. Parry was waiting.

"Nice of Camilla," he said flatly.

"Have you had any experience writing for radio?" Her fingers glittered with the potential of him. Let her speak to Job about it, they would probably try him out. She sounded encouraging, she saw him out to the left, she seemed a "jolly good sort," as they were called. An ex-chorine, she still maintained a dancer's walk.

Months after he had been installed as an assistant writer for Jobjoy, he was passing through Her Majesty's Arcade into Market Street. Camilla stepped off the escalator in front of him and they confronted each other speechlessly until she said, pleasantly, "Hello, you sweet thing," and with her strength pushed him up against a show window of bridal photographs and kissed him very firmly and wetly on the mouth. Then she whirled away in the crowd and was gone. He never saw her again.

"For Rat, with much affection,
Otto Kruger"

SEATON was so drenched in the downpour that had been going on all day that when Rat Ratcliffe opened the door, Rat said, "My dear, you look like a little salmon swimming upstream to breed." Though the invitation had read that it was to be a small dinner party, nobody else had yet arrived at the once splendid Victorian house in Yarmouth Road. It was some time before Rat conceded that the small dinner party was to consist of "just us." Seaton was dried off and told to leave his wet raincoat in the bathroom. Passing through Rat's bedroom with the outsize double bed in maroon burlap, he was drawn to the phalanx of photographs framed and hung around the gilded angels on the headboard of male Hollywood movie stars, some whose careers had faded like the photographs themselves, the standard studio portraits that usually were sent in reply to fan letters, but these, incredibly, were all inscribed in wildly diverse handwritings with loving salutations to Rat. Thus Ronald Colman had scrawled, "To my dear dear friend, Rat." Warner Baxter had asserted he was Rat's "best pal." Expansively, Otto Kruger had confessed to "much affection." But was it possible to accept Conrad Nagel's affirmation of being "yours forever"?

Possibly the limits of credulity had been stretched to the utmost when Mr. Gable had merely slashed the word "Clark" across his chest. The little duplicity was made the sadder by the mere fact that it had been intended to deceive. Even harder was it to reconcile with Rat's almost perpetually bright and often witty personality. "What a darling you are to have come through the flood tonight. I would have phoned to let you off the hook but cunningly you are not phonable and besides I was being self-indulgent."

Perfect drinks were served in Waterford crystal, the fire bubbled in the hearth, scattered around on the coffee table were fairly recent copies of *Harper's Bazaar* and *The New Yorker*. Great trouble had been taken with delicate hors d'oeuvres and the arrangements of flowers in the room; wine had been set to breathe on the table, candles lit, and Ravel's *"Alborada del gracioso"* put on the record player. But the most perfect of all was Rat's performance of himself, dry, entertaining, changing from one moment to the next in a kaleidoscope of imitations (the Prime Minister's nasal Christmas greetings, Eleanor Roosevelt, Mussolini), and all the time contriving to promote a sense of gracious distance between them, the assurance that no crafty preparations for seduction were under way, no hand was going to be laid on the knee. They sat apart in this gratifying unitedness of two casual friends and gradually Seaton was, with support from several mild gin and tonics, prompted to confide in Rat the full story of Camilla and the disgrace leading to his being fired. Rat's long peeled-banana face stayed placid.

"Got the Spindles treatment, did you?"

It was almost a tradition, then.

"Oh, it was all worked out, my dear, probably from the moment she met you. She has instincts that rarely fail her in that direction. Oh, you're not the first by a long chalk. It's got to be the running joke at her office as to who will be next."

"But why? Why would she humiliate *herself* into the bargain?"

"Oh, it's all part of the lead-up to her eventual redemption through her forgiveness, that's her orgasm. Do try a dab of horseradish with the oysters, they're a tiny bit bland. Didn't she recommend you for this job at 2XY?"

"Oh yes, I was stunned."

"There, you see?"

He couldn't see.

"Unless you know about her mania about people like us, you couldn't see, my pet. She has been on a sort of antiquated anti-queer crusade for years."

Just wait now until he fetched the cream of leek soup.

"But Rat, why?"

"In a nutshell, then, her mum died when she was eight, leaving her with daddy and an older brother, both of whom she adored. One day when she was seventeen, she opened a door. She was not expected. She found her beloved daddy and brother in bed together. See? Well, my dear, when you've caught your father and brother *in flagrante delicto,* shall we say, it makes it awkward for all of you to sit down together in the evening to enjoy egg and bacon pie, so she lit out then and there and went down onto the dark Bondi beach with the first boy she could pick up and they did it eight times. More likely only five, I think, her memory's somewhat epileptic. Anyway, from then on it all became truly tenth-rate Dickens for poor little Sophie Laye, which was her name then, Sophie the Surfer's Delight. She would do it for the price of a meal and a bed at the five-bob-a-night Montana Moon Hotel, which was only two inches up from being a bordello, and for the next year or so her life was something over which, as we say, we draw a veil until, of all people, minty Milton Dick found her working in a fish-and-chips place and took a girlish fancy to her and more or less adopted her and made her over into the lady he would have liked to be, out of the salmon-colored ankle-strap shoes and satin dresses. She learned *tout de suite,* my dear, and blossomed into the lovely Medusa we know today. It took years, but as the song goes, look at her now. Or, you might call it out of the frying pan into the *pan*sies. Wait a sec, now, while I frisk up the mint sauce for the lamb."

So, that was Camilla, but write her story with a golden pen.

When it came time to leave, Seaton blustered with polite remonstrances about Rat's getting into yellow oilskins to see him to the tram. Nonsense, dear boy, the bird's-eyes twinkled behind the gold-rimmed glasses perched on the beak nose, but there was about Rat the glinting triumph of having maintained once again the architecture of celibacy. Or had he retired from any meanderings years ago when he was still young? Had the lone life been mandated? He seemed purposely without obligation.

So they went out into the weeping night, Rat holding the umbrella, to the tram stop, not trying to speak against the wind and rain. The tram bore down on them through the torrents more like a lighted juggernaut, the conductor hanging on for dear life to the narrow footboard, his whistle in his mouth.

"—such a lovely even—"

"Get on, dear boy. Good night, dear boy."

Got the little sliding doors open and inside he was the only person on the tram save one man in a compartment further down. The conductor, under his streaming waterproof hat and oilskins, was young and somewhat dark-skinned, good-looking. After he had presented Seaton with the dampened ticket he went off along the narrow footboard of the swaying juggernaut and was seen to take refuge inside one of the forward compartments.

"Fez, pleez."

Seaton had turned to say he already had—

The beaked face at the door was streaming with rain or tears; the yellow slicker ran water.

"Rat."

"Fez, pleese."

"Rat, get in, you'll fall off, be killed—"

"I love you."

"Rat—"

"I love you with all my heart. Just want to know, is there any hope?"

"Rat—"

"Is there a smidgen? Even a smidge of hope for me?"

"Rat, if you'd get *in* and sit down—"

"No, it's written all over your face, darling, there's not the slightest hope. There never is. Well, on with the daaaance—"

The last was singing, skipping. Still hanging on to the tram as it slowed to a stop, Rat sprang off and vanished into the pitch black wet. The tram stopped, someone got on, the tram started again.

But how could one have lied? Said what? I love you? The poor long banana face, the streaming spectacles, all out of a comic film. But ugly, ugly, he knew the fact was the good-looking tram conductor any time, even soaking wet and smelling dreadfully of soaked oilskins, he would rather embrace, hug him than have Rat touch—

Thus began a train of dismal thinking (trudging up to Central Station for the Arncliffe train) about the unsuccessful men, the middle-aged and un-good-looking who had never found anyone. They were somewhat like the unsuccessful girls, the plain unwanted girls, the secretaries and office workers who went around in bunches and had Friday dinners together, bought theater tickets in groups and giggled a lot, pretending gaiety, the synthetic men were like them except that they dared not form in groups publicly.

But suppose the gradual attenuation was one's own fault? Suppose one never felt the transmutation? Fell? Imagine the poverty of never finding. The waiting and waiting.

And suppose no one ever came?

"This ancient joy of union"

*I*T READ, the embossed card, that Mr. and Mrs. Walter B. Jollivet requested the pleasure of his company to celebrate the twenty-first birthday of their daughter, Elizabeth Ann, on Saturday, the twenty-ninth of November, at seven P.M. at Romano's Restaurant. Dancing from nine till midnight. Black tie. It happened in Farmer's Men's Ready-to-Wear department. He went to buy the dinner jacket ("But Beanie," Essie had said, mouth pursing in dismay, "think of the expense and you'll probably never wear it again." But he had the money. She still couldn't get it through her head, he now earned five *pounds* a week and next year would get *seven* at Jobjoy Productions plus a small royalty from sales to New Zealand.)

Tidal changes had occurred because of "Fairyfish," because of the illness of Morris Rice (née Rosenquist) who was head writer. Could you, asked Joy Parry, do you think, manage the fairy tales while Morry's away?

Up until now Seaton had not been unequivocally successful. Two hoped-for long-run radio serials of his had not been renewed after the first fifty-two episodes. He had faltered between providing continuous cliff-hanging melodrama and awkwardness in dealing with transcribed emotions, indeed, emotion of any kind embarrassed him on paper, coupled with the crippling restraints of Australian censorship, which forbade even the word "damn" on the air, and which resulted in such circumlocutions as aghast characters having to say, "My goodness, Monica's hanged herself."

Liberated from the strictures of having to bring real people to life in "real-life" situations, Seaton took to creating for the children like the fish themselves took to water. "Fairyfish," which aired at six in the evening, was the saga of two children (played, of course, by Job and Joy) who are condemned in some rigmarole now long forgotten (the serial was in its fourth year and its age was showing) to spend a life underwater with the sea creatures, Neptune, Starfish, Whelk, Flora the Femme Fatale Flounder, and MOP, short for Queen Mother of Pearl. Poor Morris Rice, saddled also with the seven o'clock and nine o'clock shows to say nothing of the "Famous Murder Trials" at ten and "Breakfast with Job and Joy" at nine the following morning, had allowed "Fairyfish" to, in his own words, *flounder.* Seaton, overjoyed at being underwater, took to reviving it, introducing such new characters as the Artful Codger and Poor Anemic Anemone. Best of all was Crafty Alice in the Fairy Palace (also played by Joy to save money), whose machinations undid everyone and who, contrary to traditional fairy tales, inevitably came out on top, laughing.

To everyone's amazement, the "Fairyfish" ratings shot up.

Mostly because, for fun, Seaton had lately interpolated little caricatures of pompous bureaucratic members of Parliament, lampooning the latest bungling in Canberra so that last week's headline became part of the "Fairyfish" underworld. The show had begun to attract an adult audience in such a mass that Station 2XY, confronted with unexpected mail, some singing praise, some indignant, in an unprecedented decision moved the serial from six to seven in the evening. What had become lost to the juvenile listeners became grist to the grown-ups. A housewife in the dairy section of the grocery had been overheard by Seaton to say that, my dear, she was caught, captured nightly by the darn fish fairies and could not even start the dinner until it was over.

There had been another significant move: away from glum

Arncliffe to stately Cremorne across the harbor. With his new affluence came independence even though Essie's mouth cried poor (she was now indigenous to Arncliffe, prone to lean on fences talking to the neighbors, comforted to learn they too had been scandalously overcharged for beef or liver) and she was heard to say on the last day, "Oh, my poor little string beans are just coming out, too. Who'll look after them?"

To move at all in suburban Australia was epochal; people lived in the same house for sixty years. Often one of the children took it over, and kept up the same hydrangeas.

"Shifting to *Creem*orne, I hear," people said to Essie, half-admonishing. Something to do with that writer chappie, he put on airs, that Seaton. And wasn't there something a bit—you know—about him? The smiles they gave him were mixed with disapproval underneath thin-lipped kindly tolerance.

Sometimes it was not so kindly. Slipping on wet pavement outside the Ace Ham & Beef, he danced a couple of steps to stop from falling and two beefy louts behind him sniggered, and one said, "Watch out in those high heels, sweetheart."

There must be somewhere on earth where oddity went unremarked. Where one could be totally one's self without the knowing looks and the winks. He had a secret plan: he was going to move much further than to Boyle Street, Cremorne; he was going to America. Some day, some how. Fly away home, it sounded like home.

There, in a big city like Chicago or New York, one could disappear into the maw of a huge heterogeneousness. Be enveloped into a secret haven. Rat said (he knew some American "friends") there were areas of acceptance in the United States. In New York there were bars and even some restaurants that catered to such outcasts as they and very often, he had been told, there were sprinklings of handsome businessmen at these bars, even married men, hoping to meet a sympathetic stranger. Seaton saw them in his dreams, the handsome men motioning him to a bar stool, confiding.

"Just think," Rat said, "of the Statue of Liberty and that

thing she's brandishing, the biggest phallus on earth, my dear."

While Arncliffe had been working-class (" 'ow are yer, lovey?"), Cremorne was genteel ("how joo doo"). It was also afflicted with a leukemia of standardized virtue. Whenever he had the chance and the occasional invitation Seaton revived mentally and spiritually in Darling Point at the Jollivets. Every so often they had a late Sunday afternoon soiree with music, ending in a cool delightful supper of crab or lobster in the garden under paper lanterns and here mixed together the bonbons of Sydney society, the magazine editors and book authors, critics and lecturers on philosophy, a dean or two, and just people who were warm and witty and not overanxious. There was nothing stultifying about it, no bores or social climbers were permitted. Mrs. Jollivet, a tiny round woman with a large bosom and a larger heart, who never under any circumstance other than being in the shower or in church was without a lighted cigarette, took charge with little breathless asides of pleasantries and concern for one's welfare ("You're not dreadfully bored, are you? Have you had any of the fish mousse?"). Betty's father, florid, the golfer, president of a shipping line, monarch of all he could survey, was on first sight intimidating but later found to have Quite a Sense of Yumor. Prudence, the older girl, starting law school with an eventual judgeship in mind, often came down off her high horse and was even heard occasionally to tell a risqué joke. But shedding her light on everyone, gravely sweet, transparently lovely (not *pretty*, Seaton would insist, *lovely*), never aggressive, never the least sentimental, was Betty. To catch sight of Betty in pale green under the yellowing poplar was to catch the breath, to lift the heart.

"*There* you are," she said, without smiling.

"I was waiting over there, I saw you were with Hugh Lavery."

"I noticed you. I sent him to get me a drink I didn't much want. I hope he got waylaid."

"How dear of you."

"Nonsense, I needed to get rid of him."

"But you noticed me over there."

"I always notice you. Here comes Hugh back. Give me your arm and let's walk slowly away, laughing intimately."

"Like so?"

"Like so, ha-ha. What have you been doing? Writing your silly head off? You haven't kissed me."

"How remiss."

He went to Farmer's to buy the dinner jacket for her coming-of-age party.

"Can I help you?" One of the solemn attendants came forward, the others stood around like ushers at a funeral; it seemed to be a slow morning in the Men's Ready-to-Wear department.

"I'd like to look at a dinner jacket."

"Yes, if you'll step this way."

Would he care to see the new double-breasted style, perhaps the California-type white American "tuxedo" jacket, which was becoming more and more popular for summer evenings? He said, curtly, feeling the inferiority that enveloped him in clothing stores, that he would prefer something just black and formal.

"Formal, yes sir. Would that be a thirty-eight?"

A dress suit was fetched from a rack.

"This way, if you please, sir."

He was tall, this young assistant, with eyes that looked directly at Seaton with deep seriousness, but there was, around the mouth, a suggestion of some merriment that might at any moment break out with ease into laughter. "Oh, Mr. Long," another sales clerk approached, flustered, "do you know if any further two-button cheviots came in last week?" So he was Mr. Long. Mr. Long answered that the cheviots had arrived. Compared to the other gentlemen-in-waiting, Mr. Long was an eagle among a flurry of pouter pigeons, in their bored affected poses, brushing imaginary lint, gazing at fingernails; there didn't seem to be a man among them except this giant.

When Seaton was dressed in the evening suit, Mr. Long came into the fitting room with a tape measure and chalk and proceeded to fit the jacket with accomplished hands. It was pleasant, being administered to by Mr. Long's large soothing hands. He hitched shoulders here, loosened waist there. "Do you know," Mr. Long asked pleasantly, "that you have one hip slightly lower than the other?" "Would you mind telling me," Mr. Long gave a small chuckle over such a personal question, "on which side you prefer to dress?"

When it was done and Seaton was re-dressed in his day clothes, Mr. Long took the twenty-five guineas from him briskly and made out the slip, whipping the carbon paper, and asked whether they should send the suit when it was ready; Seaton said no, that he would pick it up himself, he only had to step across the street from the State Theater Building where 2XY was located. He could not admit even to himself that he wanted to see Mr. Long again.

"Shall we say Friday?"

Once or twice he thought about Mr. Long, once waking in the dead of night to the pleasantness of it.

But then again there was nothing further to be said except thank you so much when he took hold of the cardboard box on Friday and nothing more for Mr. Long to say except to assure him that any deficiency in the suit could easily be taken care of.

So then by what mysterious restraint and why did he dawdle through the men's shoe department, look at sport shirts and ties, wasting time and his lunch hour? What incalculable timing or hand of fate could have brought him to the UP lift at the same moment as Mr. Long, both of them scanning the floor indicator with intensity?

"So we meet again."

"So it seems."

"Going up," said the disgruntled lady lift operator. She was surreptitiously eating a banana concealed in one gloved hand.

"Roof garden," Mr. Long said.

Seaton said nothing. All the people in the lift stared up at the floor indicator. They were offered ladies' lingerie, kitchen utensils, leather, and china before being let off at the roof garden restaurant.

"Two?" The hostess approached them and they turned to each other.

"Well—"

"Um—I—" then, taking the bull by the horns, Seaton asked, "do you mind?"

They were shown haughtily to a table under a striped umbrella. Pansies and impatiens thrived in tubs. It was blustery. They mimed being glued with interest to the skimpy menus. Nothing was said for the longest time.

Seaton finally spoke. "I didn't know this was up here."

"They don't like us using it and keeping tables from the customers," Mr. Long said. "We have our own cafeteria in the basement, but they strain the food through linoleum." He laughed heartily at his own bon mot. He had nice square white teeth. "I'll have the salmon pie," he told the waitress. "The garden salad," Seaton said. So here they were, trapped. They stared in opposite directions and the wind blew over the salt shaker.

"Is it bad luck if it's only the wind?" Mr. Long asked.

"Aha, probably not, but just the same." They pinched a little salt over their shoulders. How ridiculous it was. Here they were, total strangers who might never again see each other in this life and Seaton fumbling with a fork and smiling vacuously while his heart was beating idiotically fast. Then Mr. Long, no longer waiting on a customer, behaved with sense and asked directly what Seaton did.

"Do?"

"You said you work at 2XY across the street."

So he explained.

"No kidding. You write that fish thing? My sister listens to that every evening." Mr. Long emphasized that he did not, thought it too silly for words. But no, it was because it was on at the same time they gave the sports results and scores on another station, so he and his sister had separate radios.

Not aggressively but emphatically Mr. Long underlined that masculinity, that taking for granted that everyone is hot for the latest cricket score and whichever favorite football team is onto a winning streak. He carved into his salmon pie with gusto. He had been, he said modestly, swimming champ at high school and later for a while a beach lifeguard at Clovelly, where his father was manager of the local Commonwealth Bank branch, but then his father had been "shifted" to Glebe where they now lived, not near a beach. He sounded offended about losing the beach. Glebe sounded lugubrious. Seaton saw rows of old gray stone houses and damp gardens.

"I sing a bit," Mr. Long said, startlingly. There was a crumb of salmon on his upper lip. Yes, he was a baritone in the St. Barnabas choir and this coming Christmas they were to do "The Messiah" with the Sydney Symphony at the Town Hall. They were already rehearsing it.

"How great."

"I like it."

"Would you want to make it a career?"

He hadn't thought about it. He wrinkled his forehead as if it might not have occurred to him ever to get out of men's ready-to-wear. "Too hard making a living," he said. "You're lucky to be doing something you like." He brushed away the salmon. "I'll have the pineapple whip," he told the waitress. About the same time as she brought the bill, Seaton had reached the point of explaining that he lived with his cousin, that his mother had died when he was a small child.

"So did mine."

For a single second they were linked in coincidence. They fumbled for change for the tip and suddenly, surprisingly, Mr. Long shot out a long arm and said, "Name's Athol."

They shook hands.

"Ethel?"

"*Ath*ol."

"Oh, pardon *me*."

Mr. Long laughed, hugely. It was a deep baritone laugh. "What's yours?" he asked.

"Seaton."

"That's an unusual name."

"My mother's maiden name."

"So is mine."

So they again had something in common. Heavens, they were still shaking hands and hastily withdrew themselves from each other and got up from the table with a show of mannish sporty grins.

On the main floor, as they got out of the lift, Seaton said, grasping the nettle, "Look, um, perhaps one of these evenings we might grab a sandwich and go to a five o'clock flick."

"I don't get off till six."

"Well, an eight o'clock, then, if you felt like it, if you'd like to see a movie, perhaps."

"Maybe so."

"Well, then, it was nice, I enjoyed it. So long, Athol."

"Hooroo, Seaton."

Athol went off on a lifeguard-on-the-sands swinging lope; it was masculine enough to be almost suspect.

Barely able to postpone it as long as the following week, Seaton bought two reserved seats in the loge at the Regent for Saturday night. Except for live theater (at seventeen shillings and sixpence on a Saturday night for a revival of *The Desert Song*) nothing could be more prestigious than the loge for the movies and at the Regent to boot, with, at the eight o'clock show, the stage extravaganza with symphony orchestra and mighty Wurlitzer organ, plus newsreel, travelogue, and "Coming Attractions." In this guileless liquorless (after six P.M.) age of antipodean primness it was as sophisticated as one could get, it was almost a declaration of love.

"I wonder," he said to Mr. Long in the men's department, which was putting it mildly; he wondered at his audacity. Was by any mad chance Athol not doing anything tomorrow, Saturday evening, because at the last minute he had been let down by "this girl" and so had two tickets to see *The Awful Truth* with Irene Dunne and Cary Grant at the Regent. Just so as not to waste them now that "Edna" had the summer flu.

Athol nodded, indifferent. He might like that, yes. Okay, he said. Agog, Seaton suggested early dinner first at the Toby Tavern, perhaps? But no, Athol said, his sister always cooked the roast "of a Saturday evening" so they could have it cold after church on Sunday. "Meet you at the Regent," Athol said. He had to go, he had a customer waiting.

Seaton bathed and dressed as if he were David for Bathsheba. Changed his tie four times.

"I have a suspicion," Essie said, twinkling, "you have a date with Wattletree."

He flushed, turned away. Wattletree was her unfortunate code word for The Girl. Some day The Girl would be brought to meet her. Lovely as a wattletree in early spring, all yellow fuzz. "When am I going to meet Wattletree?" she would ask, deliriously inaccurate, willfully misled.

"Just a chap I know."

For all her cooking, washing, ironing, mending, caring, she was given deception in return. But there was no breaking out of his chrysalis, not ever. "Don't wait up," he said and they kissed the air near each other.

Athol, wearing a heather-colored sports jacket with an open shirt and neckerchief, insinuated calm beside Seaton's too anxious business suit and tie. He took the pipe from his mouth and they shook hands. Athol was seen to have a fine neck and, surprisingly, as always, to reassemble his good looks. Cheshire cat–like, he faded from memory on parting, leaving only his smile.

He laughed throughout the movie, crossing and recrossing his long legs and on the way out he said severely, "I liked that. Now what I hate are these sappy love pictures, they give me the pip. Like Margaret Sullavan, she's always dying of something. Notice? She's always outside in the snow in an evening dress, dying. No wonder she has that hoarse voice. I can't stand her kind of picture."

The Constantinople Café was packed with the after-pictures crowd (and oh, the evening was going so fast). A frantic waitress threw down a celluloid menu. "I'll be with you soon as I can, we're going mad tonight. There's no more of the prune whip."

Perhaps there was nothing to it. Seaton became glum. Nothing, just an artificial flash of light; they were strangers with not a thing in common. Athol was looking away toward a raucous table of all girls, trying overanxiously to manufacture conviviality. Perhaps they were as hopeless as the girls were, all prettied up on a Saturday night for what? To go to their homes alone on the late trams. But after he and Athol had had their orangeade sundaes (and Athol had twice looked at his watch) Athol produced a small leather diary and pencil and asked abruptly, "Sea, what's your phone number at home?" He had to admit, shamefully, that he didn't have one. "But you can always reach me during the day at 2XY." Sea. No one had ever called him that and he liked it. Sea. The yellow paper lamps, which cast a jaundiced light on the bogus minarets and tiled walls of the ghastly Constantinople, were suddenly seductive, the rowdy girls at the next table were lovely dryads, not hopeless; they all had dates later with affectionate and attentive beaux.

"What's *yours* at home?"

"UJ2892."

He wrote it on a paper napkin.

"As it happens I'm going to get a phone put in because the office wants me to."

Athol was muttering something. What? "The noise in this place would drive you balmy."

He didn't offer to pay his half of the bill, which was six shillings for the orangeades and a stale eclair each. And when they parted outside on George Street, he merely saluted stiffly and said, "Enjoyed it, chum," and strode off.

Not that one needed to be thanked extravagantly and, perhaps, who knew, the treat might be reciprocated. But instinctively he considered what must be accepted. Athol was a taker not a giver. One surmised from the imperial gait walking away that he was a born taker.

But "Sea."

And being the sea, he floated, he flowed down into dingy

Wynyard Station underground. Here in the dirty gray atmosphere of brownish lights and sleepy people climbing on and off the arriving and leaving trams, there was a disintegration of dreams. And, he thought, severely, better not to raise any castles in the air, at least not yet. One syllable of his name spoken jocularly was hardly enough to build a sparrow's nest.

Nevertheless, in the rich early morning, turning in the bed to find each other with, as always, the exaltation of it, Athol said, "There's something I haven't told you," laying his hand gently on Sea's bare chest and—

But the bedroom door opened a slit.

"Porridge," Essie announced as Athol turned into the pillow. But in the daydreams, he was fiercely edited. No flowery amorousness, no sweet talk, and Athol in dreams never said, "I love you," but half-said things as though their understanding of each other was so proportioned that it needed no explication.

In reality, which was difficult to adjust to after the dreams, nothing happened. No telephone call came. There was no earthly reason to cross Market Street and go into Farmer's. As the days wore on, Seaton became morose, betrayed anxiety by hurrying to pick up the phone only to hear the wrong voice.

Then leaving one evening, crossing the lobby to the lifts, he saw that someone with a pipe was sitting behind a newspaper on the scarlet tubular "art-moderne" sofa and Athol put down the evening *Sun* and said, "Hello, young nipper."

"Hello." Seaton could hardly speak.

"Thought you might care for a beer on the way home. I got off early tonight."

Gathering himself together to face the real thing, Seaton asked, "But why are you sitting out here? Why didn't you ask for me?"

"I don't know whether you'll be offended, chum, but, are you ready for this? I couldn't remember your last name."

"Oh. But if you'd asked the girl at reception for the chap who writes 'Fairyfish' you'd have got me."

"You'll have to excuse me, but I couldn't remember the

name of the damn show either. Well, how about it, we've got half
an hour before they turn off the beer at six o'clock. Is the Marble
Bar OK?"

They were swept with secretaries into the down lift. "By the
way, what *is* your other name?"

"Daly."

"OK."

From a glass case in the gilded lift, the faces of Ronald
Colman and Jane Wyatt were turned in transparent adoration to
each other against creamy mountains. *Lost Horizon*, it was pro-
claimed, was coming to the State Theater.

"We ought to see that," Athol said.

We.

From outside the Marble Bar in the Hotel Australia, the
noise of men penetrated into the lobby and, pushing open the
glass-frosted door, it erupted into cacophany as they came into
the long, narrow marble-floored bar where the only women were
the barmaids, frantic with the last twenty minutes of dealing with
more than a hundred males clustered two or three deep at the bar
already awash in beer suds. The noise of male voices lifted in
coarse revelry was all-encompassing, like the sudden swirl of malt
odor that assaulted the nostrils. Under the haze of blue cigarette
smoke, dozens of gray felt hats were pushed back on sweating
foreheads, and blue serge jackets were unbuttoned over potbel-
lied waistcoats. Maleness permeated like the smell of a stable.
Men leaned on the bar, men lounged against the wall, men struck
a peculiar stance, legs apart on stiffened thighs, impersonating the
stag, the stallion, raising the heavy glass steins of Resche's ale or
KB Lager, the dark reddish-brown brew, the nectar of the common man, the flecks of foam on the lips, the cigarette burning
down to the fingers and then trodden out on the wet beery floor,
the voices raised in a chorale of masculine braggadocio. Here in
this Edenic charnel house where no female ever dare set foot was
the territory of the cocks and the rams, where freed from the
chains of decorum, Struth, a man could fucking well talk like a
man, and act like one, with his cobbers, strut, sweat, spit, swear,

get matey, line up the beers while keeping a wary eye on the clock, good on yer, Joe, good on yer, mate, give us four more, Vi love, lay out half a dozen Dulcy, and did you hear the one about the sheila who got the boy into trouble because her slip was showing? Aw, but you're fuckin' mad, Cessnock had the wrong team that game. Look out, Snow, you're dropping ash in my bloody Pilsener. Christ, I've got to take a leak, keep your eye on my drink, will you? Good on you, Blue. Are youse leaving, Ned? Hooray but.

He and Athol stood side by side on the periphery and were silent, mostly because to yell in order to be heard required there being something to say and there was the hollow feeling of estrangement he always felt in men's bars as if he had something showing to his disadvantage amongst the herd, no matter how he copied stances, legs butchly astride, quaffing down the bitter draft, brushing away the soapy foam on the back of his hand, like the other blokes, ready for a slap on the back, a dirty joke with the chaps. There was always the truth, bitter as lager, that he was out of his depth here, didn't belong.

And Athol did. Athol belonged with the men, stood easily now, one elbow on the marble bar, stein in hand, smiling slightly above his cleft chin. The fact was strikingly evident that Athol was as straight and unvarnished as a weathered barn door, as square as a perfect rectangle and innocent, and so why bother, either of them, with this preposterous proposition of friendship? If he were to be wise now, Seaton knew, the thing to do would be to put down his beer, glance at the clock on the wall, and simply say, hell, chum, I've got to dash or I'll miss the six o'clock ferry, well, so long, pal, see you around.

But neither of them moved, held together by some immovable aloneness and yet unable to reach out to each other, Seaton knowing that just the shadow of a wrong move could bring on catastrophe, just the well-meaning hand on the arm or the knee at the inappropriate moment could betray the lie of friendship, and it would cost more than thirty pieces of silver for the fatal kiss. And yet Athol, unaware, was shouting, "Give us two more,

Vi, when you've got a moment, will you?"

On the dot of six, the voice of God announces, "Time, gentlemen. Drink up, chaps, come on fellers." The barmaids begin swabbing down the urine-colored wetness, lights are turned down. But the boys can drink up the extras so no one leaves, the voices become louder and more aggressive; convivial little arguments break out into pretended fisticuffs, the line to the downstairs "dunny" extends all the way upstairs, and they're singing out, "Hurry it up you bludgers, piss on with it youse bastards."

Then in the gradually diminishing room, he caught sight of the tall man. Leaning against the wall near him, thin as tin, gaunt, the sun of years burned into the deep-lined flesh of the face, unshaven under the wide-brimmed dirty hat, a jackeroo perhaps, boundary rider from out west probably, cattle or sheep country, the ultimate in manhood, the shearer, maybe, who, drunk, would knock your head off in the country pub over a slight disagreement because his type lives in action not words, the epitome of raw, brazen, outdoor paddocks Australia. For a few moments their eyes met and then, shockingly, unbelievably, the boundary rider winked at him, surreptitiously winked, and the wink was as daring as nudity in the street, concupiscent and inviting. The wink as good as said, come on over here a minute, cobber, and I'll give you the sweetest feel of your darling little arse. Perhaps riotous imagination had taken him by surprise, the rigidity of acting his part in this male kingdom had befuddled his eyesight. But at that moment the boundary rider winked again, secretly. No doubt about it. Seaton's heart beat with the terrible admixture of aversion and, ashamedly, thrill. To be acknowledged secretly by such a protagonist of manhood was both horrifying and rapturous. He turned his back and later when he glanced around again, the boundary rider had gone.

"Shall we?"

He was still disencumbering himself from the excitement the wink had aroused, suddenly conscious of two diametrically different desires, one sacred and one profane.

"If you're ready."

They went out across the black-and-white marble lobby where the carefully dressed girls awaited tardy swains and down the steps into Castlreagh Street where he expected Athol would have an excuse for leaving, having done his polite bit, paid for the beers.

"How about a bite of something?" Athol said.

"Scotch though, only if we halve it."

"OK. Where shall we go?"

"Do you know Jacob's Room?"

"Where's that?"

"Right across the street in Victoria Arcade."

Handily. Rat Ratcliffe had introduced him to it; writers and actors went there. Since that night of rain and declared passion on a tram, Rat and he had subsided into what had always been the sweet bane of Rat's existence, a continuing friendship.

Jacob's Room, small and subdued, was maintained by two English sisters, the Misses Edith and Loraine Swansea, who had cultivated persons engaged in "the arts" as they put it, smiling demurely at their clients, one behind the cash register and the other as hostess, both gowned in faded and dowdy prints. A portrait of Virginia Woolf hung on one wall. Miss Edith greeted them ceremoniously.

"Well, Mr. Daly."

"Good evening, Miss Edith."

"What a pleasure."

"This is Mr. Long."

"Over by the window?" Pale wilting roses drooped from a blue vase onto the tablecloth; the mauve ink handwritten menu was smudged. The sisters Swansea did their best, but always there were traces of amateurishness about everything that lent a forlorn charm to the little run-down place. The regulars didn't mind. If, for instance, you were a novelist who had not had a book published since 1925, you were nourished by the proximity to another neglected writer, and across from you might be Trixie La Verne who had been the star of *Sunny* back in 1927 but who now had no place to sing, poor love, except on the Show Boat ferry. So who cared if the chicken consommé was watery?

"It's Englishy fare," Seaton explained. "Roast beef or lamb and mint sauce kind of thing. Trifle."

"I like it," was all Athol said. "Who's that on the wall?"

"Virginia Woolf, who wrote the book."

"Which book?"

"*Jacob's Room.*"

"Oh."

Quite clearly he had not yet heard of Virginia Woolf. At first it was boneless conversation and because of having the place nearly to themselves they talked in low tones as though they might be conspirators, as well one of them might be. Athol held forth about swimming and diving championships, Seaton about books, and they both strove to be interested and smiled excessively, but slowly the strictures of forced cordiality seemed to melt into a firmer sense of their being united in some understanding of each other that had been ratified. It was as if both of them had realized it at the very same moment the elderly waitress brought out the plum duff, and over coffee, Seaton was only partly astonished when he suddenly laid his hand on Athol's sleeve and said, out of the blue, something he had never said to anyone in his life: "When I was little, I was ashamed of my mother."

Athol did not withdraw his arm.

"I've never told that to anyone, but it's true, I was terribly ashamed of my mum."

"But why?"

So forgotten little Hope Seaton Daly, poor thing, was roused from the grave and dressed again in her Southern Cross flag skirt and Union Jack blouse and again she and the WAIFs marched to the tune of "Little Soldier Woman" as Seaton, carried on the flux of his astonishment at his long-repressed grudge against her, let it forth, and outside the dim window in the crepuscular stone arcade the lorn ghosts of the women came marching with Seaton at their head in his mother's costume,

Seaton waving, saluting, marching to the band, and then, momentarily stupefied by the emotion he had brought on himself and feeling the scalding tears behind his eyes, he this time had no precaution in laying a hand on Athol's knee as he said, "Sorry about all this, truly I am."

"No, don't be sorry, old chap," Athol said and ignored the hand on his knee but also graciously accepted it, man to man. "Don't be one bit sorry, Sea."

"When I was about four I turned to Essie, that's my cousin, who had brought me to see the march, and I said to her, 'Oh I wish—' and Essie said, 'Wish what, darling?' and I said, 'I wish she *wasn't.*' And you see, Athol, I wished that all the rest of her life. I just wished she *wasn't* and then, my God, one day she wasn't."

There was quite a long silence and then Athol said, "Let's have some more coffee."

Then as if they were in the same boat, on the same ocean, Athol frowned and said, "My mum died when I was eight, but I remember that she wasn't there a lot of the time, *there* but not there, if you understand."

"Yes, I do."

So gathered together in the mystery of it, they both looked away into a long distance, the wasteland where no questions are answered, and gradually came back to the reality of an empty café and of Miss Edith pulling down the blind on the door.

"I've had a good time, Sea," Athol said, and they shook hands outside in the stone mustiness of the ancient Victoria Arcade. Although it was still five weeks to Christmas, the card that came to Station 2XY two days later was embellished with holly and pictured a giant kangaroo wearing a Santa's hat and which read with unabashed jollity, "HOPPING You have a very HOPPY XMAS and New Year." Underneath, in what might be described as conventional high school calligraphy, was written, "Dear Sea, hoping the New Year will bring you happiness and cement even firmer our good friendship, Athol."

So how was it, Miss Maxwell asked, coming in to take

dictation on "Fairyfish," how was it Mr. Daly seemed so perked up, had he perhaps won the New South Wales State Lottery first prize? Oh no, my dear, Mr. Daly said, smiling, much more. Never mind, now, where were we? At lunch he bought a card bearing only a Christmas wreath and wrote inside it, "And HOW, Sea."

Although he had not seen or heard from Athol in the intervening week before the Saturday of Betty Jollivet's twenty-first birthday party, his glow like a suntan had not faded, and in the noise of revelry in Romano's ballroom and svelte as hell, he thought, in his new dinner jacket as he and Betty danced to "How Deep Is the Ocean," she asked him about it. "Something's happened to you."

"Yes."

"Can I know about it?"

They danced on for a minute while he thought about the danger and the temptation of confiding.

"I'll tell you one day."

Because how might she take it?

"Can't I know now? I'd tell *you* everything."

He nearly said that's because everything you do is aboveboard. How lucky she was, born smiling at the daintiness of life, lucky her. But then she had been prescribed right by the two loving progenitors looking on now with devotion; she had been the perfect result of a diagram made with great care and probably had known of it as a fetus and grown according to its architectural plan and would maintain her continued being in perfect accord with expectations. She had already completed her education with just the right amount of expected disappointment due girls of her status so as not to obligate her to an unnatural and unpopular intellectualism, and at just the right age she would accept just the right young man, Hugh Lavery of the Dalgetty Laverys or Peter Quentin of the Broken Hill Proprietary Quentins and be married in St. Andrews Cathedral with accompaniment of choir. She was the natural child of her natural parents, and naturally, she was perfect.

"But I adore you," he said into her ear, cradling her.

"I know," she said. "That's what's so sad."

He knew that if he had told her about Athol she would have accepted it as she did everything, without criticism. So why hadn't he? Here she had been in her pumpkin-colored dress at the approximate height of his heart and willing to take him just as he was into her everlasting comfort and he had demurred. Some misintegrated gene had interfered with his freedom just as it interfered with his physical desire of her even when, tacitly, she had many times in her generous serious way implied that he might have her; she had said half-jokingly, "You know I'm all yours" in reply to something superficial he had asked her. So now, refusing her again, he led her back to her table where her indulgent mother asked, "Oh Seaton, are you having a good time, dear? Have you had some of the birthday cake?"

So, inconsistent because of the genetic weakness he was unable to confide in the person he loved, it was possible to confide in someone he didn't. Rat had promised immediately to meet him ("Of course, my dear, I'm all ears") at the National Art Gallery where obviously they could talk privately, unobserved on a bright Sunday afternoon when everyone in his right senses would be at the beach or the golf course.

In a poorly attended wing where only a uniformed guard stultified with boredom might have overheard them, surrounded by fourth-rate Victorian paintings of woodland scenes desolate enough to dampen the spirit, they sat on a green leather bench and Seaton confided in Rat who, wearing a little porkpie hat and blinking behind his spectacles, looked for all the world like a kindly lady librarian.

"Well, darling, I don't know what to advise you," Rat said at last. "I'd be the last person in the world that *I'd* turn to for advice to the lovelorn. God knows whatever I said would be the wrong thing to do. Just look at my record. But"—Rat hesitated—"if you're so sure he's straight, then you have only two choices. You risk everything and tell him and possibly have your face smashed in."

"He's not the violent type."

"Or at the very least he'll get that deeply embarrassed look as if you had told him you have syphilis and you'll get the cold marble hand good-bye, or else you don't ever tell him and you continue to live indefinitely in a kind of unrealistic twilight where nothing ever happens and you are forced to watch him go waltzing off with girls while you must sit and wait and wait for a crumb of love to come your way, which it never will. Believe me, I've gone through it, suffered through some hopeless affairs, even when I was your age and, if you'll forgive me, not as comical-looking as I am now. Darling, you've asked me, so I'll tell you, there's nothing in it for you and there never will be, and if you'll take Auntie Rat's advice, you'll break free of him now and end it. Listen, my dear, there are manly gentlemen one might never suspect being one of us and somewhere, sometime there'll be a manly gentleman waiting for you."

"Thank you, Rat."

Seaton was careful not to say that he honestly agreed, which he did, low-heartedly.

Coming out into the clear December sunshine, they saw, as if it had been arranged for them, a tableau by a fountain: a young boy and girl were kissing.

"See that?" asked Rat. "That is what is known as real life. We are the dream."

Of course Rat was right. The thing to do was to end it.

Instead he went directly to the Town Hall and booked a seat for the next Thursday evening performance of "The Messiah." All that was left was the right-hand balcony where one was forced to look directly to the right for the whole performance, which occasioned a crick in one's neck.

When the combined choirs of St. Barnabas and the North Shore Chapel filed in under amber lights in their white surplices, Seaton was able to pick out Athol almost immediately among the baritones to the right of the podium. The choirs bowed and sat and the Sydney Symphony Orchestra appeared and last the soloists and Maestro Eugene Willmart, who took bows. The house-lights lowered and everyone stood for "God Save the King" accompanied by the choir.

Then the oratorio began and almost immediately Seaton was devoured with a sense of profound participation as though he and the orchestra and the choir were all intermingled to the exclusion of everything else around them and that sound and harmony were in a confluence with his breathing, so when during the "Hallelujah Chorus" everyone rose to their feet, the combination of the music and the scrim it interposed between him and reality was a holy sanction which anointed and purified him. He felt purged and complete; he felt, watching Athol turn the pages of the score, beatified. He was, for the duration of the oratorio, wedded to Athol.

"Hello, old bean."

In the crowded dressing room, everyone de-surplicing, Athol looked surprised, even possibly pleased.

"Thought you were all—great. I'm almost sure I heard *you*."

"You must have exceptional eyesight to be able to see my mouth open."

"Listen, how about some coffee?"

"The only thing is, I've asked this girl."

"Oh, well."

"No, but, Sea, won't you come along?"

"I don't want to crash in."

"Oh, it isn't anything like that."

Wasn't it? The way he took hold of her and introduced her was like a proclamation. "Allie Newton." He caressed her bare arm and grinned down at her.

"Howjewdo."

She gave Seaton a limp handshake. She was small and blonde with an empty cupid face; at this moment, however, she was like a little cross seraph. Someone had taken ten shillings out of her purse in the ladies' dressing room.

"You can bet your bottom it wasn't one of our mob," she said. "There's a couple of girls in the North Shore crowd I wouldn't trust with a tin butter knife in spite of all their la-di-da manners."

"Did you report it?"

"What's the use?"

Outside Athol took her by the elbow and steered her through the crowd as though she were delicate china, guiding her across the street through the traffic as though she were severely impaired, into the uproar and fiendish yellow light of the Constantinople where they were all ladled together into a booth.

Allie Newton looked at the menu crossly and said, fingering Athol's lapel possessively, "Oh, I'm not hungry, choose for me." Then, startlingly, she said she would have an asparagus omelet.

"And a chocolate malt."

Athol lit her cigarette. He seemed entertained by her, he sat with his arm around the back of her seat. Seaton just sat. For a while Allie Newton and Athol discussed the performance: here a soprano had faltered, there a bass had come in a second early, here the tempo had dragged, here accelerated too fast. Part of the blame, they agreed as Allie Newton sipped her chocolate malt, lay with the choirmaster.

"They ought to get rid of Arch," Allie said. Seaton was titillated to observe that she now had a chocolate mustache.

"Oh, Arch isn't so bad, he knows his music, Al."

"He's growing moss on himself. And you know, don't you"—Allie blew cigarette smoke from her chocolate-rimmed mouth—"he's a poofter."

Only the Aussies could have devised such an apt and terrible word for it and Seaton was almost sure, looking quickly down at his clenched hands, that Allie Newton had directed it at him.

"No kidding."

"I have it on good authority he was nabbed in Lyme Park in the men's for making a pass at a plainclothes cop."

"No kidding."

"And furthermore it cost him five hundred quid to get out of it. Old Arch is a poofter. You know, don't you, he made a pass at Kevin Bradley, you know, that basso?"

"Did Kevin tell you?"

"Not directly but Marjorie Wetland-Smith told me Kevin had warned Don Duckworth about Arch."

Now she dug, having done her best to implicate, into her omelet.

The coffee tasted of bitter vetch; Seaton allowed it to get cold. He smiled and smiled.

At last, Athol halfheartedly said to Allie Newton, "My friend here writes for radio. He writes 'Fairyfish' on XY."

"Oh yes?" Miss Newton turned a blank cupid face, unimpressed. Well, in her opinion, the stuff on the wireless was just too terrible for words. In fact, she thought something ought to be done about it, a committee or something ought to be formed to prevent the wireless stations from continuing to broadcast this rubbish which she personally did not listen to because it simply made her sick. Especially that Job and Joy couple.

"I'll have a Bananacream Bang," Allie Newton said to the waitress as Seaton rose and said, "I have to push off."

"No, no, old bean," Athol said, brushing away the pound note Seaton was offering. "My shout. Awfully glad you came."

"It was nice to meet you," Seaton lied to Allie Newton, who smiled a tight little mean smile.

All the music was gone out of the "Hallelujah Chorus" and "Unto Us a Child Is Born" was broken bottles swinging in the wind. Maybe for the best. Maybe tomorrow he could make up his mind not to see Athol again.

"Old chap, I want to apologize," Athol said on the phone almost as soon as Seaton got into the office the next day. "I want to apologize for Allie Newton. She's a joyless bitch, but until last night I wasn't really aware of it and why so many people in the choir can't stand her. But you see, she's lonely and doesn't know why. Well, I'm sorry we didn't get a chance to say a word to each other. What are you up to Saturday arvo?"

They lay on their backs, their arms outstretched and hands just touching under the shade of a Moreton Bay fig tree in the Botanic Gardens, out of the brazen sun, talked out. They had had lunch at the kiosk in the gardens and talked and talked; talk had erupted from them as if they had been released from a mandated silence and now it had left them as much spent as though they had ravished each other sexually. The talk was, in fact, a substitution for sex. They had, in effect, carnal knowledge now of each other in a more personal sense than of mere flesh because bold admissions had been proffered, lubricated by the warmth that had become significant between them, and a thawing of formality had so melted any guardedness that in the midst of discussing something irrelevant Athol had said suddenly, "I've never had a real friend before. I supposed I just hadn't the flair for it." But I feel it, Athol had said, about *you* and, stunned with the joy, Seaton had said, "And I about you," and had impulsively leaned toward Athol on the grass and taken hold of his hand and Athol had not withdrawn it and so they had lain there on their backs, apart but hand in hand, and minutes had passed as Seaton waited, scarcely breathing, while ships of white cloud passed across the sky, waited for what might come next because there was also a palpitation of divine peril in the heart which flickered like objects in a heat mirage in this physical and mental heat of day, and then Athol withdrew his hand gently and said, "Going to be rain, those are thunderheads."

But at the very moment he said it, Seaton was struck with the idea, struck dumb and electrified with it. He sat up and said, "I've had the maddest idea."

There was soon to be a new character in "Fairyfish," which had been discussed: Mussel Man, a configuration of all the muscle-man types, satyrs, Lotharios that had ever been and who wreaks havoc among the lady fish. "I have the maddest idea, Athol, why don't *you* try out for it."

"Is that how you see me, a Lothario?"

"Not entirely, but you've got the voice for it and, listen, it wouldn't interfere with your job. You're off by six o'clock and it doesn't go on the air until seven, you only have to cross the street. Why not?"

"Do you think they'd have me?"

"Well, you'd have to audition, of course, they'd have to hear you. We could do it on your lunch hour. Listen, nobody need know it's you if you don't want it, and you'd make nice pin money. They pay two guineas an episode."

Athol seemed neither appalled nor elated. He continued to lie on his back and look at clouds piling.

"What do you think?"

"I might have a go at it."

It was somewhat of a letdown, the lack of enthusiasm. Wasn't he aware that conceited amateurs stormed the office every day of the week, begging to be auditioned?

"Well, think about it."

On Monday Seaton broached the subject with Joy Parry, who twisted her diamonds and said, "Oh, we thought of John Saul for the Mussel Man."

"I wish you and Job would just listen to Athol, he has the exact voice for it, a low baritone, sexy, slightly breathy."

"Could he come in tomorrow?"

"Oh *yes*, he's just across the street in Farmer's Men's Ready-to-Wear."

Joy winked, twirled around to the mirror on her dancer's feet, and said, "I've got a feeling there's more to this than meets the eye."

"Not really."

"No? You've gone rather pink, sweetheart." But she laughed indulgently.

When Athol appeared the following noon, he seemed preoccupied. He sat in the hideousness of the art-moderne lobby and read the little scene Seaton had prepared while Seaton fussed around with the engineer in the control room. "One, two, three, four, testing," Seaton said into a mike. He was sweating. Athol looked cool; he was wearing his heather-colored sports jacket.

"We're ready now. Don't be nervous."

"I'm not nervous."

"No, you *aren't*, are you?"

It was as if Athol had done this a thousand times. He read

the scene, with Seaton cueing him, as if it were the stock market report; the voice was slightly hoarse but suitably concupiscent. Seaton went into the listening room where Job and Joy sat in judgment. It was always Joy who spoke for Job.

"Job feels he's a little on the green side but—" they both smiled at their invaluable writer. This time it was Job's turn to wink and turn a blind eye.

"But you can have him if you want him." They rose to go.

"You got it!"

He took hold of the heather lapels in his elation. Finally, generous, Athol smiled eventually.

Athol made his debut on Thursday evening, and Friday morning on the ferry while waiting for the gangplank to be let down, Seaton heard the girl in front of him remark to her pal, " 'Djew listen to 'Fairyfish' last night? That Mussel feller's got me quite a bit gooseflesh-like. I phoned up Frank and said, 'Mum's gone to a church meeting, why don't you come round and bring a couple of Pilseners."

"And did he?"

The rest was lost in an effervescence of giggles.

And later in the month it was reported by Hobart that the audience for "Fairyfish" had risen perceptibly and calls to the station intimated many middle-aged females were entranced with the Mussel Man. One day Joy Parry, twisting into Seaton's office in bold red taffeta, said, "Do you think Athol might be interested in playing the mahout that kidnaps me in 'Jaipur Nights'?"

"You'd have to ask him."

"It'd only mean coming in two nights a week."

Perhaps some sort of career was being fashioned on the behalf of a rich baritone voice and no perceptible acting talent. Athol was said to be thinking it over. It had been proposed that he give up his daytime job and join the Jobjoy Players permanently. Athol remained cautiously indifferent. No word of thanks had ever been voiced. But then Athol was not a thanker.

What was voiced eventually was couched in parenthesis:

"How would you feel about coming out to Glebe Saturday afternoon and meeting my sister?"

"Why, I'd love it."

"Say about three?"

Directions about trams were given in a lifeless manner and then a surprising reservation. "Not if it rains."

"Why not?"

Were they to have tea outside?

Oh well, Athol said, it's a long ride out if it's rotten weather.

Seaton wasn't yet to know that Athol's father never failed to go lawn bowling on fine Saturday afternoons.

Indeed it was a long tram ride out and then quite a walk. The quiet was synonymous with nervous apprehension; it was as if the suburb of Glebe had been devastated by plague and all its population fled on this fine Saturday afternoon when no lawn was being mowed, no person sat on a veranda, no dog barked; all was silence and pulled-down blinds hooding windows. Number sixteen Gallipoli Avenue, adjoining the stalwart red brick Commonwealth Bank, had a funereal air, painted a disheartening ecru. In its shadowy front garden, arum lilies clung close together as if for comfort. Seaton pressed the old-fashioned brass bell and after a few moments a woman's voice asked who was there.

"Seaton."

The door was opened by a reproduction of Athol gone awry, his nose and mouth possessed by disappointed brown eyes under a long bob of dull reddish hair.

"I'm Kay."

"How do."

"Won't you come in?"

There was a smell of desuetude, like the whiff of an old book long unopened, raincoats drooped from a hat stand like shrouds. The high-ceilinged living room was crepuscular and Victorian chairs and an oversized sofa crouched on acres of dark parsley green carpet; one almost expected gaslight. A steel engraving of

Christ in agony at Gethsemane hung on the wall to dispel any intrusion of jollity.

Kay said, "Athol's just come home from the beach and he's taking a quick shower, he'll be along in a tick."

Stranded, they sat opposite each other, he and Kay, and smiled and she picked at her nails nervously. "Found us all right then, did you?"

"No trouble at all."

"That's good."

Kay asked where did he get his ideas in order to keep "Fairy-fish" going and he wasn't sure but said that one just *kept* going and hoped for the best. Did she listen to it regularly?

"Oh, I sneak a listen now and then."

They went back to smiling and she said that the kettle would be boiling in a minute and that she guessed he must be ready for a cuppa and jumped up with relief when Athol came in and the robust tan of his cultivated healthiness enlivened this pale room like the rataplan of drums. He had never looked so prepossessing. He gripped Seaton's hand.

"Found us all right then, did you?"

A distant kettle sounded petulantly. "Give you a hand," Athol said to Kay and they went out, leaving Seaton with Christ. China rattled in the kitchen, the kettle was subdued, and the talk between brother and sister had the lukewarm agreeability of strangers' conversation. "Do you want the milk in this little jug?" "If you wouldn't mind." "Ooops, sorry." "No, my fault." "Can I give you a hand with the traymobile?" "Goodoh, if you wouldn't mind."

The traymobile, loaded with scones and pastries and a large cake iced in aching pink, was being wheeled in squeakily and Seaton was asked did he take milk, sugar? It was moving precipi-tously into a desert of horrendous politeness.

Would you care, they asked each other, for a lamington, (some coconut confection,) or another anchovy paste sandwich? Was it crowded at the beach? Kay asked her brother. Athol laughed, often heartily, at nothing much. Kay inquired of Seaton just how things were these days over in Cremorne. Seaton commented that the sultana bread was the best he had ever tasted. They were unwilling performers in a rite as old and stale as the hills but foisted on them by generations of forced civility. But the air was so cloistered that he could scarcely breathe or think that what was needed was a striking bell of confession to alert them all to reality like his putting down his cup and saying to Kay, "I'm in love with your brother." So he put down his cup and said, "How nice and quiet it is here. You can't hear any traffic."

"No, Glebe's quiet all right."

"Dead quiet," Athol said.

Then, as if abhorring the vacuum, nature interfered in a bolt from the blue. They heard the front door open and close. Light footsteps approached down the hall and Kay and Athol glanced at each other with what seemed to be sudden electricity. They alerted each other to the sounds, soundlessly.

A little man appeared in the door. He was smiling pleasantly, removing a white panama hat, the kind that old gentlemen wore bowling.

"What's this? A little feast? How delightful."

The little man had snow white hair and crinkling blue eyes. He was Dickensian, Mr. Fezziwig in modern dress. He skipped into the room and seated himself, beaming, next to Seaton and held out a miniature hand.

"Good afternoon. I'm the father."

"Seaton Daly. How do you do?"

"What name again?"

"Seaton."

"What an excellent name. And tell me, which one's friend are you? Kay's or Athol's?"

"He's mine," Athol said in all innocence and then added as if in shame, "Sea writes the radio serial I've been working in."

"Indeed?"

Kay had brought another cup, tightlipped, poured tea. "We didn't expect you home so early."

"I expected you didn't, dear, that's why I came. I had accidentally come across a bought cake partly camouflaged by dish cloths on the top shelf of the pantry, and I deduced a guest was imminent."

His smile, little pearly perfect teeth, twinkling eyes, all conspired to present the image of the darling patriarch, the favorite of all grandchildren, the pet. He could have been plucked from one of those Hollywood films in which the cherub grandfather miraculously achieves the solution to all the problems of the young people while burdening them with philosophical claptrap.

"You see, my children are wont to protect me from visitors. By maintaining the fallacy that I am frail and tire easily." The little man laughed at this absurdity. "That is why cakes are secreted and I am palmed off with white lies. Isn't that the reason, Kay?" Kay said in a tired voice, "Yes, Dad."

"Now Dad, we didn't want to get in the way of your bowling," Athol said.

"Have a meringue, father." Kay held out the dish.

"Meringues! You must be a very special guest, Mr. Seaton."

That seraphic smile. But Seaton observed that a tiny blue vein in the old man's forehead was twitching.

Mr. Long shook his head and declined a meringue. He turned his small frame, legs crossed in faultless check trousers, toward Seaton.

"Now tell me about yourself, Mr. Seaton. You write for the radio?"

"Yes sir."

"And you create this clever rigmarole I hear about that Athol has become embroiled in?"

"Well, yes."

"You must understand that at the same time it is on the air we have the overseas news on another station to which I listen with great attention because these are dangerous times. Dangerous times, Mr. Seaton. We have the shadow of a fanatic tyrant menacing our world in Mr. Hitler and so I am forced to forgo the pleasure of your, I am sure, delightful *fairy* concoction."

Athol stirred and said, "Now, Dad—"

"But tell me, what induced you to embroil Athol in it?"

"Well—"

"We had no idea that he had any thespian ambitions. We've never had any such thing in the family before—*alas.*"

What Seaton should have noticed was that the cup held in the thin-veined hands was trembling. But he said, "He has an awfully good rich voice, and we needed someone with the voice to play this Lothario character."

"Very perceptive of you to notice Athol has a Lothario voice. You must be acutely perceptive to observe *any* kind of emotion in him. God knows, I have tried to." But the laugh was devoid of mockery, good-natured. Athol had stood up and was frowning down on Seaton. And still Seaton was not alerted to any obvious peril. Old Mr. Long was now cutting himself a piece of the pink cake. He kept on holding the silver cake slicer like a dagger and smiled innocuously.

He said, "But, tell me, I'm curious, why do you take all this bother with my boy?"

In the silence while Seaton cleared his throat, preparing the pleasant lies, Athol turned away and Kay was slumped gazing at the floor. Somewhere in the hall an old clock whirred and struck. Mr. Long continued to hold onto the cake knife; his smile had petrified on his face. Everyone waited for deliverance.

"I just thought he might like to take it on, more or less."

"More or less, I see. I fancy it was more more than less. I'm a little bewildered as to why, on such short acquaintance, you would need to be so altruistic toward him. God knows, no one else ever has been. Could you enlighten me?"

"Now, Dad, I want you to stop this." Mr. Long waved the cake knife at Athol and leaned nearer Seaton.

"Well, Mr. Seaton?"

"Oh just—he's a friend."

"Just a friend, yes, I daresay he must think you're the best friend he ever had, getting him on the radio with his rich good voice and perhaps out of the men's suits basement, which is what he may have in mind. P'raps I'm wrong, but he's not always a very grateful boy, let me tell you, so what do *you* get out of it?"

"Well—I'm not expecting to *get* anything out of it."

"Only his friendship? You're remarkably easily satisfied. Wouldn't you p'raps have something more in mind?"

Athol said, "Father, I'm giving you one minute to stop this. I'm looking at my watch, Father."

Mr. Long's smile was Lucifer's. Kay had covered her eyes, leaning on an arm as though in prayer.

"I'm only asking an innocent question, Athol. Perhaps Mr. Seaton would feel repaid for all his kindness if he could count on a more, shall we say, permanent situation, would you, Mr. Seaton?"

Seaton, crimson now, reared back into his chair and said, "Perhaps."

"P'raps you and Athol might one of these days get a nice little place together out in one of the more salubrious suburbs like Rose Bay."

"Oh, I don't think—"

"P'raps you might cook him dinner. Have friends in. *Swish* in and out of the kitchen, wear a nice little apron?"

Athol leaned down and grasped Seaton by the collar of his jacket. "Come on, we're leaving."

At the door Athol turned and said toward the white head, "I told you the last time that if anything like this occurred again I would walk straight out of the house. Well, watch me."

Now, suddenly, the tableau was poignant. Mr. Long's little hunched back struck at the heartstrings, his head was lowered as if in pain. Kay, bending over him, was gently taking the cup from his trembling hand.

Outside, Athol said gruffly, "I'll walk you to the tram stop." After a silence, walking, Athol said, "My mum escaped from him by dying. It's the only way."

At the tram stop, in the urine-smelling wooden shed, Seaton had to ask the question. "Did you believe what he said?"

"Of course not," Athol's face was contused. "How could we possibly be friends if I believed *that?*"

An extremity of repulsion was declared at the very thought, so Seaton turned away from it because at the very core of Mr. Long's outrageous insinuation was a crumb of truth, the dream. The dream, wide awake and masturbatory, was of the two of them abroad somewhere and it was unashamedly matrimonial. In the dream flat they had together somewhere in New York, they addressed each other in loving words, my dear, darling, and Athol came home to him. At times it went further. Athol was the leading man in Seaton's play that all New York was acclaiming. It stopped short, for curious reasons, of bed. It always stopped short of bed.

When the city tram lumbered into view he said, "To save your embarrassment I won't say thanks," and Athol managed a grim smile. "Thanks."

When the phone rang in the midst of breakfast two days later, Athol's voice sounded a note of accomplishment.

"It's all over. I'm moving."

"Where to?"

"Found not a bad room, bed-sit. In Greenowe Avenue just off Macleay Street."

"In Kings Cross?" A transcendental move from Glebe, might as well be Paris. The "Cross" was considered sinful by some.

"When are you moving?"

"I got Saturday off. Look, could you give me a hand? Frank's lending me his car."

Who was Frank? These people, casually mentioned, Frank, Amy, whoever, seemed only to materialize in order to do Athol some favor. Oh, Frank lent me his car, I was given the tickets by Amy. Seaton never laid an eye on these people.

Outside the Greenowe Avenue house, a respectable-looking stone mansion with a wildly untidy garden and cats, Athol was unloading a rickety Buick.

"If you could take that basket of books."

He had lovingly kept his *Boys' Own Annual* and *Doctor Dolittle.* In the hall Seaton ran into the landlady, wearing a scarlet housecoat and smoking. "I'm Mrs. Atwater, love, you must be the friend. Mr. Long said he had a friend coming."

"I'm just helping him move in."

"That's all right." Mrs. Atwater smirked. "Feel free and easy with me, love, I much prefer renting to the boys, they're tidier."

The room was a narrow slit and dark; a double bed spread itself almost wall to wall with a candlewick coverlet. There was rush matting on the floor and a long-unused fireplace. Nevertheless this was now home, it was the first place in which, Athol permitting, they could be alone.

After they had carried in suitcases, clothes on hangers, a picture or two, a three-legged stool, and dumbfounding equipment for exercise by rowing, Athol opened two bottles of beer. He stretched out on the bed and Seaton sat in the only armchair.

"Cheerio."

"Mud in."

Athol frowned at the perversity of having to mention any succor.

"It's all due to you."

"In what way?"

"I couldn't have afforded the rent if it hadn't been for 'Fairy-fish' and now getting 'Jaipur Nights.'"

"Oh." Seaton had hoped Athol meant moral support, if one could dare call it moral.

"No, really. The only one I'm sorry about is poor bloody Kay having to cope alone, but she's used to it by now, she's given up her whole bloody life to the old bugger. Come to think of it, Sea, it's been you who's changed *my* whole life-style, all you, old cock, old dear."

Not knowing how long the little ecstasy might last, it might have to last till the next time Athol thought of something sweet to say, Sea said nothing, drank his beer like nectar, and they gazed at each other.

This was as perfect as their kind of reflective happiness could get, surely. In Athol's contented yawn, in the togetherness of silence. But premonition being absent, nothing foretold, warned, no sibyl bent over the clouded glass to say watch out, neither of them could have foreseen that invisible currents were moving more that morning than suitcases. None would have imagined significance in the moment outside when Seaton was seeing Athol off to return the Buick to the mysterious Frank. "Maybe see you this evening," he was murmuring when, over the car's engine, Athol said, "Someone's calling out to you."

"What?"

It was on time. It was exactly the moment for her to enter on this brightest of mornings. There she was, lovely, slightly out of breath from running.

"I *thought* it was you."

Possibly to show off, he embraced her warmly. How good she was, dear, lovable.

"I haven't seen you for eleven weeks," she said.

"Is it that long?"

"Am I a pariah?"

"No, perfect, *per*fect. Wait, wait a minute, Athol, turn off that damned engine, will you?"

Should have let Athol drive off, stupid idiot. "I'm helping a friend move in, what are *you* doing here?"

"I'm going to lunch with Angela MacArthur at the Macleay Regis across the street, and I *thought* I saw you, my darling. How *are* you, my darling?"

"I want you to meet my friend." Athol leaned out of the car, rather stony-faced. "Athol Long, Betty Jollivet."

Betty leaned down, Athol poked a hand toward her, they shook hands. How do you do, they asked each other stiffly, and Athol said to Seaton, "I'll give you a tinkle around five." He drove off. No cherubim armed with flaming swords were seen signaling to him from on high, instead pigeons alighted and dropped their leavings.

Betty said, "When ever am I going to see you again? Never?"

"Name the time," he said and caught her again and in this excess of happiness, overstating, "Oh, I'm so happy to see you, dearest dear, how lovely you look."

"Come tomorrow afternoon, why not?" she said. "We're having Nadia Tangee in to play the piano*forte* and, believe me, she plays it *forte,* before she leaves for Leipzig if Hitler lets her. Come, come." She was in a hurry now, she pushed at his restraining arm. She was all autumn leaves in her floral chiffon. "Oh, and bring your friend, too, if you like, if *he* likes."

Naturally. No four horsemen drew up now in Greenowe Avenue.

Next day Seaton said, "We're invited to Betty's tomorrow, music and buffet."

"*We?*" Athol appeared to be in a state of hauteur.

"She said to bring you if you liked."

"Are they god-awfully Darling Point?"

"Not at all, they just live there. Down-to-earth as hell." Peak in Darien kind of silent, Athol coldly looking into his cold fireplace.

"I might."

The next afternoon Athol was dressed and ready in the heather jacket, navy blue tie, but abominably huffy. He smoked more than usual and said nothing on the long walk up to the Jollivets, nor inside the house, where a small crowd of casually but expensively attired folk were talking banteringly. It was as though this were as commonplace to him as bread and butter. He scarcely glanced at the accomplishment of this room, the graceful arrangements of flowers. "Double whiskey and soda," he said to the hired barman's question. Seaton said he would have a Pimms Cup.

"That's a little old *ladies'* drink," Athol said. "Give *him* a double whiskey and soda, too. If you're going to have a drink, *drink.* If you're going to make love, take off your pants." It seemed more a determination to be boorish than a camouflage for timidity. However he gave Betty's mother a wan smile when he was introduced. "How awfully nice of Seaton to bring you. I fancy Betty's in the garden," said Mrs. Jollivet, all smiles and blowing cigarette smoke on them. As Seaton moved toward the

garden Athol said, "You go, I'll wait here." What the hell was
the matter with him? He was drinking his double whiskey too
fast and scowling. All around them was jollity and civility and
here he was, a bear having to be poked at to dance.

Then, materializing as she frequently did out of blue air,
Betty was at their side; her thin bracelets jangled, she smelled of
crushed petals as Seaton kissed her.

"You met Athol yesterday."

"Yes," she said.

"Yes," Athol said.

They were staring at each other unsmilingly and Betty had
seemed to draw aside a fraction as somebody might who did not
wish to brush another in passing. She was frowning. Athol
looked away and Betty took hold of Seaton's lapel and said, "My
friend Monica is anxious to meet you. She never misses the fish
people and she is dying to ask you if mermaids and mermen can
ever have sex and if they can why don't they?"

"Because Station 2XY and the makers of The Jolly Friar
Oats would have a conniption."

"Ladies and gentlemen, if you please. Miss Tangee's going
to play for us," announced Mrs. Jollivet, all smoke and black
taffeta.

They moved in a small tide toward the other end of the room
where chairs had been set up around the grand piano and as they
moved Athol did the polite thing, took hold of Betty's elbow and
steered her, poker-faced all the way, to a chair. He handed her into
it with all the solemnity of a priest offering the communion cup.
He and Seaton took chairs directly behind. Then Miss Tangee,
large and white as an arctic killer whale, triumphed into "La
Valse" and they were all trapped into their private thoughts of
pleasure or discomfort as people are when music takes over, and
moved fretfully, occasionally crossing legs, looking up at the
ceiling or down at their feet. After a cross rendition of the "Revo-
lutionary Étude," Miss Tangee dissolved into the calm of Bach's
"Jesu Joy of Man's Desiring" and as the room seemed to warm to
it, to respond, to deliquesce in the cleanness of it, Athol leaned

forward and put one hand on the back of Betty's chair and she, unable to feel it and yet seemingly sensitive to some clandestine touch, the brush of a moth wing in the dark, turned and seeing him, as if for the first time, communicated something with the smile she gave him, wholly secret, wholly individual, and Athol, not smiling, held up his hand in a gesture of reciprocation, of reaching out to gently touch her hair.

Perhaps then this studied indifference they had both shown toward each other had been a calculated ploy to disguise some curious feeling they had both had at the moment of their meeting, an enormity too mysterious to be hastily defined, both threatening and entrancing. Whatever it was, when supper was announced and the party began ambling toward the glassed-in sunroom porch, Athol again involuntarily took hold of Betty's elbow and without speaking they moved with the crowd, leaving Seaton to the untender mercies of Meg Fowler-Jones with whom he had gone to Miss Peel's classes in another era and who had just become, she showed her splendid diamond, engaged to John Lawson, the little boy around whom at some child's party Seaton had inadvertently thrown his arms and kissed, causing subdued amusement. And what about *you*, Seaton, Meggie Fowler-Jones teased humorlessly, come now, admit, tell her, wasn't there some nice likely lass that he had his eye on? He might have upended her apple cart by confessing that at nearly twenty-one he was still metaphorically throwing his arms around and kissing some nice likely boy, like that boy in the heather jacket now forking cold chicken in aspic onto Betty Jollivet's dish.

He and Meg had sat down, God help them, with the yachting group, and the conversation was now all jib and yaw and length and sail to cross Bass Strait with the right wind.

When eventually he escaped, making his way through three rooms without a sight of them, he came upon Betty and Athol knee to knee with their plates on their laps seated on the stairs. They appeared to be so deep in communion that, excusing himself to get past them, they edged aside to let him pass without looking up. He took a while using the bathroom and washing his hands in order to reassure himself that nothing untoward was happening, that nothing possibly could. Everyone knew that Betty was assumed to be practically engaged, certainly promised tacitly, to one of the Lavery boys or to the Carter son presently "finishing" at Oxford. Nobody in his right mind could seriously consider her even frivolously dating a men's suits salesman and part-time actor. But he was not further reassured when, finding them no longer on the stairs and nowhere to be seen, and coming finally across Betty on the lawn, she said to him in what seemed to be altogether too laconic a manner that, oh, Athol said to say good night, he had to dash off, to bed, being a working boy.

"Dear of you to invite him."

"Who?" She was all put-on mystified.

"Athol of course."

"Oh."

There was a new closed-in posture to her. "I have to go too," he said and kissed her.

"Bye, dearest thing," she said but she was elsewhere.

Sucked toward the maelstrom, in days following the boat, drawn faster and faster, the circles become narrower. Opening the front door to him, Mrs. Atwater said that Mr. Long was on the phone but to go on in, dear. Athol was sitting by the hall telephone and talking, winding the cord around a finger and smiling. He gestured toward the open door to his room and continued speaking as Seaton went into the bed-sit and sat in the armchair. Phrases reached him through the open door, something was said about Thursday evening, the Prince Edward was mentioned. Athol said, "I get off the show at quarter to eight, so don't worry."

When he came back into his room, Athol did an uncharacteristic thing, combed his hair furiously. Then, throwing down the comb, he asked, "Did I tell you what happened at the shop between me and the floor manager over the lost sales slip and what I said to him?"

It was as much a dismissal as though he might have said that to whom he was talking on the phone was nobody's business, least of all Sea's, who would have cut off his tongue before he asked, although burning at the stake. Burning with the ninety-nine-percent certainty that it had been Betty. Had she called Athol or had Athol called her? Either way it was nothing short of a betrayal and the concealing of it widened the gulf opening between them. Dates were being made, were they? Something was going on, was it? He looked at Athol and through the red mist of resentment, smiled beatifically.

Yet surely, surely Betty would not conceal it. She was as devout as any nun in friendship, inviolate, she would phone him to say, in her intensest voice, that she had been invited to the pictures by his "friend"—the word would have the quotation marks. She would assure him she had no designs on Athol.

He had no right to adjudge the two people he loved most in the world. Betty would phone him between now and Thursday. But neither Betty nor Athol phoned; their duplicity was staggering. He could barely get through work that day so painful were his accusations, so uncontrolled the passion. Conscienceless, he stationed himself at half-past seven on the steps of the Hotel Australia right across from the Prince Edward picture palace.

At the lowest ebb of pride one spies on lovers (even nonlovers) partly hidden behind marble pillars without a nudge of shame (and what did he expect to do when Betty appeared? Rush across the street screaming "traitress"?). The crowd was arriving for the eight o'clock showing of *Bluebeard's Eighth Wife,* starring Miss Colbert and Mr. Cooper whose enlarged faces and crimson lips smiled down from above the marquee. Surely enough, at ten minutes to eight Athol hove into view dressed in his Farmer's hand-tailored blue serge and stood at the opening to the lobby, lighting a cigarette. There was, Seaton was telling himself, still time to be proved wrong. Some nondescript man friend would appear or Athol's sister, Kay, and heaven be retrieved. This expectancy was heightened when at two minutes to eight and most of the crowd gone in, there was still no sight of Betty, and Athol was looking up and down the street impatiently when a cab drew up and preposterously Betty stepped out with her mother and even more preposterously Athol was greeting Mrs. Jollivet without surprise and taking both women by the elbow, escorting them inside.

Implication was now that higher stakes were being played for. Without hesitation, Seaton hailed a taxi and gave Rat's address.

Rat, playing bridge with three gentlemen, excused himself and took Seaton into the bedroom. "A crisis has arisen," Rat told them, but said to Seaton, "I don't think you have much of a case."

"I expect not."

"What business is it of yours?"

"None."

"So what on earth reprisal could you be supposed to take?"

"None."

"Then what can you do about it?"

"Nothing. Story of my life in one word."

"Look, even if you came across them *doing* it on top of the War Memorial in Martin Place you'd have no right to object unless you were a war widow. There *is* no right. Let me tell you about me. Week or so ago there was a staggeringly good-looking waiter on at the Blue Ribbon and I would have sworn he was giving me the wildest green light along with the terrine d'é-crevisse so as it was near their closing time I waited outside for him and said, 'Can I give you a lift?' and he said, 'You give me a lift *any* way,' and home we came and I should have remembered to look in the mirror first because he was all too much sweetness, sweetness was not the word for him, he was like experiencing music physically. In the morning, he was gone and with him a valuable little eighteenth-century pill box, my Burberry raincoat, and twenty quid out of my wallet."

"The bugger."

"Yes, that part of him was nice. Dear, *we* are vulnerable, there's no excuse for us under the sun. What I'd do if I were you is be nice to him, nice to her, too. Kill them with niceness."

"Trouble is I hate them at the moment."

"Yes, but they possibly love you."

"Possibly."

"Be a good sport about it, darling, it's all you *can* be and you might as well start getting used to it, you're going to have to be a good sport about it for the rest of your life."

But how to be a good sport when one is not even told the glad tidings? For two weeks or more darkness hung over the situation and people moved surreptitiously in and out of it, people were "tied up" or would "give you a ring soon." Athol outwardly remained the same. Betty, when Seaton saw her, was immaculate and sweet but noncommunicative. A cloud of preoccupation distanced them from other people, they seemed not to be listening to conversation but more to a secret joyful song.

Then Athol said over dinner at Jacob's Room, as if asking might one pass the bread, "The family are going up to Bowral for the long Easter weekend and—"

"The family?"

"Yes, the Jollivets."

So it was the family already and he a part of it.

"—and very nicely they included me, but for one thing I don't, as you know, golf and for another I'm being lent a beach house for the whole of Easter at Haddock Bay near Palm Beach. Sylvia's lending me her house."

Who is Sylvia?

"And so Betty decided to stay in town as she's not keen for four days of golf and we thought we'd ask some of the kids on the show and, of course, you."

"To go to the beach, you mean?"

"There's two bedrooms, boys and girls. We thought we'd ask Arnold Betts and Gwen Riddle and someone for you. Who'd you like?"

"I don't know yet."

All this arranged so as quietly to introduce him to the inevitable? And he couldn't stand Arnold Betts, a big roustabout bully who played Neptune in "Fairyfish" and was said to have laid every young actress between here and Fremantle, and Gwen

Riddle was an over-made-up nondescript girl who played Flora
the Femme Fatale Flounder in contralto tones. For a long weekend beginning Thursday evening and not ending until Tuesday
morning and all of it a purgatory for everyone involved except
the two lovers basking in the delicious disguise of it while no one
else had a good time. He was expected to enter into this deception
with joy?

But indeed it was the inevitable that was unfolding like
destiny's backdrop of the stage and better to roll with it than to
stay away, visualizing them rollicking naked on a darkened
beach.

"Sounds appetizing," said the good sport.

"Who'd you like us to ask for you?"

"It's of no consequence."

Which it wasn't. But it wouldn't have occurred to him to say
"Anyone *but* Peg Leggett." For Peg Leggett it was, sitting in the
backseat of the car when he arrived at Greenowe Avenue on
Thursday evening. Hopeless Peg who played Queen Mother of
Pearl in the series and who would have been least likely for
anything, poor thing. Her oversized top, buttressed by prolific
breasts, dwindled away into thin spindly legs hardly able to
support the load, surmounted by the face of an iguana. Yet she
had exquisite skin and a horse's eyelashes into which drifted
occasional blobs of fluff. Against her formidable drawbacks, Peg,
dear, brave old Peg, waged continual war, dressed like an exotic
concubine, hung around with beaten silver and gold, lavished
with unguents and rouge. She assumed a sinuosity in her movements, heavy with sexual innuendo, and a husky voice, impreg-
nating every mild thing she said with Salome-like carnality. Poor
hopeless Peg, when she was a lettuce sandwich. So she had been
chosen for him!

"I'm your date," Peg said huskily and moved aside on the
backseat as though drawing aside seven veils. "Dear, sweet, Sea."
From around her rose a heavy scent of cinnamon or tuber roses,
enough to make him drowsy.

"How great, Peg," Seaton said, not even trying to soften the blatant lie.

When Betty, radiant as morning in blue-and-green cotton, was picked up outside her gate, she got into the car and without a word turned in toward the backseat and kissed Seaton on the mouth, long and silently, which meant she knew that he knew.

"We're *off*," Athol said too boyishly as someone else's borrowed car leapt forward. Arnold Betts and Gwen Riddle, it seemed, were driving down separately in Arnold's convertible.

Now they all said pretty to the flash of trees, the first sight of sea, wildflowers, as Curl Curl, Dee Why, Newport flashed past and Athol, aged twenty-six, one must remember, bent over the wheel, driving it seemed in a fury to catch up with the life he'd never dreamed was around the corner with Betty waiting on it.

Sylvia's little cottage crouched apologetically in a clump of saltbush and mulga and was compensated for its ugliness, stained a sullen utility brown, by the unexpected onrush of ocean beneath it enveloping and devouring the continent. The deepness of ink blue was all-encompassing and the balcony that ran the length of the house seemed to be thrusting with all its might against gravity, combating the sea's entreaties to fall into it.

Kookaburras laughed in the stunted gums, perhaps at Arnold Betts's grotesque jokes, all of which dealt with sexual encounters of dinosaur proportions. Arnold and Gwen Riddle had found the hidden key just where it was supposed to be and made themselves at home, Arnold now wearing only khaki shorts so brief as to be censorable and carefully maneuvering the splendidness of his lifeguard body into positions that called for acclaim. He constantly accosted Gwen with his muscular arms, snapping her bathing suit straps or tickling her around the navel, grasping her in a headlock from behind, but Seaton was aware that all the time what Arnold was really taking in was Betty, silently and in great depth. Betty was quietly inviolate and all charm. There was a contrasting parallel between the two couples, Arnold and Gwen all flamboyant sexuality, all touching arms and legs, all wriggling, shrieking, and Athol and Betty all silent, untouching but sensate adoration. In between these two hemispheres of contrasting passion lay the doldrums, Seaton and Peg. Their function as chaperones showed in their seminakedness on the beach as much as in the whiteness of their limbs among the other tanned young bodies. Only in the water were they merely heads bobbing.

But miraculously things worked, if only on the surface. Thanks to Betty's inborn talent for sly and pretty management of things meals were prepared, beds made, drinks concocted, towels hung up to dry, and at bedtime what could have held the seeds of intemperance that invited debauchery, the jokingly promiscuous leading to the serious and orgiastic only moments away, was muted seemingly by mutual consent, and like children they parted at the separate rooms and went their separate ways to bed and innocent sleep.

All was pure as the salt air, nothing was more pungent than remarks about fly swatters, about who had last had the mayonnaise. Someone asked to switch on the radio so they might dance, and their touching of one another's bodies had no more intention on their part than to soothe their sunburn with the scented oils they helped rub onto one another's backs. At times a dullness settled on them like the sea fog and they slumped in hammocks or on benches in a bored silence, only to awaken from it and run zestily down the twiggy sandy paths that wound down to Haddock Beach and into the loving ocean embracing them.

Nothing infiltrated on their assurance of propriety until the moonlight came on Sunday evening, putting whitewash on the tin roof. Every thin gum leaf outlined, one could read a book in the moonlight if that was all one could think to do, Peg said invitingly. She was overdressed pathetically in ruffled white lace that withdrew alarmingly below the cleavage of her breasts and she had coquettishly embedded a silver Spanish comb in her thick, dark, oily hair. Across the veranda dinner table the harsh perfume like peppermint that arose from her made it seem as if she had doused herself with poison flowers. She talked gaily and no one listened, spellbound by the moonlight and the barbaric sexual insistence of Borodin's Polovtsian Dances on the radio and quickly after dinner they disappeared, Arnold and Gwen into the dark hammock that hung between two banksia bushes and Athol and Betty God knows where, vanished into the opalescence of this the brightest night any of them could remember.

Seaton was left at the dinner table with Peg. Unguarded, the conversation or rather her monologue had drifted to food, one of her sources of consolation, and now with her back to the moon, the shadow blessedly blurring the inconsistency of the iguana face and the illumination brightening her hair and catching her silver comb in a radiance, she was telling Seaton that she cooked fish in a little white wine and water, salt, pepper, and a sliced onion. What she did, she said softly, was cook it first over the top jet as if frying it and then in the oven, turning the fish over so that both sides were generously done.

"I see," Seaton said, watching Athol and Betty, lying down now on a soft grassy patch or even in the sand, warm underneath its top strata from the day's sun and now they kissed gently, almost with diffidence, but gradually more lustfully and began twisting, stretching out and searching for each other's wantonness in the silverness of white night around them.

Now Peg had come around to his side of the table, he could feel her breath as she sat close to him on the bench and almost see in the moonlight the rise and fall of the big breasts under the froth of lace.

"What I do then," Peg said breathlessly, "is add a little chopped parsley and a cup of white sauce which I've simmered separately and pour it over the fish."

"I see."

Now Athol was undoing the top buttons on Betty's blouse and she allowed him, she touched his face and drew him down to her, kissing his eyes—

"But it's important to keep the fish piping hot until the moment before you serve."

"Of course."

There was silence now except for the distant sea, a slight zephyr stirring the gum trees.

"It's too bright even to see the stars," Peg said, hopeless, looking up, and recklessly out of pity, not want, he put an arm around her soft yielding waist. She didn't respond, perhaps not daring to scare the bird away.

"Another thing I often like to do," she said, "is plain old pot roast."

The sorrow and anguish were translated into pity for her, for the loneliness of her, of them both. He turned toward her and took her mouth in his. At first she didn't react, stunned, perhaps, or dismayed or too innocent to know what to do next and they kissed until her tongue darted into his mouth and quick as lightning she seemed to be all around him, all over him like an anaconda while with one hand she snatched off the silver comb and let her long thick hair fall. She was making small groaning noises and rubbing herself against him fiercely until he attempted to pull away from her, which only heightened her frenzy and, clinging even more tightly to him, she pursued him and as he turned his head away from her searching, famished mouth, she began to whimper softly and say "please, please" over and over and then, "My God, how marvelous you are."

"Oh Christ, yes, yes," she begged as he forcefully pushed her away from him and she fell back on the wooden bench and into a sudden complete silence as if mortally wounded.

"I'm sorry," he said. "I didn't mean to hurt you."

The silence continued, she might have died; only the chirping of night crickets was heard above the sea.

"Well," he said, fully aware of the cruelty, "bedtime, I think, if you'll excuse me."

"Coward," she said softly.

There was no arguing that, no further need to amplify the shame done to her, poor girl, so he went into the boys' bedroom and shut the door, stayed awake long after he heard Arnold come in and undress in the dark and there was still no Athol and even the moon was down before Athol came. Athol bent over his bed

and asked in a whisper "Are you asleep?" but Seaton didn't want
to be the postscript to whatever had taken place in their be-
witched moonlight so he feigned steady breathing.

In the morning, containment being the key word, there
seemed no need of expiation. They had their coffee and tea all
together on the veranda without obligation except that Peg Leggett seemed more Sheba-like than ever in a skintight yellow
bathing suit over which she had regally cast a terrycloth robe
which fell in folds to her feet. There was nothing unusual in what
passed between Athol and Betty except for his solicitude, which
was perhaps a little strained. "Do you want toast, dear?" Athol
asked. "Can I get you any jam?" But not *in* to any, one hoped.

Slight restlessness was fraying the edges of them as though
this the fourth day was already one too many and it flared into
a little sniping fit between Arnold and Gwen Riddle, ending
with Gwen saying that, oh, he was always so *big* and *tall* and
loathesome. But he merely laughed and tickled her naked back.

"Who's for the sea?" Peg asked. "I want to stay in all day,
I may never come out."

It was Seaton's turn to clear up and sweep the veranda after
they all departed with their tubes of sun oil and their paperback
novels, leaving the house to the noise of the kookaburras in the
banksia and the squawking of the fat locusts, which reminded
him of school mornings at Miss Peel's a thousand years ago. He
swept.

Taken utterly by surprise, from behind, strong, warm arms
pulling him backward and Arnold laughed and said, "Didn't
mean to frighten you, pal."

But this was one of Arnold's heavyweight jokes. Wasn't it?

"I thought you'd gone with the others."

"I thought you thought that."

Queer funny tick in Arnold's left eyelid, strange cold grin,
ugly smile, and now there was no doubt about it whatever, he
was embraced and felt for inside his swimsuit, the big warm hand
took hold of it, all of it in Arnold's quite gentle hand and Arnold
was saying, "Let's go down into the laundry room." Cold as ice

water, no feeling except incredulity as he and Arnold went, Arnold slightly ahead and him following in a parody of obedience like an Oriental wife.

Nearly knocked off his feet in the cool dimness of the laundry room by Arnold's plundering of him, his swimsuit ripped off him, hands reaching for him; there was nothing reticent about Arnold, no fragility or graciousness, it was like being let down into a pit with a frivolous gladiator; in a sense they fought and Arnold won, which was perhaps the lie Arnold maintained to justify such an aberration. It was strangely masculine and satisfying after these months of platonic subterfuge, the hot mouth, the lips bitten, the strength of the naked body that held him in a protective grip and even the standing-up erectness of them, like wrestlers in the ring circling each other, then the purging of the release between them, the spurting forth together as if they had momentarily declared a love for each other within these few seconds and then Arnold drew him close, putting a fist playfully against his cheek, and said, "Now we won't ever mention this to anyone, will we, or we might get a bloody big black eye, by God, feller." Arnold kissed him on the forehead and they put their swimsuits back on and walked back up to the house.

And thirty years later it would be Arnold he thought about in moments of tender loneliness, not Athol.

So it was curiously inconsistent of him when Betty Jollivet phoned to ask him could he meet her and have drinks at the Australia, that she had something to tell him, to hope shamefully that something was wrong between her and Athol. But he hoped it shamefully and thought about gentle scenes of consolation, because who else would Athol turn to?

She was sitting in the lobby in a black dress and had on a big black straw hat; something about her severe dress prompted the thought that this was going to be of significance, there was a calmness about her sitting there with her white gloves on that intimated decision. It was going to be catastrophic.

"Look, darling, I don't feel like a drink in there, in the

bloody Wintergarden with all those *women,*" he said, kissing her. "Do you mind if we just talk out here?"

"No, of course not. Let's go over there where it's quiet." And when they had sat down she removed her gloves and looked him right in the eye. "Athol and I are going to be married. On the fifteenth. St. Stephen's in Vaucluse. No bridesmaids or groomsmen."

Just as if she had said it in a telegram.

"I see."

They looked at the black-and-white marble floor. Mr. Some-one-or-other was being paged.

"You're the first person we've told, apart from Mother and Daddy."

"I see."

She leaned over and touched his knee.

"I know that you love him."

"Yes, yes I do."

"I hope you're not terribly broken up about it."

"Oh, no." He turned away so as not to show his eyes. "It never amounted to much anyway. I mean—you know it wasn't anything *real.*"

"It was to you."

"Oh, I suppose so. Let me give you a kiss and wish you the bestest ever."

Oddly, the very first thought was frivolous. Athol's role would have to be written out of "Fairyfish"; the full impact, the shock would come later. Or had he been fatalistically preparing for it? The Mussel Man character had been missing for a week already. Had he anticipated this disconnection?

"You see," Betty was saying, touching his arm in an urgent manner, "at least, I hope you see, darling, that it was while we were at the beach that we discovered we had always been meant for each other, I hope you realize that. But the reason that it's going to be so sudden is because Athol is sure there's going to be a war and he may have to go overseas, we might not have that much time anymore and the family has been marvelous about it.

Daddy was a bit against it at first, the thought that we're too young and so on, but Mother made him see the light. Oh, darling, it's all worked out as if it really *was* meant. Athol's going to be the new tour director for the shipping company in Brisbane, for Daddy's company."

So everything was arranged, their lives, neat as piles of washed linen on a shelf and it had all happened through him, Seaton. He had been the catalyst or at least had fitted the pieces together. How curious, but in a way, planned. If Betty had not invited him to her birthday dance, he need not have had to buy the dinner jacket that introduced him to Athol who now lived in the house which Bet built. Some people, he thought, and I am one of them, are servitors, without knowing it, and go through their lives implementing other people's fates, which is all they are intended to do. But surely one can expect *some* recognition for it?

He burst out with it. "Oh, but why didn't *he* tell me himself?"

"Because he had to go home very suddenly to his family. His father is dying."

Oh well, in that case—

"Oh, I see."

That alters everything. Athol would always have an excuse for getting out of anything.

"I see," he said dully, helplessly. He wanted suddenly to be alone, not in this crowded lobby with good-looking happy people greeting good-looking happy people.

They sat silently for a bit.

"Would you like a drink?" he asked eventually.

"Not if you don't."

"I don't, really."

They were holding hands and he now withdrew his and stood up, but Betty was looking up at him from under her big hat with wide-eyed concern.

"You *are* upset, I can tell."

"Not really."

"You *are*, there are tears in your eyes."

He brushed at his eyes impatiently.

"Not anymore."

Because how can you cry over losing something you never had to begin with?

So again he kissed her and they held each other tightly as if to allay any suspicion that they might have been rivals and with arms around each other they walked out of the hotel lobby as though it were he that was about to lead her down the aisle of St. Stephen's.

Which Athol did the following month with an overtone of proprietorship, escorting her down the aisle past the smiling faces as if in rather a hurry to get marriage started and she, in her simple gray street dress, holding on to her lilies of the valley with her look of utter compliance while Seaton and Meg Fowler-Jones, the witnesses, followed behind with the organ pealing Mendlessohn to the three-quarters empty church, and then to all the kissing and congratulations in the afternoon sun while he and Meg, their duties done, stood idly by like appendages. It was, thank God, over and done with as was his obligatory dinner with Athol (grandly at the Carlton), strained with goodwill and laughter sounding like the dubbed-in laugh track to some weak radio comedy and Seaton dreading that Athol might feel required to make some bleak affectionate move or statement that would have been as embarrassing as if they had kissed. Never had they seemed so mismatched as friends and both knew it, both of them, it seemed, wanted only for it to be over and to go their separate ways, so good night, good night, and inwardly Seaton thanked God that it had never become so maladroit as it might have had he ever said to Athol, "I love you."

But coddled by the sunshine and Verve Cliquot, even the skeptics were smiling as the wedding feast got under way in the garden at the Jollivet house, even those who had disapproved the haste of it and warned of repentence and who, if they lived that long, would live to eat more than their words when this celebration would be repeated for a silver anniversary and on

the cake in sugar icing "Made for each Other" would be inscribed by as yet unborn children who had occasionally felt
isolated by a great love.

Now Seaton, on a nod from Mrs. Jollivet just prior to the
appearance of today's cake, rose and said, "Dear friends, we are
here today in the company of two people who have just made the
most solemn and exalted promise two human beings can make
to one another. This promise is as old as life itself and this ancient
joy of union touches us all, all of us, married and unmarried, are
deeply moved by it because it is the embodiment of the most
human necessity, to love and be loved, and so its miracle sheds
light on all of us and we are made the more whole because of it,
and so, darling Betty, dear, dear Athol, we raise our glasses to you
in love and in our joy we send you our everlasting blessing."

In the confusion of chairs being pushed back and glasses
clinked, he hoped nobody had heard the slight tin crack of cyni-
cism; he would get now honorably and peacefully drunk. He
waved to the waiter.

By the end of the wedding breakfast he had become slightly
raucous and had twice kissed Meg Fowler-Jones wetly on the
mouth, once assaulted her aristocratic rump, and she seemed to
have loved it. He had greeted distant Jollivet family members by
their first names and upset a full bottle of champagne over Betty's
sister's mauve taffeta. "Oh, Seaton darling, you were so moving,"
Betty's mother said and then anxiously, "Are you having a good
time, dear, what did you think of the poule blanc, was yours a
little dry? Mine was a touch dry."

Things were flying by pleasantly in a colored kaleidoscope;
now Athol and he were standing alone together in the profusion
of shasta daisies around the old gazebo, thanks to the tactfulness
of Betty, who saw Seaton approach unsteadily.

"Thanks for standing up for me, old man," Athol was saying.

"Have I stood up for you?"

Athol gave that laugh of his, his salesman's take-in-the-waist-
a-fraction laugh.

"Mostly always, old cobber, one way or another."

For some reason they were shaking hands. Good-bye?

"I expect Betty's told you we're moving to Brisbane. I'm to take over the tour office there."

"Yes she did. Well, good luck."

"So we won't be seeing much of each other for a while."

"Prob'ly not."

Were they going to shake hands forever? He said, "You know what I wish you."

"Think I do, yes."

"Always and always."

"Yes."

Athol was frowning, he had something to say, had for some time, and now here they were almost at the end and no more time for procrastination.

"You know, don't you? I've always known."

"Known?"

"About you."

"Have you?"

"Always."

"Oh."

"I just want you to know now I've never minded, it never bothered me."

It sounded as though he expected congratulations for not being a bigot. He waved his hand as though brushing them away.

"I'm *so* glad."

"I never cared in the least, old dear, that's the truth."

Yes, old dear, it *was* the sorrowful truth, but in another sense, there it was, old dear, the actual difference between them but now that Athol had spoken the truth, no matter that it was misrepresented as a compliment, he deserved the truth back.

"I love you, Athol."

So Athol, sanctified by his tolerance, buttressed by marriage, at last took him in an embrace that contrived at the same time to impress upon him Athol's autonomy. He felt himself caressed and repulsed. He broke free and said thickly, "I've got to go."

"So long then."

"So long."

"So long chum."

Seaton made his way through sudden waters over the lawn. The absolute best thing in the world was that it was over; the second absolute best thing was that a taxi was letting someone out across Darling Point Road. He gave the Carlton as his destination, there was still time for a drink. The Saturday race crowd was right up to the door of the Blue Room. He ordered two gins and ginger ale, light on the ginger. In the distance a small band was playing at the *"thé dansant."* "Tonight I mustn't think of him, music maestro, please, tonight I really must forget," the crooner's beseeching voice wailed.

He drank the gins down quickly and ordered another two.

Think of *him?* Bugger him.

Now, anyone but him. Go for broke, old dear. The taxi driver had had a sensuous neck, rather full. Think of the taxi driver. Think of the lifeguard in the shower in the men's dressing shed, no one else there that afternoon a couple of years ago, what a surprise. Whatever else he thought of tonight it had to be that, flat-out reality, here in this bar full of smoke and lonely chaps drowning in lager and mooning over girls, most likely, with one or two of the "brethren" as Rat would have called them, middle-aged aunties or thin desperate striplings wearing glasses and with prominent Adam's apples. "Think this nice weather'll keep up?" Couldn't stand *one* of them, not tonight. If it was anything it was going to be as lustful as it would be for *them* in the honeymoon bed wherever that was going to be, rather have some grizzled tram or truck driver, how're yer goin' mate, want it? Grab it, fat, getting fatter, delightful, rollicking naked in the hot sand dunes with big hairy Squizzy Taylor, his science master, who activated thoughts like that when he bent over you, lighting the Bunsen burner with virile hands but wearing natural nail polish. Tonight it would be flat OUT.

So Gomorrah. Gomorrah was the underground station Men's at Wynyard, all that subterranean white-tiled netherland of yellow lighting and where the men assumed monumental nonchalance, standing around the white porcelain fixtures like mannequins, heads up innocently, pretending not to be looking down or sideways, but wanton, taking unearthly time buttoning up, darting lightning glances at one another with faces as immobile as marble but playing the game Rat called "a tisket, a tasket, let's see what's in your basket." Others less daring were lined up at the wash basins, washing and rewashing their hands, all the time watching in the mirror what might be going on behind their backs and late in the evening when few were there it often could be observed that there were two pairs of feet to be seen under the door of one of the pay toilets. But there was an unspoken code of behavior and once it had been violated by an ugly little dwarf of a man with a huge head who had danced a little obscene dance in the middle of the room with his exposed Goliath-like equipment jiggling, causing a flux of hasty departures, flushing water, and a hurrying off like outraged deacons. One never contravened the myth of sanctity that hung over the washroom like the reek of disinfectant. Outside was different, in the margarine light, men dawdled, pretending to read newspapers, leaned on the tiled pillars; others paused and sometimes asked the time or for a match and then often as not two strolled away together.

This night it could be instantly seen to be unrewarding; the long known faces, the hopeless hungry ones were the only prospects but coming out there was a man leaning on the closed tobacco kiosk whose quiet observance of the comings and goings and whose questioning eyes were noticeable a distance away. He was bulky and had large powerful shoulders forced into a tight suit made of some cheap material that was blatantly foreign, could have been the shore mufti of a sailor from a freighter; his felt hat was or had been a gray homburg of some elegance. "Want to take a walk?" Seaton asked, without a fraction of hesitation, and the man smiled, showing large uneven teeth. The silence as they went up the back escalator was more likely an admission of linguistic failure than diffidence; each time Seaton glanced up at him he smiled his uneven-tooth smile, but when they emerged into the dark steepness of Essex Street, it appeared to be more than gravity pulling them downhill to where there was a small truck bay safeguarded from the street by a high wall where a breathless middle-aged businessman had once taken Seaton and surprised him by adding that he did not have much time because "I have to meet my daughter."

Here in the safety of the minimal light from a streetlamp they stood, getting their breath, and Seaton had turned a pace sideways when the first blow struck him on the side of the jaw, knocking him slightly backward, and in his unsteady tipsy state halfway to his knees. The second blow caught him full in the face and he went down on his back into the hard asphalt. Words were being spoken in what sounded like Swedish, curses and reprisals, he assumed, for some similar action taken against the bulky man.

He may have lost consciousness for a second or two because he was only aware of quiet sleepiness and could not take in the huge welted shoes beside his eyes but then he was booted and booted in the face and it was clear to him, again without fear, that he was being killed. Scrambling up, he managed to dodge the blows coming at him, one so savage that missing him and passing through air, it shook the Swede's balance and he stumbled backward and in that second Seaton got by him and out the open gate. The hill in amber streetlight was mountainous but the terror now beginning at last to dawn gave him the adrenaline to run to the top without stopping and then into the lighted underground entrance and to skim down the escalator two steps at a time, never daring to turn around and never to stop until safely on the waiting tram where he got into an already crowded compartment and where his heart continued to pound and he continued to be drenched in sweat until the tram started and pulled away safely into the tunnel.

By morning, peering still affrighted into his bathroom mirror, his face had swollen to a puce football, his eyes had narrowed orientally, and he had difficulty even speaking, let alone being able to eat. Fortunately his front teeth, though slightly loose, were in place. His Essie, his dear, bland, unimaginative darling, believed his story. It was an allergy he had somehow contracted the evening before at the wedding breakfast, very likely the cold salmon. He had, he said, once before been similarly affected by salmon.

All she said, drying a dish, her dear plain face, believing the moon was green cheese, was that just fancy, she couldn't imagine *anyone* serving cold salmon at a wedding.

Poor little orphan, watch out for Her

T HE WELL-DRESSED WOMAN lay flat on her back outside Hordern's in Pitt Street, her hands in white gloves at her side, her
little hat pushed slightly forward on her unconscious face. The
woman kneeling beside her and wearing a black beret and a long
tweed coat was trying gently to lift up her head while a small
sullen crowd looked on without any expression, even surprise, as
though numberless women fell on Sydney streets every few minutes. One girl was chewing gum. As Seaton paused on the edge
of the crowd, the woman in the beret looked up and said, "Will
someone get an ambulance," and when nobody moved she spoke
directly to Seaton. "She may be having a heart attack. For God's
sake go into Hordern's and ask them to call the ambulance." He
turned and went into the store where a floor walker in striped
pants and tail coat was standing officiously by a rack of ladies'
topcoats. "There's someone lying on the pavement outside, could
you call an ambulance?"

"Fourth floor," the floor walker said. "Turn left and ask for
Sister Macintosh."

"No, I want an ambulance."

"Fourth floor, sir, customers' first aid."

"God's sake I want an ambulance," Seaton said and turning,
perhaps to find someone with sense, noticed that outside the
prone woman was now sitting up. He went out and stood over

158

the girl in the beret and the recovering woman. "Hang on to my arm," the girl was saying, "someone's gone to phone for an ambulance." "No, I'm all right," the woman said and then, floundering around, "Where's my bag?" Seeing her bag in the girl's hand, the woman asked sharply, "What are you doing with my bag?" "I was trying to put it under your head," the girl said as the woman now scrambled up and practically snatched it from the girl's hand. "I want to see if my purse is still in it," she said and hunted in the alligator bag. Seemingly satisfied, she closed it with a snap. The incident was over. "I'm perfectly all right," she said. "I must have just had a little fainting spell." She brushed her skirt with her gloved hands, never once smiling. "Perfectly all right," she said. "Thank you just the same." She straightened her little hat and walked away.

"Gratitude," the girl said grimly.

She was odd-looking. Her tweed coat reached nearly to her ankles, and looked as though it had been loaned to her. It was hard to tell if she were twenty-three or close to forty; she was as innocent of makeup, even lipstick, as a Mayan Indian. Below the black beret, her dark brown hair was fashioned into buns over her ears and her plain black shoes, laced up the front, were the type usually worn by housemaids or elderly women.

"Thanks for trying to get the ambulance."

"I wasn't able."

"Least you tried."

They had begun walking toward King Street; he honestly did not know what on earth was prompting him to walk along with her except that the girl seemingly needed to be reassured that she had performed a kindness. She was more vulnerable than the woman who had fainted.

At King Street, outside Proud's the jeweler, they stopped and she said, "Anyone would have thought I was trying to steal her stupid bag. Do I look that needy?"

"Some people are unexplainable."

"Inexplicable," she corrected him primly.

He held out a hand to bid her good-bye, but she ignored it,

glowering at the traffic. Not glowering, exactly, but expression-less. In the nearly thirty years they were to know each other, he never once saw an expression on her face of delight or rage or even indignation; she was as implacable as stone. There was something oriental about her neutrality. The only indication of any emotion was in her eyes, which turned into darker black spots when she was displeased, caught light from occasional plea-sure. She was given to sudden vibrant opinion. "Outrageous" or "impeccable." Once in a great while she let her armor slit open an inch. "I have," she told him, "looked into the black pit." She held a certain arcane record for nonconformity; once she had been married for twenty-three minutes. Now she said abruptly, "I'm on my way to see the Macquarie Prize portrait. What are *you* doing?"

"What is it?"

"You mean you don't *know?*"

The Macquarie Prize was the most prestigious in the art world and this year it had been won by Theodore Steinbaum, an unknown artist, and had been violently opposed by a group calling itself "Art for Australians." In their attempt to disqualify the painting they had declared it a caricature and not a genuine representation of the human body; they had even called in a doctor who had measured the upper limbs and testified that no human being could have arms of such length.

"They're fifty years behind the times," the girl said. "All they can think of is gum trees in the moonlight, the sick stock-rider's daughter, Burke and Wills in their deserted camp, *sheep.*"

The portrait, simply titled "Fleming," was electrifying, nod-ding to Modigliani and Dali; even from a distance as they came into the gallery the strength of it reverberated, its grotesqueness leapt out of the frame, the huge head, the tiny neck, the tarantula arms, all in a compactness of a plaid suit. The man was being crucified the great eyes told.

"Faultless," the girl said and although Seaton didn't alto-gether agree, he could unfortunately see what the AFA Commit-tee had complained about; nevertheless, it was not to be lightly dismissed—in this deplorably mundane society it was an alarm bell.

Only as they went down from the gallery in the tiny lift did the girl admit an identification. "I'm Gin."

"Gin?"

"Ginette Spaulding. Who are you?"

He told her. She looked to be a trifle discomforted with his name, better it had been George Thomkins.

"What do people call you?"

"Sea."

"That's better. Would you care to have a crumpet with me?"

On this cold July afternoon with a bitter wind circling them, it seemed appropriate, hot crumpets juicy with butter. They had them with pots of China tea in The Jam Spoon in polite little Bligh Street. Gin unexpectedly smoked strong Turkish cigarettes which she got, she said, from a men's barbershop. In staccato revelations delivered in bone-sharp emotionless economy he learned that her late father (the angry dots of eyes melted into warm grapes) had been Mr. Justice Spaulding of the State Supreme Court who had died when she was still a child of unattended pneumonia following an uncared-for chest cold, caught while lake fishing in cold weather. Her mother (the eyes snapped back) had been killed the year before in a riding accident when her horse had bolted, striking her against a low tree branch which had almost but not quite decapitated her. Gin had then been parceled off by relatives to Foote, a rarified girls' boarding school in Armadale, from which she emerged only at Christmas to spend a stultifying yule in a cousin's home in Moss Vale.

So they were alike, Gin and he, both orphans, both superintended by cousins he informed her approvingly, but her only reaction was to demand a jug of hot water from the waitress.

But there was something of infinitely more relevance to him about her; that was her sexlessness. He could not remember meeting a girl (she had taken off her beret and it was now obvious in spite of her middle-aged aspects that she was in her twenties) with less feminine preoccupation and the absence of it was restful. Not needing to cajole with expected male responses, or even respect her made him respect her more, the desire to touch her untouchability made him want to touch her. When he helped her on with her gigantic coat he made a motion of tenderness with his hands on her sharp shoulders. But he felt the tendons move in rejection of any familiarity. It would need four strong men to hold her down and separate her legs in order for one other man to rape her. She was passionate about being inviolable.

"I'd like to see you again," he said.

"I'm in the book," she said, "Spaulding with a *u*. Ocean Avenue."

And was gone through the door out into the wind.

Had he never really listened to the sound of water? Never read a decent book in his life? Had he never known what a treat Corelli was or realized the little lovelinesses of Giotto sketches? She would now call him to account. "Don't read that awful trash." "Look at the peace on the Virgin's face." "Never *heard* of Fra Angelico?" "People matter less and less, believe me."

There was no doubt that she knew what he was and that she was neither pleased nor outraged, merely complaisant. But not compassionate, she was rock-bottom hard as flint and he liked that too. After the long months of pale artificial love and longing, the ice cold bath she offered was wildly rejuvenating.

She had the nicest little flat on a pleasant hill on Ocean Avenue. In some respects it was as bare as a monk's cell with its cedar floors on which only oatmeal-colored mats were strewn, on the pure white walls were only a Goya print and a Van Gogh church quivering in terror among spinach trees all agog with his marvelous insanity. Here in the quiet of her room they had tea with the exquisite little cucumber sandwiches made by Mrs. Wycomb who came and went, mouselike in carpet slippers to ease the pain of bunions. Mrs. Wycomb seemed to be something of a miracle housekeeper-cook. Hardly a word ever came from out her mouth, hardly ever was a teaspoon forgotten or the kettle not boiling. The fact that democratically she was not required to wear any uniform and her distinctly upper-class bearing might have led to the mistaking of her for another guest or friend rather than a live-in servant. So he was astonished and moderately shocked when by accident, once returning a tray to the little kitchenette, he came upon Mrs. Wycomb having her leftover dinner in her room, which was not much larger than a walk-in closet, so cramped that she needed to sit on the cot in order to eat off the washstand, obvious also was that were she to pull open a drawer she would first have had to close the door. "Something you wanted?" Mrs. Wycomb asked him coldly, discombobulated at being spied upon and he had apologized and quickly withdrawn.

Now. How Gin would kill Hitler.

She had it worked out to the last detail. She was already proficient in German, told her accent was Bavarian. She would perfect it. She would dye her hair a lighter shade, she would get herself to Munich, there to become a member of the Hitler Youth, fanatically loyal, fanatically anti-Semitic. Surely it would not be impossible to obtain some menial position in Berchtesgaden and once there eventually to be sent upstairs on some errand that would bring her into the same room with the Führer. She would have a small revolver capable of being hidden in her khaki shirt and—

"You'd be immediately assassinated."

"What would that matter? I would have saved the world from his war."

She had briefly been captivated by Communism, worshiped Lenin and the five-year plans but word of the leftist violence in American unions and pressure on her here in Australia to vote not according to sense had disspelled the romanticism of the Marxist dream. Staccato admissions were fired. Like a bird she edged closer to him through them. Long silence would be followed by confession. "I have always despised Christmas and everything to do with it." "I am anti-God."

Once, looking down through blue miasmas, "I was married once for about twenty-three minutes. His name was Glenn Hawcroft. I must have been momentarily blinded by his seeming kindliness and by a moment or two of the terror of never being wanted. We were married by a justice of the peace, it took about five minutes, two paid witnesses were present to whom neither of us were introduced and afterward we went off for a honeymoon somewhere in his little car. I was sitting beside him and suddenly he put his hand on my knee and said, 'Now I've *got* you,' and I said, 'Stop at the next corner a minute,' and he asked why and I said, 'Never mind why, just stop,' and he did and I got out and I said to him, 'If you think you've got me, you've got another big think coming,' and I walked away. He looked the most astonished man who ever breathed. I never laid eyes on him again. I imagine, being Catholic, he was immensely relieved that he could legitimately obtain an annulment."

Sometimes she receded, not into silence, but into deeper evasion. On these days he learned to curtail his visit and often just to get up and go.

Perhaps, he thinks, this is the nearest thing to love that I shall ever know, this understanding, this utter undemanding. Perhaps, he thinks, this is the nearest to happiness that I shall ever deserve.

Even though it was fatiguing sometimes to try to measure up to her standard of perfection. It seemed as though her existence was dependent on it. She could detect the one wrong note in a crescendo passage of the "Pathétique," she would wince at it. You could not always enjoy a film because of her deep sighs at any triteness of dialogue; dramatically even Garbo might not measure up. Occasionally he protested, "You're too finicky." "Well"—her hopeless arms thrust out—"to see the mediocre being ravenously eaten."

Poor Gin, fighting with all her strength to maintain a semblance of impeccability. And to set things straight, even physically. She had been known to cross a dentist's waiting room to right a picture gone awry on the wall. Yet she condemned symmetry for being banal; the Taj Mahal, she maintained, was altogether too balanced. On the other hand there was the transport of her delight when something pleased her. "Mrs. Wycomb has composed a walnut cake that is perfection," she would declare, cutting into it, and Mrs. Wycomb, receiving her crumb, was hard put not to show her crooked grin, had to cover her mouth, hobble from the room pretending something was running over on the stove as was her cup.

But when what Seaton thought of as "the glint" showed, it was better to abandon ship than stay to fight. The glint narrowed the face and brought the dots of eyes to boiling point in seconds, the hands groped as if she were fumbling for the hidden dagger in the skirt, the voice grew low and threatening, and then when the verdict was given it came like forked lightning. Reparations would be undertaken, she would write to the Prime Minister (and frequently did in effortless syntax) or to the *Sydney Morning Herald* (ditto).

Sometimes, unable to right the situation, unable to bear the scourge of its wrongness, she took out her vengeance on it in the form of cleanliness. She would clean house from top to bottom. Often the vacuum cleaner would burst the middle of the night silence and awaken Mrs. Wycomb, but there was no stopping it. Gin would pretend she didn't hear protests. Finally toward dawn, the last brass object having been polished to perfection, the last never-used china tureen scalded and buffed into radiance, she would submit to daylight and sleep the sleep of the justified.

They were standing on the little balcony overlooking the crystal harbor one night over which the winter sky was clear as glass and from inside the living room was coming the voluptuous climax of *Der Rosenkavalier* and without precaution, thinking only of the virginal pleasure of being with her, moved suddenly by the small immaculate containment of her in her dull gray flannel skirt and inevitable white blouse and by the sweetness of the bother she took to concoct her old-fashioned hairdo with the buns of dark chestnut over her ears, he drew her to him (she was as light as a tin plate) and put both his arms around her, drawing her back into the encumbrance of this delight without a word. She hesitated only moments before removing herself and then, turning, as if she had the gun to kill Hitler in hand, said, firing the bullet into his heart, "Don't be *absurd.*"

It was a wet woolly August Sunday afternoon when he left rather earlier than usual. She was alone, Mrs. Wycomb having the afternoon off to attend a Christian Soldiers for God service. Gin had been discovered on hands and knees, scrubbing the kitchen floor. ("Mrs. Wycomb doesn't always get into the corners so I take the opportunity when she's out.")

It had been one of those days of restless silences, peculiar glances, and even intervals when she went out of the room, leaving him alone with the vexing enigma of their friendship. When he rose to leave she didn't bother to come with him to the door.

Halfway up the hill of Ocean Avenue in a strong blustery wind, he was startled when somebody stepped out from behind a giant Moreton Bay fig tree in his path as though she might have been waiting for him, but it was a minute or two before he was able to recognize Mrs. Wycomb in her imitation astrakhan coat and a little violet straw hat that she was holding by the brim to prevent the wind from snatching it off.

"Blowy day, Mrs. Wycomb."

"I saw you coming out, so I was waiting for you, Mr. Daly. I wanted to have a word with you."

The wind had caught and blown her light scarf across her mouth so that what she had said was partly muffled. Had she said she wanted a word with him? She tugged the scarf away from her mouth.

"It's about *her.*"

"I see." He didn't, also didn't like her approaching him in this stealthy way, coming out from behind a tree.

"I'll be plain. You want to watch out for her."

"Well—Mrs. Wycomb, I—"

"You're a nice young man but you're a bit naive."

Now already this was impertinence.

"Now Mrs. Wycomb—"

"I mean this kindly. Don't get in too deep with her, she's a manipulator. I've seen several people she's manipulated to her own ends. You be careful, now."

"Mrs. Wycomb, I'm sure this is well meant, but I have to tell you I think it's most inappropriate of you to discuss Miss Spaulding behind her back with—"

"It's not inappropriate."

Again the scarf blew across the words.

"I beg your pardon?"

"I said, it's not inappropriate. I have every right."

"I think that most certainly you do *not* have the right to—considering she's your employer—speak to me behind her back like—"

"She's not my employer."

"Mrs. Wycomb—"

"I don't receive a penny salary from her."

"Mrs. Wycomb! *Truly?*"

"Just bed and board and you've seen the kind of bed and board I get, hardly room to turn around."

"Well, I can scarcely believe—"

"She's punishing me."

"For what?"

"Being her mother."

The wind had blown a strand of hair across Mrs. Wycomb's face, slicing it in half. She struggled to keep her hat from flying off, and in this moment he struggled to take it in.

"I daresay you've been told how her mother was thrown off a horse. As you can see, it's only true because she likes to believe it. Can you understand why she's never once admitted I'm her mother, she's never called me by anything but my second married name. I can't blame her altogether. I left her as a child, I left the judge, her father, left them both for the person I loved and I had a few years of perfect joy, Mr. Daly, until he died, and then I sort of died myself and I was only just breathing, living from day to day, when I had a phone call from her lawyer just saying that Miss Spaulding wanted a cook-housekeeper and asking would I consider the job. She wanted me back. Well, I took the job and never a private word's been spoken between us in four and a half years. I cook and clean and that's the end of it."

Mrs. Wycomb's eyes were streaming now from the wind.

"But why," he asked, "do you go on with it? You could get a legitimate job, hundreds of women would hire you in a second and pay you a decent salary."

"I'm aware of that."

"Then why don't you?"

She raised both hands to her face to avert this cruelty, the obvious question.

"Can't you *see?*"

Now her gloved hands were fumbling to open her bag, get out a handkerchief.

"Can't you? At least I'm *with* her."

He saw. Right down into her disgrace, the disgrace of both her and Gin in their mutual need and their shame of it, the dreadfulness of their wanting, their outward repudiation of it, all white gloves and merciless politeness. "Mrs. Wycomb, would you bring the bread and butter plates, the cake knife, the cyanide capsules?" "Right away." And Mrs. Wycomb, waiting hand and foot on her, waiting also for the stray reward. "The lamb's the best you've ever done." Mother. Now Mrs. Wycomb took a step toward him, entreating.

"I'm relying on you not to let her know I've told you."

It would be like tearing off Gin's clothes, the rape, the four husky men holding her down and her screaming. What a lie, she would say, what utter bosh, the woman's mad. Because it was Gin who must be a little insane, playing this game.

"Of course," he said.

"Poor thing, poor little orphan," Mrs. Wycomb said. "But you watch out for her." She went off down the windy street.

See if we can pick off a bush turkey

*B*OOTS GREATLY HELPED his transformation into a man, the solid Aussie army boots, cedar red, thick-soled with iron cleats on the heels, and stamping across the bare boards in them it sounded like three men crossing over to hand in today's Standing Orders to Captain Smollett (known to all as Vince the Vile) and clicking to attention. Captain Smollett took the typed orders and without seeming to glance downward said, "Corporal Daly, one of your socks is falling down."

"Sir!"

Yes, sir, thank you, *sir*, thank you, you frog's arsehole, you fucking lizard's gallbladder.

But Corporal Daly pulled up the offending sock, about-turned smartly, and returned to his desk.

Captain Smollett was the most hated officer at the Eighth Advanced Ordnance Depot in Butcher's Creek in the Northern Territory, seven hundred miles north of Alice Springs, two hundred miles south of Darwin, and exactly in the center of nowhere. Captain Smollett had eyes in the back of his head and a sense of timing that was extrasensory. Should you still be wearing your daytime khaki shorts at one minute past eighteen hundred when it became mandatory for you to be in your long dress pants, you could be certain to have Captain Smollett run into you coming from the latrines or on your way to the sleeping hut and

169

instantly you would be put on a charge sheet, given extra guard duty or mess service.

Vince the Vile Smollett was young, stocky, and boasted a bristly brown mustache. Impeccable in exquisitely pressed khaki shorts and laundered shirts, he directed the camp commandant's office with the iron precision and military flair of an earlier era as if this were still the Boer War and he Lord Kitchener. Here in this dust bowl where for eight months of the year no rain fell, it was Vince who ordained that everyone's boots be burnished for Monday's dress parade so that a lot of Sunday afternoon had to be occupied with polish and brush up and down the rows of sleeping huts. Vince's hawk's eye could pick out the indifferently buffed boot a yard away. He was obliged to submit to nature during the wet season.

He was one of those men who seemed to have had no life before the war; as if he'd been taken out of a military "Q" store, spat on and polished, already in uniform, his horizon no larger than a rifle range and with a mental capacity unable to comprehend anything not spelled out in the military manual; one could readily imagine him waking in the night in a sweat of fear that one day this war might end and he would be put back into storage.

In order to nourish the sense of battle here in the desolation of emus and aborigines he maintained a strict wartime footing. Now in 1944, long after the last Japanese had retreated north as far as Milne Bay, the guard was stood every night from six P.M. to six A.M. even though all there was to protect from enemy attack were Soyer stoves, mess kits, boots, cooking utensils, and mosquito netting. Captain Smollett was the only duty officer who requisitioned a driver to take him around the guard posts during the middle of the night in order to catch any poor bugger who had lit a small fire against the desert night cold. Corporal Daly had seen the distant headlights approaching and quickly kicked out his fire but was apprehended on a more minor charge when Captain Smollett's flashlight caught sight of an unfastened button on his tunic. Next time, Corporal, the whiny Australianized voice had warned, there would be more than being severely reprimanded.

It was a shock to discover that someone on this earth actually loved Vince the Vile. When Seaton, class A typist in Headquarters, had painstakingly finished typing the twenty-two-page report on the inquiry into drainage and maintenance of septic tanks and grease traps and taken it over at sunset to the officers' tents and had been directed to Captain Smollett's tent by a cursory nod (the Captain was not much liked even here, it seemed), he had found the tent immaculate and empty, paused a few seconds to look around, and there on a wooden box beside the army cot was a framed photograph of a young girl wearing an evening dress and a wan smile. Her big dark eyes, mournful in sepia matte, seemed reproachful as though she had recently been severely reprimanded, perhaps for having a bra strap showing, and across her bare shoulder was written "Always your own Brenda." Her limp hands in her lap were turned to the camera as if to show his ring on her engagement finger. Even to manufacture the idea of being ravished by Vince the Vile caused one to close one's eyes and shudder.

Until Pearl Harbor there had been no need to finagle one's way out of military service and indeed so little actual effect had the distant war had on life, apart from the troops who had sailed off to the Middle East and the getting of good imported whiskey, that sometimes it was difficult not to think of it all as some fiction in the evening papers. Even the fall of France and Hitler's invasions of Holland and Norway only constituted mild dismay; the Australian fortitude and well-known cheeriness never-mind-what were the prevailing attitudes. Old "Winnie" would get them through if the Germans didn't cross the Channel, and even if they did (in the pubs everyone sang along with Vera Lynn that there'd always be an England) and when, to everyone's surprise, Hitler turned in the other direction and attacked the USSR, that monolith, like a wasp on an elephant, the more dreamily optimistic even saw an end to the war in possibly six weeks.

Then out of the blue in Hawaii came the little beasts.

Seaton, temporarily on a reserve status with the occupational excuse of keeping up the morale on the home front by entertaining it nightly on radio, found himself called up and denied any further exemption. Pronounced hastily by an overworked weary physician as "A One," his application for continued immunity was stamped NOT APPROVED by a stratospherically uppish lieutenant who looked him down, not up, and said, "Work on the wireless, do you? P'raps you'd like to take a signals course now that you can't get out of it."

"I'm not trying to get out of anything," he had said hotly.

"*Sir,* when you address me, cobber."

Into the unpleasant-smelling, horrid-to-the-touch, shit-colored khaki and clamped onto the head went the absurd Digger hat, not much changed from when the Aussie infantry had been mown down by the Turks at Gallipoli in 1915, on went the boots with the heavy iron cleats, and he was presented with a poorly put together sewing kit and a dog tag bearing his blood type to be worn constantly around his neck to remind him even in the dead of night that he now belonged to the army.

Then, when he was dragged from his safe job at the Victoria Barracks (courtesy of a friend of Rat Ratcliffe who had rescued several trembling privates from the fate of New Guinea jungles and set them up in comfy stay-at-home jobs in the spick-and-span commandant's office where they giggled with the WAAC girl secretaries and lunched out wherever they liked with a dry sherry to boot) and carted off to the Show Ground and put on a draft to Butcher's Creek away up in "the Territory," it hit him for the first time that there was now nothing for it than to become one of the mob in order to eradicate any trace of himself.

"Oh, you poor miserable drongoes," the sergeant said, lining up the seven of them bound for "the Creek." "You wretched no-hopers. You'll only get pink lolly water where you're going and the grub's said to be the worst in Australia. They've got blokes what haven't had a leave for two years and they say many poor bludgers have gone off their rocker. They take 'em up to the loony bin in Darwin and leave 'em there, you can hear them wailing all the way down to Daly Waters. Oh, you poor miserable arseholes."

The seven shuffled their feet and smirked ruefully. Corporal Daly took the lead for them forthrightly. "Shit," he said and there was a laugh.

"Ta-ta you bloody no-hopers, see you when the war's over," the sergeant said gloatingly, waving to them as the old wooden box train wobbled out of Central Station.

They were indeed a wretched lot, the seven; one slept all the way north to Townsville, the others stared moodily out the window and occasionally spat out the same lifeless obscenity. They might have learned only four words since birth, fuck and shit varied only with Christ and cunt. Their dull eyes accepted the uneatable food served them on station platforms while the train waited; their souls were embedded in damp khaki wool while they stood in the rain waiting for their chow. At Mount Isa on the border of the Territory they were taken off the train and put into a truck. Nights they slept on the dirty sand with a tormenting wind blowing grit into their mouths. Cunt of a wind, they told one another. Aroused by shrill blasts on a whistle in the half-dark, they assured one another that one day they'd get that bastard by the arsehole and belt a big "woolly pup" up him, an expression instigated by the artillery men who cleaned out the big guns.

There was a difference in the air now, a cleansing wind blew across the stunted trees gnarled into shapes of people bent over in agony. But the nights were pure with cold air and lit with stars; it was the northern winter, dry from April until October, hot by day and chilly at night; they wrapped themselves, wearing their heavy boots (not taken off once since Sydney), in gray army blankets and slept with their heads on their pack bags. Shit, they told one another good night, and fuck, they said, greeting the morning; their language was as impoverished as that of a nomad tribe awakening after the ice age somewhere near Ararat.

The first indication of Butcher's Creek (they arrived at twenty hundred hours in the dark) was the smell. A sickly sweet powerful smell of disinfectant oil poured down the latrines and set on fire. The tents and huts were lit with kerosene lamps and shadowy figures came and went. The cries of those betting on the "swy" game, played with pennies shot in the air, came through the sharp chill. The first news was there was no supper for them, the cook and kitchen detail had gone off for the night. They could, if they were starving, get a chocolate Violet Crumble Bar and a bottle of "lolly water," that pale mouthwash that passed for a soda, at the Red Cross hut. "Shit," said Corporal Daly for them. "Up them," he said. By now you couldn't tell Seaton from the others; he had a slouching male walk like a wrestler leaving the ring in triumph. Only his deep blue eyes occasionally registered a cry for help.

Well, commandant's office (because he was a Class A typist) in headquarters wasn't bad, at least he was out of the broiling sun at a clean desk and except for the wretched standing orders that he was required to type in stencil to be run off in dozens of copies on a Roneo machine, the work was not arduous. Of course, there was Captain Smollett nearby, always waiting to slap you onto a charge sheet or order you to retype a whole page because one word had been omitted (and generally at one minute to five just before stand-down), but there was also Grudge. Grudge O'Brien, the pay sergeant, was a quiet balding man in his thirties (most of the troops were under twenty-five) who was barely known to say a word except "mate." "Goodoh mate," Grudge would say and wink kindly at you as if to ameliorate your bored melancholy and once or twice to pinch his hand when Corporal Daly handed him some memo from NORFORCE about restriction of payment to a long absent-without-leave private (in desperation, some had been known to hide in the dark along the railway line and jump the weekly night train that went through with troops from Darwin on leave to Alice Springs, never to be heard from again). But the softness in Grudge's eyes signified nothing more than plain humanity.

Perhaps something was put in the tea they drank, perhaps it was merely the superfluity of male bodies walking naked to the evening shower wearing only untied boots, nothing more useless than the dozens upon dozens of deactivated organs going flip-flop, flip-flop to the showers. No one looked, no one cared. After a period of such mutual abstention it became a virtue, like an oath of chastity. Yet the more they were sexually restrained by some nitrate, the more they exercised their right to copulate by obscenity; fuck him, you, it, they said. Get it up the flaming cook, they said, reviling the food. Up Vince the Vile they chorused when he canceled the Saturday football game for an "emu" parade.

Get it up! Always up.

At the picture show on Saturday night at the vast open-air screen, where they sat on log seats with their blankets and lolly water, they incited the male star to molest the female (the more that showed of Lana Turner, the wilder the shrieks). "Do her over," a voice would yell from the dark, and after a moment another voice, "Or I will." This was inevitably followed by such laughter that the usually prudish dialogue was drowned out for several minutes.

Bereft of communion with the flesh, they claimed their long-distance rights to it with feverish abandonment; they were engulfed in nostalgic wantonness, but in the soft lamplight over their evening poker, their faces were like those of innocent children.

Seaton was unable to remember when exactly it was that the old feeling of exclusion had vanished. He had become one of the mob, browned and red-dusted, thin with the daily portions of dry mutton and boiled potato (cold at lunch, hot at supper), gritty with the constant blowing sand, loquacious on beer nights (Thursday and Saturday they were doled two bottles of warm lager), satisfied. Here in this scorched-earth exile, amidst five-foot-high anthills like ancient Inca cities against the sunset, here where only once a week a train whistle was to be heard in the night, reminding them of the outside world, here was a peace. No one knew.

No one cared, he was one of the poor bludgers who'd copped "the Creek." On guard duty one dawn (bad luck to cop the third shift, which started at four A.M.) he watched as the stars faded and the fuzzy yellow light confiscated the eastern night. As the dawn broke he realized the utterly improbable: he was at peace, not happy, but more peaceful than ever so far in his life and being devoid of the precaution constantly forced on him by his sexuality or peculiarity, whichever it was, was as refreshing as early morning rain; the acceptance of him by "mates" and the continuous serenity of their peculiar brotherhood made it a singular appeasement.

So it was, going to mess, say, that one automatically put an arm around a cobber and he around you; they needed to and that was all there was to it. For a few moments his unutterable desire was for it to continue for life, that he need never again want, and not wanting the dubious pleasures of his left-handedness, the forbidden delights, taken with care, with the blinds down, touching fingers under the table, disguised with girls present and only imploring eyes to imploring eyes to witness, no longer a prey to any of it, would be the awakening of a reality and a trueness of himself. When the guard truck came to relieve him, he put his arm around the driver's shoulder in this new morning joy.

"How are you, mate?"

"Not bad, mate, how's yourself?"

"Fuckin' nice day."

He kept it a dream, his secret.

"Corporal Daly."

"SIR."

To instant attention, iron heels clicking.

"Can you drive a Ute?"

"Yes, sir." Captain Smollett's little cold blue eyes. Thinking he might as well get something from the army gratis that might be useful in what they jokingly called the After Life, he had signed on for a driving course while at Victoria Barracks and all he'd driven so far had been small trucks. He knew how to handle a Ute.

"My usual driver's got a touch of dysentery and I have to be up at the Katherine camp, they're having a review of the new two-button slicker, which is going to be issued next March, just in time to miss the Wet, of course. Here's your requisition for the Ute. Be in front of the officers' mess at fourteen hundred."

"Yes, sir."

Well, a run up to the Katherine was a breather away from the typewriter and the bloody stencils, even if it had to be with Vince. And maybe he could stay on for mess; rumor had it the blokes at Katherine had a superior mess to the Creek. Might even be a movie if Vince stayed overnight. Rumor was the Katherine blokes had already had *Casablanca*, whereas the Creek got Deanna Durbin week in and week out.

"And bring your rifle, Corporal. We might see if we can pick off a bush turkey for the cook."

"Sir."

Captain Smollett was waiting outside the mess at two minutes to fourteen hundred, smoking a cigarette.

He climbed in beside Seaton and they rumbled out a little uncertainly (not absolutely at home with the gears) onto the long North–South road and nothing was said. Captain Smollett stared ahead at the monotonous red dust and stunted gums.

"Ever been to the Red Lily Lagoon?" he asked.

"No, sir."

"Worth a trip, good shooting there. Crocodiles. Big ones. Come out after you like buggery. Got one right in the eye; she threw a fit, landing on her back, but the chaps said don't go near that lashing tail, so we left her there to die in peace." Captain Smollett chuckled. "About fifteen feet she was, the bugger."

"Fancy."

"Big bitch."

They drove in silence; the road spun endlessly before them; once an artillery truck passed them going south and tooted its horn.

"Bloody Territory," Captain Smollett said, "goes on forever."

"Yes, sir."

When they were passing a greener patch of what looked like

mulga and wild wattle, the Captain said, "Drive off here a moment. This looks like possible turkey territory." They left the road and bumped a few yards into a low sandy basin surrounded by brittle thorn bushes and some abandoned anthills. Big birds hovered in the blue, but there was no sign of turkey.

"Stop here a minute, Corporal."

"Yes, sir."

He cut off the engine and they sat there until the Captain, pointing, said, "Watch over there a minute, something's stirring behind those bushes. Got your rifle?"

"Yes, sir."

He brought out his rifle and lowered the side window. They waited.

"Watch over there to the right."

"I am, sir."

Nothing moved, they sat silent, so close that he could hear the Captain breathing. When nothing moved for endless minutes, he said, "I don't think there's anything there, sir," and turned back right into the Captain's warm mouth and then arms were around him tightly and he was pressed against the Captain's faultless shirt.

"Drop your bloody gun, Corporal." The Captain, chuckling, said, "Relax, sonny boy, it's all right. You know, I had you pegged from the start. And do you know how I got the idea? You buckle your belt the wrong way, from left to right, the way girls buckle a belt. I never reprimanded you because I was waiting to find out."

Later the Captain said, "Lie back a bit," and then, even later, "Do you know something? You're a little corker, that's what you are, a bloody little corker. I'll tell you something, corker, I like you. Do you like me a bit?"

"Yes, sir."

"Don't be formal for a few fucking minutes, it's all we've got, it might be all we'll ever have."

Holding him down on the seat, legs twisted under the steering wheel, Captain Smollett kissed him lengthily on the mouth and then said hoarsely, "I don't think I have to tell you that if ever a word of this squeaked out the results would be very serious for you. I don't have to remind you that the word of an officer against a soldier is generally taken without question. Just a word to the wise, corker." Sitting straight up now, the Captain rebuckled his belt and said, "Drive on, Corporal."

They drove on.

It was as fleeting as a quick dream during a five-minute nap; he couldn't yet accept it as real, glancing at the Captain's composed face, the bristling military mustache, the cap set at a perfect angle, it was a little snatched dream during an after-lunch nap.

The review of the new two-button issue slickers took less than an hour. When Seaton stood to attention and opened the door to the cab, Captain Smollett said curtly, "Don't bother."

Driving back along the darkening road, the Captain sniggered and said, "Somebody's authorized them to spend a couple of hundred thousand to issue a new slicker that isn't as good as the old one. You can bet somebody's cousin is benefiting if I know the War Department."

And "Good night, Corporal, you're dismissed," marching smartly away.

Not a vestige of anything having happened. In the office, orders were still barked out, typing errors discovered just before stand-down; not by an eyelash did Vince admit anything more than that Corporal Daly's desk was next to his own and hand him orders to be typed in triplicate. Once on an A8 Form of Inquiry into Ullage, he had scribbled "Four copies X." The *X* was tiny and infinitely discreet or could have been meant as a period. The only hint of a possibility of recollection was that Corporal Daly was mysteriously left off the guard duty roster for nearly ten days.

Then "Bring this report to my tent, Corporal."

"Sir."

The order was given at ten minutes to seventeen hundred.

Seaton took his time typing it, annoyed at the silliness of having a noticeable heartbeat.

The flap of the tent had been left wide open as if to minimize suspicion of anything untoward. Captain Smollett was sitting on the cot in stocking feet. His fiancée in the photograph beside him looked more glum than ever, as though she might have suspected something.

"Stand over there, Corporal. Stand easy."

"Sir."

Anyone passing the tent would see an officer reading a report while the NCO waited. Captain Smollett read the report, reread it, reread it again in silence while from across the way sounds of the early cocktail hour reverberated in coarse male laughter from the officers' mess.

Eventually Vince said in a low voice, "Can you hear what I'm saying? I don't want to speak loudly."

"Yes, sir."

He spoke without raising his head from the report, knuckling his forehead. "Something extraordinary and unfortunate, unforeseen has happened. I have fallen in love with you. I realize that this places both of us in an untenable and extremely dangerous situation. Discovery could mean the end for me of my military career, almost certain dishonorable discharge, and possibly six months at hard labor up at Daly Waters Correction Camp, very likely considerably worse for you. On the other hand, the prospect of never once again being close to you even for a few seconds is infinitely worse. Are you hearing me?"

"Yes, sir."

"I've been informed there's been some breaking in and stealing from sheds at Number Three Sub Depot, and I intend to make some late-night raids there in the hope of discovering the culprits. I intend to make these inspections alone after lights out. I am hardly in the position, nor is it permissible for me, to make this an order, Corporal, but if a certain person were to be there— do I make myself clear?"

"Yes, sir."

"You know where. A little after lights out."

"Sir."

"That's all, thank you, Corporal."

In the moon shadows behind the grim corrugated iron sheds at Number Three Sub Depot where there was no sign of attempted night ullage, the two spectral figures became quickly merged into one.

"Quick, we don't have long. Keep your eyes peeled. See anything?"

"No."

"Thought I heard something." Whispered. "Over there."

Waiting.

"I didn't."

"God, you sweet, you sweet little bugger. Look, would you do something for me? Would you?"

"What?"

"Say something sweet to me, even if you don't mean it."

Toward August, the winter turning, the long-awaited, plotted transfer came through. Corporal Daly had been accepted as chief writer for the newly created First Commonwealth Broadcast Unit to produce a weekly propaganda radio program titled "The Army Show" and not only had the approval of the transfer come directly from General Blamey's headquarters in Melbourne and so was automatically counterapproved by NORFORCE in Darwin and therefore could not be disapproved by anyone, even Colonel Plank, but also specified that Corporal Daly was to be transported by plane from the Larimah transit camp as far as Brisbane. No NCO had ever before been flown out of the Territory.

"Good on yer, matie," dear old Grudge said in the shower line, he who had not had a day's leave for what would be three years in September. Handshakes and backslaps came all the way down the naked row of boys in only boots in line for their fifteen thousandth tepid shower with the yellow soap tossed about like a football and the only thing they had to look forward to on a non-movie night, God bless their warm generous natures. Seaton felt a glow for them.

"Report to my tent at stand-down," Captain Smollett said, shifting papers and not looking up.

This time no precautions were taken. He was naked to the waist, washing himself with a sponge out of a tin basin; he merely gestured toward the camp chair and Seaton sat although it was improper for him to be seated while an officer stood. Was there going to be trouble? Could Vince have discovered some arcane loophole in the army manual that could preclude the transfer?

Vince wiped his face and chest with a towel and said, "So you're going back to a nice safe cozy job at base, are you?"

"Sir."

"Don't be formal."

"They need experienced radio scriptwriters. I'm one."

"I see."

Captain Smollett smiled glassily, the smile that invariably preceded a verdict of guilty, bringing with it a punishment of draconian severity. Then still smiling he tore the towel he was holding completely down the middle. It was as biblical as the rending of clothes. In a strangled voice he said, "This place is going to be unthinkable without you," and as Seaton rose to go to him, barked, "Sit still. Anyone might come in." He bent over the tin wash basin as if in pain. "I shouldn't complain, it's not that bad of a posting for a somewhat uneducated bloke like me. The officer chaps are not bad, they're not my type, but they try, the boys do their best, it's just that"—a very long pause and then in almost no voice at all—"I'm so fucking lonely. Not only here, everywhere. Back in Melbourne. Everywhere. Oh, I shouldn't complain, I've got a good dull job to go back to. I'm engaged to a fine girl. Got my mum and dad. A bonza sister. They all think I'm the berries, poor boobs. I've never told anyone about myself. You're one of the four people on earth who knows. I wanted just to tell you that and to tell you one last time I love you." He picked up the tin basin and, moving to the flap of the tent, threw out the soapy water onto the dirty sand. For the first time, he looked at Seaton. "That's all, dismissed!"

On Wednesday morning, the truck waiting to take him

down to Larimah in-transit camp, Seaton took his transfer papers
from Captain Smollett, who appeared not to be noticing him.

"Good-bye, sir."

The voice was a live electric wire. "Corporal."

"Sir."

"Your bootlace is untied."

What'll I do with my rubber?

NOBODY was really prepared for the peace that came with such suddenness following the fire over Hiroshima; no one was adjusted after nearly six years to being without the war and to be expected to join in the celebration of the bomb, which to some was a horrendous jollification. After two false alarms when misguided folks rushed into the street blowing whistles, when the sirens finally announced the real McCoy, in the late morning, at first there was a curious stillness before the thunderstorm of joy.

Mrs. Dolly Hollingshead went immediately down Macleay Street to The Gin Cask and purchased six bottles of Gilbey's gin and two of Penfold's sherry, one sweet and one dry before they ran out. In the street people were already slightly tipsy and smiling foolishly at strangers. Strung around her neck on a mock gold chain was her air-raid precaution gear: a tin whistle, a toy flashlight, a wee penknife, and a large flat pink India rubber eraser to be slipped into her mouth to prevent her biting off her tongue even though, goodness knows, she often had need of it being bitten off, with the unfortunate and funny things she said. In the last few years she had entertained (less charitable people might have said enticed) numerous American servicemen to her second-floor apartment. Among them Captain Orville G. Bentley from Oshkosh, Lieutenant Ward Q. Applegate from Racine,

184

Staff Sergeant Willis J. Nutley from New Canaan, and Major John Phillip Sousa MacElroy from Kalamazoo. She had also entertained with less enthusiasm Lieutenants Betty Jean Kirkwood and Delphine Weinstein of the U.S. Navy. Currently there was Lootenant (as he said it) Lloyd C. Manville of Grosse Point, Michigan, for whom she had secreted a preciously saved bottle of Johnnie Walker whiskey given to her by Captain Mick Leatherbee of North Hollywood, said to be a close friend of the character actress Cora Witherspoon, who, oddly enough, greatly resembled Dolly.

Dolly naturally had been on the stage, her height and nose contributing to her comicality, and she had specialized in the kind of run-on, run-off socialite ladies wearing floral chiffon who contributed to the piffling plots in musical comedies. None of the comedy dialogue forced on her was one-tenth as witty or original as the things she said herself, the little barbs and acerbities that came from her. Her comedic self was said to have had many catastrophic effects on her love life; many partners were said to have fallen out of bed laughing at her and not gotten back in. Something about her nose perched beakishly over her small mouth and the glasses quivering on the bridge of it set people to laughing even before she delivered her punch line. When she was seriously and deeply in love, which was continually, she would want desperately to communicate in as simple and truthful a way as she could muster, the emotion she felt to the man, but oftentimes before she reached halfway into the simple declaration of love, her wretched nose would appear to grow even larger and her small mouth to curl up in exquisite disdain at herself and lo and behold instead of being in each other's arms, she and the paramour would be rolling on the floor and holding their sides because she had transformed the situation into a moment of comicality so rich and true that it could not support any modicum of emotion, let alone sensuality. Gentlemen, on the point of eloquent lust, would be unsexed by something she said, usually in a low aside, about their deportment or underwear and, unable to maintain their lustful stance, wilting, would take her in their arms, chortling that never in their lives had they encountered her equal. God almighty, they said, you are the berries, they told her. They told her that she took the cake.

Which had made for a lonely life on the whole. Being followed by gusts of laughter instead of guitars, reviving the bored, succoring the melancholy. Some of the gentlemen were not always gentlemen. During the New Zealand train tour of *Roberta* in which she ran-on, ran-off with the skimpy plot, her current adoration, a tall good-looking chorus boy, had tried it on with one of the night porters who made up the sleeper berths, tried to get the porter into the upper and was assaulted for it, loosening two front teeth and getting a black eye, when Dolly burst into the compartment and began beating the night porter. How dare he make approaches to her *husband,* she demanded to know and, hand on the emergency cord, threatened to stop the train and hand him over to the authorities for making lewd and obscene advances. Nothing more was heard of or from the night porter.

Who Mr. Hollingshead, her real husband, was and where he was remained a mystery, and Mr. Hollingshead remained silent in an enamel frame on her dressing table. Alongside him was the small oval framed picture of a little boy in a sailor suit and occasionally when her eyes lighted on it, her nose swelled and her glance moistened. Someone knew and passed on the information that her little boy had died at age seven from acute mononucleosis; more likely, a less-kind person opined, he had died laughing at something Dolly said.

Well, if this was the end of the war, it was going to go out with a whizbang as far as Dolly was concerned. By the time Seaton got out of the lift, the small flat was already spilling out into the hall with people and Dolly's store of drinking glasses had run out; several people were drinking out of Horlick's Malted Milk tins and jam jars; the noise of talk and laughter was uproarious. Saying excuse me, pardon me, Seaton pushed his way into the crowded living room and embraced Dolly, who was weeping with laughter. "Too awful to tell," she said and introduced her American love.

Lootenant Lloyd C. Manville (all Americans, it seemed, were born with a middle initial) was so young and boyish that he could have been a twelve-year-old dressed up in an army uniform for some school play. He blinked behind gold-rimmed glasses, his baby-smooth skin might never have felt a razor. "Hi, Season," Lloyd said and gave a warm child hand. He was amiable to the point of caricature. Yes, sir, yes, ma'am, he said, smiling, and offered to get drinks, give up his chair, move the lamp so it wasn't in your eyes, get you a napkin, ask after your folks. When congratulated on his country's bomb, he smiled modestly but stood to attention and murmured that people would now have to recognize that America was the greatest country on earth and such was his innocence and genuine pride that to discountenance any such statement would have amounted to treason. "If you don't mind my saying," Lloyd C. Manville, said, blinking.

One person who emphatically did not agree with him and who was becoming drunker and louder by the second was Julia Montrose, British to the core, or as she was now, on her ump-teenth gin, obliged to pronounce, "Brish-ish." Thank God, she said for the Brishish. "I'm proud to remind you tonight it was the simple Brishish folk in their bloody little fishing boats at Dunkirk that got us through, not the bloody Yanks and their detestable bomb." "Oh, Julie," Dolly said, "when you get smashed you get more and more to look like Disraeli."

The party swayed back and forth from the hallway to the kitchen as more people arrived and some left. Some, Dolly said, she had never seen before. "Darling," Dolly said, pulling a face, "this sherry's as thin as tin, get me something robust to drink." Lloyd C. Manville ran to get it. Dolly drank and laughed, laughed and drank, but it wasn't until after midnight, when most of the crowd had gone, that Seaton found her alone in the kitchen, crying.

"Damn their bomb," Dolly said, mopping her eyes. "Light me a Philip Morris."

She had been metamorphosed by the war; all the years of feeding off Hollywood films had translated her, unbeknownst,

into a vicarious Yankee Doodle and then suddenly the avalanche
of GIs and officers had transcended the cinema; the huge mysterious country known only on black-and-white film where lustrous
people moved and lived in unreality became suddenly as real as
the corner grocery, and there in their beautiful pink-and-beige
uniforms were the prototypes of John Hodiak and Dana Andrews; the American girls, the WACS and WAVES spoke and
behaved like Gene Tierney or Jeanne Crain. America came to
Kings Cross, Sydney, and just around Dolly's corner was New
York or New Orleans, the pure childlike GI faces, pleased to
present you with a carton of Lucky Strike or a pair of precious
nylons if you'd give kindness in return and not syphilis. Dolly
was a born mother and she mothered the army orphans, gave
them drinks, and made them laugh and in return they admitted
her to the United States or the nearest approximation of it.

Now in one fell swoop of atomic fission, the Mardi Gras was
over, the boys and girls would be going home to Omaha and
Bakersfield, many boys with brides from Oatley and Strathfield,
none would be taking Dolly back with them to the old folks at
home; she would be left stranded on the beach with only the
poignancy of them and a see-through plastic cigarette case left
her by Private First Class Clarence B. Rosenquat.

Now, as Seaton put his arms around her and squeezed her,
she fingered her air-raid precautions kit and said, "Now what'll
I do with my *rubber?*"

That set them off giggling like nincompoops. The way she
said "my rubber," sounded so suggestive and they knew about
the "pro" stations and what was handed out to the boys on
furlough (they now never said "leave," always furlough; vacation, not holiday; ketchup, not tomato sauce; and Dolly would
say wait a sec till she looked at her "skedule"—without being
conscious of it Seaton and Dolly had become imitation GIs) and
being, both of them, exclusive, Dolly because of middle age,
Seaton by nature, they looked askance at the eagerness with
which the Australian girls took in the bewildered aliens in more
ways than one. There was, of course, xenophobia, the natural

hostility aroused by the invasion of these substantially funded foreigners with their marvelous teeth and crew cuts (the well-worn joke was "oversexed, overpaid, and over here"), and there had been at least one terrifying incident in a Brisbane bar in which a harmless American GI had been savagely beaten to death by a mob of drunken Australian bullies incensed over some triviality, and there were complaints from the unbearably prudish North Shore Liners that Wynyard Station underground was becoming a honeycomb of prostitution at night. Still, everyone sang along with Bing, and Dolly took to eating American-style, cutting her meat and then laying down the knife and transferring the fork to her right hand. "I'll be hornswoggled," she was heard to say.

"Go and see if Lloyd's all right," she said. "I'll be there in a minute. I want to put on some eyebrows so I'll look bold enough to face the future."

Lloyd C. Manville had been taken over by Madge Trimble, who, Dolly said, was known to bend over backward to be raped. Sure enough, Madge Trimble was leaning over backward in an attitude of presenting her private commodity to Lloyd C. Manville. She was wearing a black openwork lace dress over a flesh-colored slip that suggested she had nothing on but cobwebs and she was by now lavishly "shickered" and unable to stop talking. Back and back she leaned, one hand on the fake fireplace mantel, until literally she was all but pushing what Dolly called her "credenza" into Lloyd's crotch. While Lloyd, glass in hand, stood in his immaculate uniform as motionless as a sentry and stupefied with boredom as, makeup-smeared, hair awry, she drove relentlessly on with some pointless anecdote. When he caught sight of Seaton, relief flooded his prep school face and he reached out and put an arm around Seaton, drawing him into the conversation. "Oh, hey there, Season," Lloyd said and smiled a message that read "For God's sake, don't leave me alone with this dame."

And so on, my dear, and so on, Madge went on, seemingly unaware of Seaton, all about how she had shaken off the unwanted advances of some "Lootnant Colonel." She laughed at her artifices and poked Lloyd Manville in and around his confidential parts. "Not that I'm any f-f-finicky little virgin, as anyone will tell you," she said, catching hold of his lapel and spilling her drink on him, wiping him off and pushing up her ravaged face into his with a gargoyle smile, revealing expensively re-created teeth. "You betcha bottom dollar, sweetheart." She was one of those drunks who reach a plateau, never passing out or actually falling down, but beyond accountability. "Bet your arse, sweet-art," Madge said, swaying toward Lloyd who, to avoid her, swayed back and in doing so hugged Seaton. In a very low voice Lloyd said into Seaton's ear, "Are you going to come home with me?"

"If you want," Seaton said, surprised.

"Oh, please, I want you to, will you, will you, please?"

When Seaton nodded, Lloyd laughed pleasantly and poor Madge mistakenly thought she had spoken some witticism; her unfocused glare changed to one of pleased acquiescence. "Tol' you so, I'm *fun*, you wanna know something, I'm fun, more ways 'n one, darling." Now she dropped her glass on the carpet and, coiling herself around Lloyd, she attempted to put her teeth around his earlobe while he smiled, sweating slightly, holding her at arm's length while she mooed incomprehensibly into his left ear some garbled nonsense about not being a common whore because she cared about those she loved, like Lloyd. "I car 'bout you, you darling boy, see? How big's your *ontraynoo*, swee'-heart? I'll bet you're no midget."

Lloyd was scarlet now, holding her away from him as if he had been lewdly groped in church. Come to think of it, he was rather like a pleasant young Sunday school teacher out on a picnic treat with his pupils. "I think, ma'am, you ought to sit down," he said and firmly put Madge in a chair where she dropped into a glum silence, the beginning of what would become the outraged virulence of the often-scorned. But Dolly would have to cope with that, and could.

As they went down in the lift, Lloyd's fingers brushed Seaton's.

"Thanks an awful lot," Lloyd said.

"For what?"

"Rescuing me. That poor unhappy dame."

He was putting up at the Oriental Hotel. Putting up "with" would have been more likely. It had had a loose reputation even before the war and since the American invasion it had deteriorated to a new low only a notch above a bordello; its tawdry lobby was a hive of tarty girls trying to pick up the army and navy officers who couldn't get in anywhere else and now two of the tartiest approached Seaton and Lloyd as they came in. "Yew boys look a bit *laoe* nly," one of them said. They were inches deep in rouge and both wore chandelier paste earrings and tight, livid green imitation silk dresses. "Excuse us ladies, good night," Lloyd said and pushed Seaton past them toward the lift. "Oh, they want to be excused," the other girl said scathingly. "They want to be alone, the dear things. Whoo-oo, whoo-OO," the tarts chorused and they swished into an imitation sissy walk, hand on hip and loose-wristed. "Oh, you sweet things," they sang derisively and some sailors laughed with them.

In the narrow talcum-smelling little room lit with only blatant ceiling light and with only one three-quarter bed covered in raspberry terrycloth, Seaton asked to use the phone and awoke Essie to tell her the crowds in the streets had gotten out of hand and that he was safer being put up on Dolly's sofa, what with the carryings-on. Essie, more than usually woolly-headed because of being awakened, asked seriously was this because of the war being over. "When will they let you out, pet?" she asked as if it might be Tuesday.

Lloyd had a bottle of warming champagne sitting in melted ice.

"I didn't want to welcome the peace in all on my own and so I went downstairs in search of a friendly face but all there was was what we've just seen and the thought of having a drink with any of them was too depressing. Now let *us* drink to the peace, Season."

"To the peace."

"Long may it last."

"Long may it last."

"God bless America."

"America."

"And us."

"And us."

They sat side by side on the bed and sipped the tepid champagne, an Adelaide brew more like lemonade. It was somehow appropriate to the harmlessness of the situation, more like being sequestered with the vicar, and when Lloyd leaned toward him and said without a trace of irony, "May I?" before kissing him quickly and dryly on the lips he almost expected that the next thing Lloyd would say might be that the scriptural text for today's Bible lesson was from Thessalonians. Everything was so unlustful and highly proper that their proximity to each other seemed accidental and even had Lloyd's mother come into the room, entirely moral. But then Lloyd put an arm around him and kissed him emphatically and said, exactly like a boyish scoutmaster, "Shall we proceed?"

They undressed in silence and Lloyd, naked, wound his watch and placed it on the bedside table and then took off his gold-rimmed glasses, which left a pink mark on the bridge of his nose and made him seem nuder than the taking off of his clothes, and younger. The smooth hairless adolescent body suggested that one could be contributing to the delinquency of a minor.

Off went the ceiling light, leaving them in the neutrality of the glow from Darlinghurst Road streetlights as though Lloyd reasoned that there was less sinfulness in the opaque. Sinfulness was hardly the word for the boyishness of his behavior, waggish was more the word for the flip-flopping gymnastics that went on as if it were taking place in a rubber boat shooting the rapids, their heads bumping on the headboard (Gosh, did you hurt yourself?); it reminded Seaton of his schoolday afternoons with sex mates (Quick, in case Mum should come) in toolsheds and cellars, seeing who would be first.

Yet there was an overall sense of simplicity and innocence in Lloyd that made it, in a sense, endearing. Completed, they lay side by side in silence like stone effigies and Lloyd took hold of Seaton's hand and said, "I just couldn't have borne to be alone tonight on this wonderful night for the world. Thank you, Season, I deeply appreciate it, I do indeed, guy. Thanks a heap, Season."

"The name is Sea*ton,*" he said. But in the silence that followed he heard only deep breathing.

Over greasy eggs in the Kings Cross Hot Cross Bun, Lloyd said, "How long do you have off?"

"All today."

"And I have till seven this evening when they *say* they've got a transport for me to Manila. Let's spend the day together. Would you like that, or am I taking up too much of your time?"

"No, Lloyd."

Even after all that fumbling and touching last night, Seaton couldn't quite be obvious in the daylight; Lloyd was too polite to make approaches to, too manly to be told that he was sweet. He merely smiled a lot.

They went to the Botanic Gardens; there might never have been a war, they might have been actors dressed in uniform for a film. Right off, doing the right thing, Lloyd rushed after a speeding child headed pell-mell for a pond and scooped her up in his arms, presenting her to her grateful mother with a salute. He half-bowed, half-lifted his hand to his cap to people who passed by. He was dead serious about the telling of himself and it was not all wildly encouraging. He was with a small law firm in Detroit, he liked a good basketball game, he had seen *Bambi* nineteen times (said without a glimmer of embarrassment). Hold on, he would say at the sight of a banyan tree, I want to remember that. Stand there a minute so's I can remember you there, too. And once, in a secluded bamboo garden, he stopped still and said,

"Do you mind, while no one's around?" And kissed Seaton. Remember me, he said out of the blue, dewy with the warm day and with good-natured affection. He was so absolutely decent, taking off and polishing his glasses and smiling up at Seaton, the young American lieutenant doing his bit to save a world for the very same decency of himself that Seaton wanted to take him in his arms. In the quietest way possible and in dead seriousness, as if he were now taking an oath on his mother's Bible, he said, "If you ever want to come to America, I'd be honored to be your sponsor, Season."

As they parted in front of the Grace Building U.S. headquarters, he gave Seaton a wilted personal card left over from his prewar days. It read "Lloyd C. Manville, Attorney. Lord and Tomkins Attorneys at Law, 200 Edsel Square, Detroit, Michigan." On the back he had written in high-school handwriting "Don't lose me."

"So long, pal," he said as the cab whirled him away forever.

PART TWO

They must think I'm one of the Vanderbilts

No ONE SAID MUCH, on the road to Mascot airport, Rat Ratcliffe driving his new Holden mini with Seaton and Essie sitting in the back, partly because of the noise of rain pelting down on the roof but more because they seemed to be stunned at the actuality of what was taking place on this Saturday night in cold, wet July. The rains were perhaps weeping at his leaving, Essie said, all she could think of to say, poor wretch being left, perhaps forever. Had on a new hat from McCathy's, altogether wrong for midwinter, a white straw with a mosquito netting veil ornamented with little pink rosebuds.

Because why? Why on earth was he going? He was going to America, that land of cars and movie stars and night baseball, where, according to some recent survey, somebody was fatally shot every eight minutes.

Even he didn't seem to know why. His correspondence with the American lieutenant, Mr. Manville, had gone on now for three years, and indeed it was Mr. Manville out in Detroit, who, good as his word, had put up all the necessary papers for the U.S. consulate. Essie had not been told until it was, as Seaton put it, a "fate accomplee" and he was on the waiting list for a quota number from Washington. Miss Annaheim at the consulate had been most amiable and totally unhelpful except to say to him only to come in if he had a change of address, and so much

197

time had gone by that Essie had become accustomed to it, until out of the blue last May a terse note had informed him that a quota number had become available for him and that if he still desired to emigrate, he must do so before three months was up. No ships sailing any longer, he was now booked on Pan American Flight 211 to Los Angeles leaving Mascot at midnight. The fancy had become reality; three large suitcases, an overnight bag, and portable Smith-Corona were in the trunk and they were speeding through the rain-washed traffic to the airport, not too late yet for him to say turn around, he had changed his mind, that it worried him that the elderly Miss Liggins who had rented his room might not be a harmonious lodger for Essie and that anyway he could, at the last moment, not be parted from his beloved foster mother, his friends, his country.

From time to time he patted Essie's knee and she turned to him and smiled wanly.

Not yet, by some years, the international airport it would become, swept by lights, implemented with moving walkways, inundated by flights arriving from and leaving to all points on earth, the overseas departure lounge was situated in a corrugated iron shed in a field of paspalum grass and litter. A cardboard sign read PAN AM FLIGHTS: LEFT, which could have meant they had departed.

In the tin shed "lounge" they were met by a Pan Am superintendent wearing a name plate that read "Miss Shields" who looked at Seaton's ticket and said, pointing to a door, to go on in to processing and be weighed in. Rat helped carry the heavy bags as far as the scales and then said, "We'll be in the lounge as they call it, darling." Someone who had traveled abroad had said that when you get to Mascot, ask for Mr. Dodge and slip him five quid and then if you're a smidge overweight he'll just wink and put you through. Mr. Dodge turned out to be a weighty man with muscles enough needed to lift heavy luggage on and off scales. "Don" had said to say hello, Seaton told Mr. Dodge and pushed the five-pound note into his hand, but Mr. Dodge neither winked nor put his baggage through. Mr. Dodge scratched his head and looked sad. "You're nearly forty pounds over," Mr. Dodge said. "It's going to cost you a bit."

"How much?"

"Say around a pound sterling a pound weight, let's say thirty-five, thirty-six quid."

No, they could not accept a check.

Well, all he had now was American dollars, hard to get these days because of a dollar freeze. He was lucky to have been able to scrounge eight hundred; they had to last, not one could be spared. Who could have envisioned this ridiculous impasse?

"I'll have to see if my friend has any money."

But all Rat had was about four quid and some change. "Welcome to it, darling." Who would think to bring thirty or forty pounds with him just to see someone off on a plane? Essie had eleven shillings and ninepence.

The line at the check-in was already dispersing. "Could you leave one bag behind and the airline will forward it?" asked Mr. Dodge. But what was in what bag? Scripts, most necessary to show experience, were in both suitcases; which had in it his clean underwear? Which his good gray suit?

"I can't, really."

The clock above Mr. Dodge's desk now showed it to be a little before eleven.

"I'll get it somehow."

Back he went to the waiting lounge where Essie and Rat sat like immigrants themselves on a wooden bench.

"They must think I'm one of the Vanderbilts, able to lay my hands on any amount of cash at a minute's notice. Who on earth would carry forty quid around with them on a wet Saturday night out here in the rain forest?"

"Dolly would." Rat said.

Dolly Hollingshead would indeed. She kept her money under the mattress and hidden under coffee beans in jars; she was nervous that the banks might close again as they almost did in '32.

"Get her on the phone quick, tell her Essie will pay her back with a check on Monday morning."

Rat ran.

Dear Dolly, port in any storm, demurred only to say she hadn't any makeup on, looked like a little piece of fluff in someone's eye. Dolly would have to call a cab, sometimes they were busy on a wet Saturday night. Hang up and *come*, Rat almost screamed.

The clock said four minutes past eleven. Most of the passengers had been processed through and now were laughing with friends and relatives, were having drinks out of paper cups.

But Seaton, Essie, and Rat sat dumbly, aware of the clock's minute hand and calculating the time it would take Dolly to get a cab and of how long it might take to get from Kings Cross to Mascot in driving rain. Let's hope, Rat said, she doesn't wait to put on mascara. Every now and then Rat squeezed Seaton's knee in a generous gesture of encouragement although it was crystal clear he hoped beyond measure that Seaton would indeed miss the plane, change his mind, never go. It seemed as if Essie might be hoping this unforeseen to-do about the luggage might be God's way of keeping her boy in the country.

At eleven-twenty-nine a voice on the public speaker announced that Pan Am Flight 211 would be ready to begin boarding in approximately five minutes.

"Can we get them to delay the take-off?" Rat asked.

"I wouldn't think so."

Some of the passengers even now moved slowly toward the only gate that read "211 Pan Am to Nandi, Canton Island, Honolulu, Los Angeles."

In another five minutes, sticking to schedule, the voice of God told them that Flight 211 was now ready for boarding and asked them please to have their boarding passes in hand.

"Go and tell them someone's on the way," Rat urged and Seaton went into the processing room where Mr. Dodge and his assistants were leaning on the desk.

"They can't hold open the baggage compartment indefinitely," Mr. Dodge warned.

Minutes ticked by; it seemed that there must be twenty

before Rat appeared, screaming, "She's here, she had to get a friend to drive her."

A disheveled Dolly appeared, waving a little American flag and behind her a bald middle-aged man almost up to his chin with manila envelopes and little canvas bags.

"Oh, darling, we feel like Jimmy Stewart and Carole Lombard getting the serum through for the baby. This is Phil Chips, my dear neighbor who drove me out. I haven't got any lipstick on, precious, I look like a salted almond."

"Passengers only in here," Mr. Dodge said, seizing hold of the envelopes and bags.

"Just wait for me in the lounge. Thank you, Dolly, darling," Seaton said, accepting the Old Glory she was putting into his hand. Now some of the envelopes held a pound note, some only ten shillings, some of the canvas bags were filled with shillings and sixpence, one even had threepenny bits. An old Protestant hymnal had pound notes scattered here and there between "Rock of Ages" and "Lord of God, the Trumpeter." Mr. Dodge and his two assistants had started to sort out the money into little hills and meanwhile a pretty blonde Pan Am stewardess had come in asking for passenger Daly.

"Here."

"Are you ready to board, Mr. Daly?"

"Just the minute we have the money paid for my overweight, it won't be a minute."

"Don't be long, Mr. Daly, will you. Everyone else is aboard."

Good God and Jesus Christ, Mr. Dodge muttered, they had come across some Dutch currency and even a few buttons. One envelope contained "stage" money that had been used by Dolly in "Hot Millions."

From the distant lounge the voice on the loud speaker was announcing that this was the final call for Flight 211.

"Good Christ," groaned Mr. Dodge, holding up a pound note that had been torn in half and stuck together with gum so that the halves were back to front.

The last ten minutes became a crucifixion until Mr. Dodge, panting, said, "Thirty-five. We'll let you go at that," and the little pink LA paper tags were attached to the bags and the bags were whisked away on a motor barrow by the ground staff.

And now the little Pan Am stewardess was back, holding open the door to the runway and saying, "Come with me, please, Mr. Daly."

"I have to say good-bye to—"

"You have to come right this minute, Mr. Daly, they're closing the doors *now.*"

"Only take a—"

"They're ready to wheel away the steps."

She had picked up his typewriter and was out the door before he could quite take it all in. He flew after her, beginning to dry retch. Sure enough two ground crewmen were standing ready to wheel away the aluminum staircase and another stewardess was standing in the lighted doorway of the plane.

"He's coming," the first stewardess called.

This couldn't be happening. He tried to wave into the window to the visitors' lounge, but as he paused one of the men waiting to wheel away the steps leaned forward and, taking his arm, propelled him onto the stairs.

He went up, coughing and retching. As he stepped into the plane, the other stewardess said, "Good evening. May I see your seat number? Yes, you're the seventh to the left, the window seat."

This couldn't be happening.

But the plane door was closing, the huge locks were being swung into place.

"Could I have a brandy?"

"I'm sorry, we're not allowed to serve while on the ground. Get you one once the plane is airborne and the seat belt lights are off. Please fasten your seat belt, Mr. Daly."

Now it wouldn't be so terrible for Rat and Dolly, they would make a spiteful joke about how he never came to say good-bye, they would party out on it. But Essie had no sense of humor to bolster her grief, no grasp whatever of the malignant comedy this was.

The giant silver room they were in shuddered and moved blunderingly, its four huge propellers turning. He realized for the first time that he was sopping wet. Also he had regurgitated down the front of his shirt and tie.

"Good evening ladies and gentlemen, or rather, good morning, as it is now twelve minutes past twelve A.M., and welcome aboard Pan Am Flight Two-Eleven for—"

Lights moved in a blur outside, little red lights dotted the ground.

Once when she had thought him asleep, early one morning, Essie had paused by his door and for some secret reason of her own she had said, "I love you, Beanie," and he, burning with anger at this declaration made so inconsistently, without recourse or reason, spoke out cuttingly, "Don't be *silly.*" Merely a reflex, as if she had caught him naked, but cruel.

She had come down from the bush in order to make a life for herself, she hoped, as a secretary, and fate had conspired to assure that never in that life would she touch a typewriter. She had been left heiress to him by the Little Soldier Woman. She had cooked ten or twelve thousand meals for him, made his bed, washed his dirty underwear, sat up when he was ill, praised, sympathized, loved.

And I am a prick, he said aloud, no one in the seat next to him to hear. A real prick, he said and cried.

The titanic bird shuddered and then roared down the runway and a moment later, tiny lights below showed where the airport had been flung away into darkness. Stars were glimpsed sideways beyond the rain clouds.

What he would do would be—

"Your brandy, Mr. Daly."

"Thank you."

"Very nearly left you behind, didn't we?"

What he would do the minute he got to Los Angeles would be to go to one of the big stores in Hollywood and buy her one of those new see-through plastic purses, a big one. She would love that, show it to everyone, an American plastic bag that she could see through. If she was unable to see through him.

For a while you're somebody else

WHEN Seaton got off the Greyhound bus, he saw that Lloyd Manville was standing in a small clump of people wearing a summer weight navy blue suit, a polka dot tie, and a button reading "I'M FOR DEWEY." It was hot as hell even at nearly ten o'clock in the evening.

"Well, well, here you are," Lloyd said heartily and they shook and shook hands as if they were not sure how to proceed. Slight deafness and a feeling that iron sheets were closing in on them; a fog of fatigue. He had boarded the bus in Los Angeles last Sunday evening; it was now Thursday and in that time he had crossed America, breakfasted in Cheyenne, eaten lunch in Omaha, changed buses in Chicago, showered in Pittsburgh. Sleep, when it was possible, was with his head pressed against the window. Often the passengers had to get off the bus in the middle of the night while people came on to sweep it. Nobody had spoken more than a few words to him the entire trip and his own voice sounded disembodied. Now that they were in a taxi with his dreadful luggage stowed in the trunk, racing across town to the New Weston Hotel somewhere on Madison Avenue, New York was not possible to take in nor believe, no matter what Lloyd said about this being Broadway, this being Sixth Avenue, that *there* was Radio City, there Rockefeller Center.

"And how have you been getting on?"

Hard to say. Both wonderfully and disappointingly. The magic of it, the smell of coffee mixed with early morning smog, Hollywood Boulevard with its red electric trolleys going up and down, women wearing gold platform shoes early in the day, seeing Percy Kilbride in the post office and Cesar Romero in a white convertible at a stoplight, becoming accustomed to American politeness, nice no matter if feigned, but also the impression that in spite of overstressed assurances to the contrary, being entertained by strangers to whom he had been given notes of introduction was fatiguing both for him and for them. "Now be sure and call us," they said, on parting, but departed in their cars with a rush. "Anything we can do," they pleaded, backing away. He had been taken to a Hollywood Bowl concert by a girlfriend of Rat's, a former Sydney model, now married to a "sound mixer" out at Warner Brothers, and to the Brown Derby for lunch by one of Dolly Hollingshead's WACS, now a second assistant in makeup to one of the Westmores. Brushed, combed, polished within an inch of his life, he had proceeded to Columbia Pictures on Gower Street with an appointment to meet Mr. Jaime Lopez, proffered by Tommy Loomis, who worked in the Sydney office for Columbia. He had brought scripts with him in the unlikelihood that they might be asked for and had been told Mr. Lopez could be found in screening room A, where he was checking a movie dubbed into Spanish and, groping his way past the dazzle of projection light, he had shaken hands with this diminutive man and repeated his name twice and that of Tommy and that he was from Sydney and been asked to sit and watch the rest of the film, which, alas, had only just begun to unreel. It was *The Fuller Brush Man* dubbed into Spanish for Mexican audiences and therefore was incomprehensible except to Mr. Lopez and his assistant, who laughed heartily at it from beginning to end. The ending seemed to arrive not much before evening when, lights being turned on, Mr. Lopez also turned on and asked what it was that he might do for this young man and on being told that he had been a radio scriptwriter advised him that radio was just about to become as dead as mutton because of the advent of television; even the movies were in dire danger, screenwriters at every studio were being phased out like horses and buggies when the auto came in. "You'd better get yourself to New York," Mr. Lopez said. "It's all dead out here." On their way outside to the gate, they almost knocked over Glenn Ford, who waved to Mr. Lopez in a tired way. "Well, now you've seen a *star,*" Mr. Lopez said as if that might suffice for coming such a distance on a fool's errand.

"Not too bad. *Badly,*" he now told Lloyd. "I liked Hollywood."

When he came out of the shower at the New Weston, Lloyd was talking on the phone and gestured for him to sit down. Lloyd was speaking at length to someone he addressed as "Peach."

"Did the man come about the roaches?" Lloyd was asking Peach. "Well, if they don't come tomorrow, call them up. I left the number on the little yellow pad in the den. Hot out there? Hot here too. Yes, Peachy. Me too. Now is *he* still coughing? Well now, listen honey, listen dear, I think it would be perfectly all right to give him a teaspoon of that cough medicine they gave me when I had that April cold. Listen, honey, it's at the back of the medicine cabinet behind where I keep the stuff for my scalp. Honey, don't give him more than a teaspoon. What? Yes he's here, he got here all right. Oh, he's just fine, we're just going out to hear Ella Dell." Kisses were given into the phone and seemingly returned.

Now a snapshot was proudly produced from a wallet showing Lloyd and his wife Edna, who presumably was Peach, standing in front of a brick porch, Lloyd holding a largish child who was holding a Donald Duck. Leaning against him somewhat coyly was Peach, her shorts revealing oversize thighs. The baby, Junior, would be two next June, Lloyd said. His good-natured face was lit with the gratification of fatherhood.

Going out to the elevator, Lloyd put an affectionate arm around Seaton. "Got to get you some dinner, old chum," he said and that they served a nice barbecued steak at the Stardust Trail, if he remembered right.

What he did not remember was exactly where the Stardust Trail was located. Somewhere in the Forties between Sixth and Broadway he told the taxi driver as they threaded their way across Forty-Ninth and then back along Forty-Eighth, back and forth from the blaze of Times Square to the seediness of Sixth Avenue, mostly shoddy streets of closed shops and tacky ill-lit bars until Lloyd yelled, "*There* it is," as they caught sight of the electric sign, its *S* missing.

The enlarged photograph of Ella Dell was so airbrushed and retouched that the face might have been drawn on a baby's bottom. "Solo Attraction" the legend read. A bored woman looked up from her knitting to tear off two tickets, which at twenty dollars each seemed to indicate that the Stardust Trail was what used to be called a clip joint and the dirty uniform on the ticket taker confirmed this.

Inside the dimly lit room fashioned to resemble a Western saloon, four couples sat at tables drinking. A hostile waiter took their drink orders and said that only the supper menu was now available, which consisted of a cheese omelet with french fries and garlic bread or a bowl of chili. On top of the outrageous entrance fee there was a minimum drink charge.

"But Ella's worth it," Lloyd said. He had met Ella first in Detroit before the war. "You'll never forget her," he said. Possibly hoping against hope for a couple more customers, the eleven o'clock show was delayed long enough, unfortunately, for Seaton to be able to see the glutinous omelet he was eating until a spotlight hit the small bandstand where a melancholy trio had assembled and a voice on a speaker announced that the Stardust Trail had the honor to present in person Misssssss Ella DELLLLLLLLL! A sorrowful sight, the assaulted face, perhaps many times surgically resuscitated, fringed in enormous false eyelashes and enameled into a frozen painted smile, looked out hopelessly on the threadbare audience. Her emaciated body was a sack of bones thrust into green satin. Her turkey neck was secreted in a rhinestone choker; she was seventy if a day. "Dream lover, cast your arms around me," she sang in a whiskey mezzo. "Thank you, thank you," she said to the pat of applause at its end and then said that she would like to dedicate her next song to her friend and beloved coworker Libby Holman and launched into "Moanin' Low." After four nights sitting up on a bus and now three drinks, Seaton was so overcome with sleepiness that he had difficulty keeping his eyes open and saw three Ellas from time to time as she went relentlessly on about when the "midnight choochoo leaves for Alabam" and then that she had a "sand in her shoes, sand from Havana." One couple rose and left during "April in Paris"; the others seemed lulled into somnolence and scarcely to be listening. Only Lloyd applauded as though it were Sophie Tucker in person. For her signature song Ella Dell sang, "I Only Have Eyes for You," going with her microphone from table to table. She took two bows, blowing kisses to the scant applause, and the lights came up again on the disgrace of the shabby room, the scanty audience paying their overcharged tabs and leaving.

But (dear God, *no*) Lloyd was saying that he knew her well, that they must go round and say hello. A flap of dirty curtain was pulled aside to show Ella cramped into a tiny space between the kitchen and the toilets. She had taken off one of her eyelashes and she seemed blindly unable to attach identity to Lloyd, calling him Barry and, waving sticks of arms toward the ceiling, said, "Eleven people at the nine o'clock show, eight at this. I've reached rock bottom, time to call it quits."

No, no, she hadn't, Lloyd was insisting gallantly, she was still a marvel, she had such presence, she had such poise, she had *grace.*

"I'll tell you what I have, honey," Ella rasped, "I have a great-niece in Altoona P.A. with a spare bedroom."

"That's the way along the Great White Way," Lloyd said as they walked back to the New Weston. He seemed deflated. "Everything changes," he said. "New York's not the same as it was before the war. I guess *we* also change." Crossing Fifth Avenue he took hold of Seaton's elbow as though to steer him. It was the first affectionate gesture he had made since Seaton arrived. Waiting for the elevator, he smiled the remembered innocent sweet smile. "Good evening, ladies," he said to two middle-aged frumps riding up with them.

In the bright bathroom, Seaton changed into the new pajamas and touched his hair with a comb, preparing. He wished that he had some provocative aftershave. He was wide awake now with the prospect of reunion; he was, ridiculously, even a little nervous. Here he was with the man who had opened the door to America.

Lloyd had already got into his bed and was sitting up reading the *Journal-American*. Seaton switched off the bedlamp over his own bed and, bending over, put his arms around Lloyd and lightly kissed him on the forehead.

Had he slapped Lloyd, spat on—

"What do you think you're *doing?*"

What?

"Just what do you think you're doing?"

The newspaper went on the floor. Lloyd took off his gold-rimmed glasses, perhaps ready for fisticuffs.

"I just—was saying good night."

"I'd have thought you had enough common sense to know I'm not built that way, son. You surely must know by now I'm happily married to a wonderful wife with a blessed angel of a child and that I'm just not that way, Seaton."

Lloyd's jaws were clenched in outrage. Seaton sat down on his bed so stunned that he could muster up nothing to say but to speak the apparently awful truth.

"Lloyd, we were lovers in Sydney."

"Good God, man," Lloyd said, "that was the *war.*"

As if Seaton could not comprehend, Lloyd repeated it. "That was the war, feller. All kinds of guys did all kinds of things because we didn't know what day might be the last."

"The war was over, Lloyd."

"Just call it the need for someone that night."

"I see. I'm sorry."

"I should think you *were*. Very sorry."

Lloyd turned out his bedlamp and lay down. Muffled by sheets he said, "The war did queer things to people, for a while you're somebody else." There were sounds of getting comfortable. Then, serenely, "Good night, chum, sleep well."

Welcome to America.

He sat a long time on his bed in the dark, churning with thoughts of being perhaps condemned to an everlasting defeat with only sporadic implications of love or a substitute for it. It took a long while for him to go to sleep while the utter silence from the other bed made more convincing the impression of being alone.

He was about seven years old, some child's party and he suddenly threw his arms around little John Lawson and kissed him. "OOOOer," the little girls sniggered, "you kissed a *boy!*"

Awakened in the early light by the sounds of Lloyd speaking with premeditated softness into the telephone. "Operator, I want to make a call to Detroit," and giving the number. Then, "Did I wake you? I had to, Peach. I haven't slept all night worrying about little Lloydie. Is he better? He did? All night? My God, you'd better call Doctor Lewis right away. You did? What did he say? Not till *then?* Honey, I don't think we ought to wait that long, you had better take him to the clinic. Listen, honey, Peach, I'd better come home *today.* No, no, *he'll* understand. Honey, I've made up my mind, I'll get the first flight out I can this morning. Do you, dearest? Are you, dear? So am I. And it may only be a bronchial cold but we can't take any risks. No, no, I'll call from the airport when I get in. You too, you too." Kisses were given. He then made a call to United Airlines. Following that there were sounds in and out of the bathroom and then of a suitcase being packed and zipped.

Seaton feigned sleep until he was gently shaken.

"Got to wake you, feller, sorry. Listen, my little boy is ill. I made a call home and he's been coughing all night. I'm sorry, chum, but I'll have to go home today. They've got me on a flight at eleven so by the time I get out to La Guardia—you do understand, don't you, how upset I am and sorry to leave you. Listen, the room's reserved for two nights and I'm paying them for the second so you can stay on tonight rent free. Oh, and I had got us seats for tonight for a Broadway show, *High Button Shoes,* it's supposed to be a big hit, but if you wanted you could return one ticket or sell it to someone. I'll leave them here on the dressing table, old man. I sure hate to walk out on you this way, but you understand, don't you? No, don't get up, stay and sleep some more, you must be tuckered out after that bus trip across the country."

Good luck, good-bye. Lloyd was edging to the door, they obviously were now at the point of permanent severance. But, Lloyd was saying, if Seaton was ever in the Detroit area, well, they only had a small house, nothing posh, but he could have a shakedown any time with the Manvilles. Glad you could come, Lloyd said in parting, as though coming to America was crossing the street.

Afterward the room was silent and lonely. Seaton got up and looked out of the window and saw Rockefeller Center beyond the spires of St. Patrick's. Beyond that somewhere was his new life. On the last lap of the plane trip between Honolulu and Los Angeles he had sat next to an ex-army nurse who had served on Guam and had volunteered to stay on in the service after the war but now discharged, she was on her way home to Oklahoma City. She had asked him where he aimed to settle in the States and on being told New York City she had exclaimed in horror, "That cesspool. They're so heartless there, if you dropped dead in the street all they'd do would be to step over you to hail a cab."

But somehow he knew better, it was going to be all right, he was going to make good here, take it one day at a time. The hotel was paid for another night, he would find cheaper lodgings tomorrow, he would go see *High Button Shoes* tonight, the tickets were each seven and a half dollars. He would sell the other one or return it and seven dollars might well buy him a decent dinner. He went down in the elevator whistling, feeling freed from any further necessity of gratitude to Lloyd. The young desk clerk gave him a shrewd guess of a look when he handed in his key and then the suggestion of a wink. Outside the heat had mellowed into a fresh miracle of morning with breezes from the river. New York soared, roaring into the sky. First he would go to see the Metropolitan Museum.

He stepped over Lloyd Manville's dead body to hail a cab.

They have good breadsticks here

THE NIGHT *A Very Pleasant Lady* opened on Broadway there was a fierce rain, which the old-timers said was a good augury; hit shows invariably opened in the rain. *Oklahoma* had opened on a wet night and it did nothing to dampen the well-dressed crowd swarming into the Lyceum. However there was no disguising the fact that they were in their satin and furbelows to welcome back Beatrice Tree after an absence of nearly six years rather than because of any curiosity about the play's unknown author.

Beady Tree was considered in a stratum only a little less exalted than the Misses Hayes, Fontaine, and Cornell. True, she had never had a ringing triumph, her longest-run appearance being less than a year. Her Saint Joan had gone widely unseen due to a bus and subway strike. She had made the mistake of turning down both *The Little Foxes* and *State of the Union,* the latter in order to go to Hollywood to make five quickly forgotten movies in a row. But she was the darling of the elite with her tall dark good looks, her grace, and above all her celebrated mezzo voice, which was consistently referred to as a bass cello and which could give the most inept line virtue.

To some who knew better, the thing that might have given her away was her walk; even though she dazzled in Mainbocher peau-de-soie, her stride was that of the Duke of Wellington at

Waterloo. That masculine slouch, however, endeared her to the large clandestine horde of Sapphic ladies who followed her every move. She had married her leading man, an Englishman named Hugh Toomey, which had provoked some of the more spiteful members of her clique to intone "How Come Hugh Toomey like Hugh Do Do Do." The faint marriage had endured only three years, but they had never divorced and continued to appear together on the stage. He now lived with a set designer named Fritz and Beady had acquired Loraine "Huck" Bonvard, whose family owned seven lumber mills in Wyoming. She was a small etiolated blonde with white eyelashes who never wore makeup and looked readily prone to underwrite a mulititude of disasters but in reality was shrewder than a truckload of Rothschilds.

After settling down with Huck Bonvard in a gargantuan apartment on Central Park West and a fine house in Watermill, Beady had lapsed into a divine lassitude. Her slightest need was Huck's command. No longer need she strike a match to light her own cigarette, the click of Huck's gold Dunhill lighter was heard all day and night although Huck herself did not smoke. Was there an itch just out of Beady's reach, Huck was there to scratch it; no clink of ice at the bottom of the glass was ever heard before the fresh drink was at her side. Huck ran the house, paid the gardeners, argued with repair people, shopped, drove, went for the mail, answered the phone, quarantined the bores and nuisances, organized the many dinner parties and the weekend guest list. Nowadays, Beady's only voiced complaint was "I can't find a play I like" and many people rightly thought it was her excuse for this lengthy retirement into laziness. "I can't find a play I like" was what Beady said to Seaton in the Algonquin and that was how it had all started. Beatrice Tree needed a play.

She was sitting with four or five ladies of her conclave. She had on a man's fedora and a severe suit of perfectly tailored trousers and jacket over a soft lemon yellow silk shirt and she looked ravishing. Moving her chair a little apart from the chatter of the girls, she concentrated her attention with her great blue-gray eyes on the young man who had been introduced as that clever boy who had written such intelligent little playlets on "Omnibus," that really classy Sunday afternoon television show, and had also garnered plaudits for his adaptations of certain classics for the prestigious "Hallmark" specials.

So he had told Beatrice Tree his idea for the satiric play about Helen of Troy and she had responded enthusiastically. "Come and listen to this," she had bade Huck Bonvard and encouraged Seaton to go over it again.

This was no different than anything that had happened in the last four or five years; everything in New York led to something else. The nice woman in the dry cleaners who happened to know that old Mr. Samson wanted a quiet well-behaved lodger, the bare acquaintance's recommended dentist who also attended to the teeth of the story editor at CBS; the anonymous woman at the cocktail party who was living with the director of the most-watched daytime soap, "Another Man's Woman"; person led to person, opportunity to opportunity, success to success. Alas, there was no one to advise on where to locate the needed loved one.

Timing was also a condition of this alchemy; had Seaton and Judy Jensen (one-time child star back in the twenties, now chubby and a manicurist at the St. Regis) not left an unendurably boring play at the intermission, Beatrice Tree and her gang would no longer have been at the Algonquin and the confluence would not have taken place. As the middle of the evening was generally the drab deserted hour in their beloved "Algonk," Seaton and Judy were not surprised to find only one large group surrounding, of all people, Beatrice Tree, who, gloriously, Judy knew slightly enough to impose on with clucks of extreme overadulation. Beady Tree acknowledged her with quiet nods and as Judy interposed Seaton, he said, grasping the lily of a hand, that he had seen every one of her movies. "You must be," the star said from a distance of the Milky Way, "a glutton for punishment."

But shortly afterward, perhaps bored with the female spite that was being shucked around the circle like corn, she had moved her chair around to face him and said in the famous voice, "Tell me what you write. I know nothing about the television world." So it had happened. Before even the after-theater crowd bombardment, gathering up her herd by simply standing up (chairs were pushed back instantly, Huck attending to the check), she had said to Seaton, "Give Huck your phone number."

Incredibly, a week later, in the evening whilst he was watching Miriam Hopkins essaying Becky Sharp on the Channel 5 late movie, he was instructed by a voice on the telephone declaring itself to be Loraine Bonvard to hold the line for Beatrice Tree. He would have held a live electric wire for her. "Hello" was all he said. The Helen of Troy thing was declared a possibility; money was no object, Huck Bonvard had only to make a few telephone calls, Miss Tree's name and six-year absence from the stage would guarantee a desirable theater and interest the "theater party" people. As it was still early spring, perhaps they might even be able to announce a late-fall opening.

The cup, full to the brim, ran over when Beatrice Tree suggested that he spend the summer at their country place in Watermill where peace and quiet could guarantee a healthy working atmosphere. Tomorrow an agreement between them would be drawn up by Beady's lawyer for Seaton's agent to look over. Seaton's agent, Matty Sawyer, merely said, "Bit long in the tooth, isn't she, for Helen of Troy?"

"Far Reaches," the Tree farm, was large and gracious among rolling hills and remained solitary and rural during the week. But on the weekends, ladies descended from coupes and convertibles in large numbers from Sagaponack, Bridgehampton, Sag Harbor, and even from the North Fork; ladies dressed in faultless trousers and tinted shirts and with an air of slight conspiracy—someone was always bursting with the worst to tell about someone else. Mostly Seaton tended bar, became adept at concocting perfect bullshots and vodka stingers but sometimes, to be the only male present, was tantamount to being a lone monk in a seminary. Oddly enough it was the big husband-girls, the bulls, who were the most friendly, gave him rough hugs and boyish kisses; the wife-girls usually were etiolated and bland; they also were the more brutal when slaughter was called for.

The lesbian world seemed to be in a continuous flux, an undercurrent ran through it that furred the surface of what looked to be still waters. If Nancy and Phyllis were about to break up, then might it not have been because of Joan's leaving Geraldine after finding out she had been playing around with Clare who had been Nancy's original mate but had left her for Rochelle who in turn had dumped her for Shirley who, everyone knew, had been the fancy mate of both Phyllis and Geraldine and who now lived with one of the three Lizzies, another of whom had renounced the sisterhood and was now a Queens housewife and mother of three and pretended she had never known any of them. One might receive the impression that this game of musical chairs could become so complicated that nobody would honestly remember with whom they'd coupled beyond a week or so ago. Because these ladies were frequently all in the same room together and passing around the shrimp and clam dip even if Terese and Lola never addressed a word to each other and though it was rumored that Patty still owed Betty Jo five thousand dollars that she was finagling for Louise to pay in return for favors given.

Throughout this Laocoön-like mingling of flesh and serpents, Beatrice Tree remined aloof and uninterested, waited on, adored, listened to, and advised. The strength of her calm remoteness seemed sometimes to weigh on Huck Bonvard who grew thinner and paler and drank so unobtrusively that it surprised and comforted others when she had to be carried upstairs to bed, which was frequently.

Away from the ebb and flow of Sapphic passion, Seaton, celibate, inaccessible in his attic room, wrote and wrote, the play poured out like cream from a pitcher and was finished except for minor revisions by the end of August so that Beatrice invited Hugh Toomey (who was to play Paris) and six other thespian friends to read it aloud to an audience of carefully chosen ladies, all of whom fell about with laughter and clutched at each other with the delight of it, roared at every clever riposte and applauded at the end until their palms hurt.

The one person who was not laughing was Huck Bonvard, who held three-quarters of the investment in it. Under the roars of approval someone might also have heard Hugh Toomey murmur that, traditionally, guffaws at a first reading usually predicted disaster.

The reviews in Boston were mainly taken up with rapture at again seeing Beatrice Tree on the stage and sorrow at her costuming, all of which was hurriedly and expensively changed. One repetitive scene was cut and a supporting actress replaced. It all passed in a dreamlike worshiping of Beatrice and a whitewashing of the play because it had been her choice, but "paper thin" declared Letitia Gibbs of the *Boston Herald*.

The opening night party was to be in a suite at the Astor, superintended by Skinner, who was Beady's lawyer. Maxim A. Skinner had never been known as anything else but "Skinner." Maximillian Alexander Skinner, born Kraskinski, in Odessa, Russia, maintained a faintly czarist air about him like a whiff of a once-rarified perfume now gone to vinegar. Only eight years old when the revolution swept Russia and when his parents were rounded up in the middle of the night and hustled into a truck along with a dozen other landowners now considered enemies by the "Bolsheviks" and driven away to be summarily executed, the child was brought up by a peasant family who had been servants at the summer dacha now in ruins by fire, and the child would have ended up a woodcutter like themselves if it hadn't been for the perspicacity of his mother's sister, his aunt Anyuska, who had escaped to London and who had had in her possession a golden Farbergé egg that once belonged to the czar with which she bribed a succession of influential persons to get little Maxim out of Mother Russia and safely to London.

In England he was sent to private schools where he quickly picked up the language and an air of convincing superiority that was to be his for life. When he was fourteen he was buggered by a gymnastics master and rather enjoyed it. After graduating from Cambridge he quarreled ostentatiously with Aunt Anyuska and set sail for the United States where he made a propitious loveless but quite convenient marriage to a girl whose family owned much of the soft coal in Pennsylvania and who quite agreeably saw him financially through law school after which she saw daylight and divorced him. He was now a junior partner in the firm of Terhune, Mirror and Rackabee where he specialized mostly in theatrical contracts and cases involving plagiarism or libel. Legally he represented Beatrice Tree, so here he was, overseeing, along with some of the VIPs from Olympic Artists who were her agents, the opening-night party and being as condescending to waiters as if they were serfs from long ago.

"Oh, he's behaving as if it were a smash hit," said Emily, sitting down by Seaton. Emily White was Skinner's secretary and had introduced herself and brought Seaton a much-needed drink. "He's always at his most ducal at a flop," Emily said calmly as if it were already a fait accompli.

"You think it is?" Seaton ventured.

"Well, with such a bad review in the *New York Times,* honey, there honestly isn't much hope except that if Kerr likes it in the *Tribune* you might be able to hang on." Emily looked around. "Oh, there's Julian MacNaughton, Judas, they call him. He's always at a flop opening party, he can smell them like a buzzard."

Emily kindly kept providing Seaton with drinks and after the third, his head had begun to swim. "What are they watching?" he asked Emily, pointing to a group around the television. "Jock O'Brien's review on NBC," she said. "I wouldn't go over if I were you, they're smirking."

A while later Andrew Tighe, the press agent, called for attention. He was waving the early edition of the *Herald Tribune.* Walter Kerr had opened his review by saying that there had been a lot of laughter last night at the Lyceum Theater but that unfortunately nearly all of it had come from the stage. Then Richard Watts in the *Daily News* lamented that he feared the welcome return of Beatrice Tree to Broadway would only be a matter of the shortest duration.

Already there was a steady stream of people going out the door; nothing is more profoundly unsettling than a flop play. Even to be present at an opening night of a flop is to somehow connect one with failure, and failure is insupportable in the Broadway lexicon.

From what Seaton and Emily could hear coming from the bedroom, Skinner and the agents from Olympic were being notified on the phone by Huck Bonvard of the imminent closing. When they emerged their faces told the story.

"Saturday," Skinner said, sitting down by Emily. He was not a tall man but excessively wide like an armchair without being obese and with a wide Slavic face and flat cheekbones. He had coal black eyes that lit up when he laughed and turned an opalescent dark green like the underside of a wave in a late afternoon sun. There was a magnetic quality to them and to his sudden fitful concentration which, when he turned it on, swept over one like a cold draught of air.

Now he turned it on Seaton, leaning toward him and saying, "Don't be downhearted, chik-chik, it's not your fault, your play was *originally* very fine, very witty. I read it. It's what happened to it that was unfortunate."

It was the first and only compliment Seaton had been paid all evening long.

"Stars are idiots," Skinner said, laughing. "I ought to know. Beady Tree should never have done your play, she has no idea of comedy. She doesn't know why they're laughing even." He glanced around him and lowered his voice. "And you see, the lesbian thing comes through, which was fatal to your play, chik-chik, you almost expected her to carry *Paris* off. When it comes to playing Helen of Troy, you might just as well have had Edward G. Robinson." He laughed heartily at this and Emily joined in.

"Now then," Skinner said to Seaton, "be a gentleman and take Emily down and put her in a cab and then you come back.

I have things to say to you." His eyes were liquid green with the implication of corruption.

"You needn't come outside," Emily said in the lobby. "You haven't got a coat on. She kissed Seaton lightly and then, narrowing her eyes, she said warningly, "Be careful not to be lured up the garden path."

When he got back to the suite, the door was ajar and the room empty. Skinner's voice could be heard talking on the phone in the bedroom and it was something of a shock to find him sitting cross-legged on the bed, naked. He signaled to Seaton to sit down and went on talking to someone, presumably in California. Skinner was quoting from the reviews in his hands. He made a gesture of smoking and pointed to a cigarette pack on the dressing table and when Seaton lit a cigarette, the Turkish oval kind, and brought it to him, he curled a naked arm around Seaton and pulled him down beside him on the bed, all the time casually agreeing that very likely now the motion picture sale would be abruptly terminated, nobody in his right mind would touch it. The sound was of vast sums of money going down the drain, some of which would have been Seaton's.

Eventually, having disposed of Beatrice Tree, Seaton's play, and those responsible for the debacle, Skinner put down the phone and without further ado drew Seaton to him and immediately engaged him in a total foreplay that was so intrinsically skillful and experienced that it seemed to instill a kind of feeble amateurishness in Seaton as though he were the country boy of sixteen being seduced for the first time. Everything Skinner did, he did with the utmost concentration, ferociously, and when finally they climaxed within a few seconds of each other, he seemed almost to dust off his hands with satisfaction, as if he had just won an important legal battle in court. He then went immediately to sleep, leaving Seaton, still in the whirlwind of this exercise in love, to stare at the ceiling.

Around ten o'clock the following morning they were awakened by the telephone and there was a lengthy series of commands given by Skinner to someone, perhaps Emily: flowers to be sent to

Beatrice Tree, to the leading man, to the director, with a card delicately suggesting better luck next time. At one point, quite obviously, Seaton's name must have come up because Skinner laughed and said, "No need, he's here," so obviously the playwright was to be omitted from the consolation awards. The playwright showered and dressed and Skinner being again on the phone, he gestured good-bye and let himself out. It was cold and bleak on Times Square. The morning *Times* reported in Sam Zolotov's column that mindful of generally negative reviews *A Very Pleasant Lady* would end its run on Saturday.

Now there was nothing to do. His apartment seemed unusually quiet. The phone remained obdurately silent, not a call from any chum broke the silence with a cheering word. In New York failure consigns one to the valley of the lepers. But at four that afternoon a large package arrived by special messenger. It contained a turkey lying nude on a bed of parsley with little blue ribbons tied on its truncated limbs and with it was a card engraved M. A. Skinner. It stated "Dear Misguided Author, the critics have labeled and libeled your play a turkey. Let us cook this and invite them to eat their words. Come at six to 211 East 90th Street, apartment 9A for a cheer-up drink. S." It was an old nondescript building put up in the twenties with an ancient elevator that moved arthritically upward and stopped with a groan.

Several people were laughing around the big red leather chair where Skinner was sitting with a ravishingly pretty girl on a footstool beside him. This was the first shock.

"My daughter, Trish."

She was unlike him in every way except for her coal black eyes. She was nineteen and going to Bennington. Everything her father said delighted her and she laughed and sometimes leaned forward and pulled at his velvet lapel. He kept a hand continually on her knee, sometimes massaging it gently. The unspoken bond between them was such that people obviously felt intrusive. Among the other people were some of Skinner's West Coast clients, the movie actress Nina Foch, and a writer whom he had recently successfully defended in a plagiarism suit, the actors' agent Miriam Howell, and Marian Seldes.

Seaton sat and said nothing, letting the theater and movie talk swirl around him. Trish Skinner frequently turned and smiled on him as if she had been favored with some inside information and this disquieted him. How deeply intimate were father and daughter? When she rose to go, kissing Skinner on the forehead, he asked, "How's that fool of a mother of yours?" Trish's departure set other people to glancing at watches and a general exodus seemed to have been deliberately ordained by fate or cleverly and subtly designed by Skinner in winking at the Philippine barman, who then disappeared, leaving the drinker languishing. The departures having been neatly effected, Seaton also rose and said, "Well—"

"Don't be such a nitwit, I've been waiting for them to go so that I can take you in my arms, chik-chik."

Everything Skinner did managed to operate to his advantage and there was no alternative; if Seaton were to be the next court favorite (God knows how many there had been, male and female), then the fact had been handed down as a judgment in favor of the defendant, M. A. Skinner. Had Seaton said at that moment, "But I am deeply involved with someone," he would have been told nonsense, poppycock, told to get on his coat, that they were going to dine at Quo Vadis, which, as it happened, they were. Far from being presumptuous and mechanical, the friendship, if it could be so called, was often impromptu and entertaining. It was gratifying to be in the know about important people, how much they were making, intimate conditions of a divorce; it was satisfying to have the house seats to the smash musical nobody else could get into, to be waved obsequiously by the maître d' to the best table.

There were squalls; ferocious storms might erupt over the most minor delinquencies—a lost umbrella, being seated in the wrong row and having to move once the curtain was up—terrible fates were threatened for the unfortunates who disrupted Skinner's serenity, but the storms passed, the grim frown, the clouded-over eyes melted with the charm of his melancholy Slavic smile. "Let's go home and forget everybody." Little by little Skinner's life ran into Seaton's like dye spreading across a pure white cloth and it became usual to make no plans until Emily White had called in the morning to say be at such-and-such restaurant at one o'clock.

In early March Seaton had to fly to California to oversee production and attend rehearsals for the live television broadcast of his adaptation of *Paris Bound* for "Hollywood Playhouse," which mainly constituted sitting around, taking credit for Philip Barry's witty dialogue, and every so often squiring the lady star to lunch at La Scala. One night about midnight the phone rang in the Beverly Hills Hotel and the voice said "I miss you" and hung up. Seaton had enough discretion not to call New York; it would have somehow dislodged Skinner into anticlimax, but there was a small globule of sweetness left in the air. The next day Seaton spent fifty dollars on a massive volume of Mondrian's work to take back to the midnight voice.

After the telecast he decided not to take the red-eye flight home but to wait and take a nine o'clock flight the following morning, and once home decided against calling in lieu of just arriving at the apartment bearing the Mondrian.

What?

Was he at the wrong apartment? No, 9A and there was "Skinner" in the card slot.

"Can I help you?" the young girl asked.

"I—um—Mr. Skinner?"

"He isn't home yet, may I be of help?"

She might have been eighteen (he found out later, twenty-four, but she looked younger) and she was the neatest thing you ever saw, rather posh Lord and Taylor brown cashmere sweater and a dark gray and blue wool skirt and tan loafers and her glossy clean brown hair might just have been shampooed, it bounced above her little white Peter Pan collar; she put one in mind of June Allyson only more authentic, there was nothing in the least ingenue about her, in fact, there was more than a hint of the spinster as if she were already making severe plans for her unwed future.

"Yes?" she said.

"I'm Seaton Daly," he pronounced, somehow now in high dudgeon.

"Oh, you're back, then," she said and held the door open wider. "He *will* be pleased. Won't you come in? I'm Patience Godworthy."

The name sounded as if it had come off a mossy tomb in Salem, Massachusetts, and indeed she came from Peru, Vermont, he soon found out. He followed her into the living room and immediately noticed that organic changes had taken place. It was neat beyond credibility. Where stacks of books had stood on the floor and windowsills, now there were pots of gloxinia and African violets. Skinner's old leather chair had been covered with a dark paisley shawl. Two or three new watercolors of flowering chives and rosemary hung on the walls.

"What might I get you to drink?"

"Vodka on the rocks?"

"Think we have some, let me see. Maxim and I haven't been drinking much more than a glass of Armontilado lately."

First time anyone had ever called Skinner Maxim, and Armontilado! Ye gods, what had taken place? Patience Godworthy was heard in the kitchen getting out ice, she was humming. Was she *living* here then? What in God's name had been going on?

She came back with a fat squat glass generously filled with vodka. She herself had an eyedropper glass of some flame-colored liquid.

"We saw your show, liked it," Patience said.

"Thank you, we had some technical problems."

Sitting down on a low ottoman, she was more than ever sophomoric. Ruthlessly endearing, he decided unfairly to her, her very spotless appearance, her perfect teeth, and unvarnished nails, she was like the Christmas cover of *Ladies Home Journal*, the young girl on the doorstep in the snow presenting the basket of goodies to the old apple-cheeked couple. But there was more to her than that, although she smiled readily, there was a solemnity to her, a feeling that she could quickly assume the role of governess and crack down on an unruly pupil. Now, however, she smiled, she smiled.

"I ought to explain to you, Seaton, that Maxim and I are living together."

"I had observed."

"It is quite the most unexpected and beautiful thing that has ever happened to me. And to him."

Thus she spoke of some miracle but without astonishment. "It's changed our lives."

The grave certainty with which she said this, the calm pronouncement, was alarming in its placidity. To take Skinner for granted on the basis of a night or two, even to a virgin, was one thing, but to presume that this had changed his life to coincide with hers was surely dangerously naive. Skinner had come up to her at a party on Sutton Place (she barely knew the people) and asked her if she was alone; he had already clearly identified her, she said, with somebody he had once loved. He then never left her side all through the party. Automatically they left together and it was magically ordained that they should come back here to his place and it was here, she said (she could have been speaking of two stamp collectors) that most beautifully they became one. Anyone listening to this adolescent romanticizing might have now cut her mercifully short with one word, balls, but the manner in which Patience Godworthy told it demanded respect; she might have been telling of the first consummation ever to take place in the early heat of this earth in that fatal garden, her calm eyes assured you of her utter faith, her unpleading hands lay in her lap, everything about her was secure. Maxim, she said, had never told her who it was she reminded him of and she had never asked. There was no need, they were one.

That might be, but it still did not explain this abrupt change in the life-style of M. A. Skinner, fussy, selfish, sybaritic, who would never ordinarily have opened his bedroom door on a long-term basis to a child romanticist, no matter how fresh as dew. There was something dark and unholy about it and her side of the story was the expurgated version.

A key was in the door and Skinner was with them. Skinner and Patience kissed long and lovingly, then when he spotted Seaton, Skinner's face darkened and, having been uncovered in his new role without warning, he resorted to attack as usual.

"That thing you perpetrated the other night on CBS was the worst outrage I have ever seen, dreadfully acted, appallingly directed and so badly lighted that most of the time they all seemed to be in the Holland Tunnel and why anyone would cast heavyweight Marsha Van Oppen in a lightweight comedy role is beyond me. And why are you titivating around adapting stale old stuff from the thirties when you should be risking your life writing something daring and unusual for the theater, you milksop."

Patience had brought him his drink. He settled in his chair and immediately she squatted on the arm of it and together they looked at Seaton, and it was manifest, here were two mates, in total agreement. Together they could rule the earth. Skinner rested his hand on Patience's knee.

"You've met my new companion."

"Yes indeed."

"The only girl I've ever met who can whistle Boccherini."

Among other talents.

Patience leaned restfully toward him and he continued massaging her knee. And where was it then, recently, that Skinner had been massaging someone's knee, another young girl's? He and Patience spoke in terse sentences as though an excess of words would be ambiguous; there was talk about a lost book found, about a telephone call she had had from her sister, she had bought oranges. He massaged. She leaned. No term of endearment crossed their lips; there was no need. They thrived on the understanding between them, they fed on the idea of each other.

The scene repeated, Skinner's hand on the girl's leg, her eyes lavishing him, occasionally her hand passing across his forehead. All more sexually explicit than if they had been squirming with lust in bed. "My daughter, Trish," Skinner had said, introducing the girl.

Seaton tried to control the paroxysm of conviction that passed from head to toe in him like electricity. Patience was the substitute for deeply suppressed dark dreams, sweet nightmares of desire, quickly, subtly repressed, never dared admitted and on seeing Patience standing alone at this party, it had all gathered itself together and forced him forward into capitulation to divine and unspeakable longing for the uttermost obscenity and Skinner was not yet aware of it. But he was too bright a man not to reveal it to himself one day and then the judgment would be terrible, the Damoclean sword would fall on the head of the wrong person.

"I have to go," Seaton said and remembered the heavy Mondrian book on the floor by his chair. "For you," he said.

"Why, how very sweet, chik-chik."

"How nice of you, we love him," Patience said.

The two faces looked up at him, the innocent faces of the two felons.

"Yesterday," Skinner said, "she walked eleven blocks to get me an avocado because our little greengrocer didn't have any. She cleans my shoes, I don't ask her to. I have to be careful in mentioning anything I fancy. The other night she cooked us an eight-pound turkey, just for us, with all the trimmings, I had said something about Thanksgiving. It is perfection, perfection but sometimes—I have even been driven to deliberately engineering some small spat between us to try to make her mad. It is no use, I am always right, she is always wrong, she says, black is white, day is night, it is no use. Another thing is—she hums."

"Hums?" Skinner and Seaton were having drinks in Le Paz.

"She hums going about the apartment, in the kitchen, in the bathroom, she hums. Not that I mind her doing it but this constant state of geniality is—I want to say to her, aren't you ever depressed, irritable, downhearted? She is sweetness itself, she is thoughtfulness personified, she is—like my shadow I can't get rid of. She washes my *combs!* I'm going to get drunk and be late home this evening, let's have another drink, it's so good to see you, chik-chik. Waiter."

Then the following week on the phone, the voice sounded desperate. "Can you come over right away?"

"Why?"

"I need you, I need you this evening, you know what for."

"What about—"

"She's at Hunter at a class this evening, come as soon as you can."

And Skinner, trembling almost with this fever of want, opened the front door wearing only a bathrobe and immediately drew Seaton to him in a fierce embrace; immediately Seaton felt himself being unbuttoned, unzipped, felt for, while his clothes dropped on the hallway floor. "Quick," Skinner impatiently said while Seaton paused getting out of his shoes and began picking things up. "Never mind, leave them, we haven't got long."

In bed the fury continued and there was a nagging get-on-with-it urgency to everything; they performed like seals, there was no joy to it, not an ounce of caring, only hurry, and all the time Skinner's one ear on the possible homecoming increased his ravenous haste to get there. Seaton's lips were bitten raw and he was oppressed by the weight of Skinner's body on him. Once or twice Seaton was about to cry "don't" when, appallingly, footsteps were heard in the hall.

"Lie still, perfectly still," Skinner said as the footsteps approached the bedroom and in a flash, stupid him, Seaton grasped that it had all been laid as carefully as any fox trap, that Patience should discover them and brutally be told the truth, but once again Skinner had not counted on Patience Godworthy, who opened the door, looked swiftly in at them in their nakedness under the blazing bedlight. "Oh, excuse me," Patience said, closing the door. Footsteps walked away.

They lay there for some time, taking in the full meaning of it. There was no way of alienating her, she was imperturbable, she was iron, possessive beyond accounting, and in her sweet-girl way as ruthless as Skinner.

There might be no getting away from her.

"Jesus Christ," Skinner said.

After Seaton had dressed and while he was quietly crossing the hall, he heard Patience Godworthy in the kitchen, humming.

Weeks went by with no word, no telephone call, then:

"Meet me for a drink at five-thirty, the Tapestry Room at the Alexander Hamilton."

Skinner possibly was into his second bullshot, his black eyes had flicks of gold in them.

"Hello, chik-chik."

"Has something happened?"

"Indeed it has."

"What?"

"Here's Andre, tell him what you want to drink."

"Just a Smirnoff on the rocks, Andre."

Skinner leaned forward; his lips were very pink and wet.

"My little lass has gone."

"How? What happened?"

"I took the law into my hands."

"How?"

"On Sunday I just looked up from reading the paper and I said to her, 'I want you out of this apartment by five o'clock,' and she just stared at me, she was crocheting, so I said, 'Do you understand what I am saying to you, Patience? I want you packed and out of this apartment by five o'clock.' "

"What happened?"

"Nothing at first, she bent sideways as if she had had an attack of appendicitis, holding her side and wincing. 'What have I done?' she said and I said, 'Nothing, it's over, that's all,' and I went on reading the paper and there was silence for the longest time and then she said, 'But I love you more than something-or-other life itself,' and again I just said nothing and went on reading the paper and about half an hour passed and she said, 'I wanted to have a child by you,' but I just coughed and turned pages and she sat there silently and then eventually she said, 'Have I disappointed you in some way?' and I said, 'No, you're perfection and I've had enough of it,' and then I put down the paper and looked straight at her and said, 'You know, don't you, that I can obtain a court order to have you removed forcibly if you go on resisting me,' and this time it seemed to have struck home because she bent over forward as if she were having some spasm and she made this ugly noise rather as if she were going to vomit and were unable to and a minute later she got up and ran into the bathroom where I could hear that she really *did* throw up and she was in there a long time and then I heard her go into the bedroom and drawers were pulled in and out and she came back carrying her two suitcases and with some clothes on hangers and she was as white as anything, her lips were white as paper and she put her apartment key down on the coffee table and all she said was 'Your laundry will be back on Thursday; tomorrow the people from Bloomingdales will be coming to measure the couch and chair for the slipcovers but I've arranged with the super to let them in.' Then she turned and went to the front door and she had some difficulty unlocking it, it sometimes sticks and you have to thump at it, and she was thumping and pulling, trying to hold on to her coat hangers at the same time and I just sat there watching her and finally she got the door open and got out with her bags and shut the door behind her and I heard the elevator doors open and close. That's all."

It was his not helping her open the door that shocked. More than the cold-blooded manner he'd gone about the whole thing.

"That's all?"

"That's all, you can't believe how easy it was. Andre, bring the same again."

Skinner sank back into an armchair of self-satisfaction. "Just always tell the truth. I told the truth, it was over. It's not as though she had any claim on me and she knew it, she damn well knew it."

Skinner's smile was not congenial. Seaton looked away as the drinks were brought.

"*Now,*" Skinner said, "let's you and I put our relationship onto a better foundation and here's to it." What did he mean? They clinked glasses. "I've been giving it some thought," Skinner said, "and I've come to the conclusion that it's time now that you retained me as your lawyer to look over contracts, advise you, attend to your needs, your tax problems, all that. You can easily afford me, they're paying you ten grand now for those ladylike adaptations of old plays you do like falling off the proverbial log. What do you say?"

"Well, I—don't know."

"It's time you did."

"How exactly do you mean?"

"As I said, I'd manage you."

"But I have an agent. Matty Sawyer is my agent."

"She's moribund, pet, and most of the time all she does is read through the contract and miss seeing the traps."

"Well, but—"

"First thing I'd do is get you in touch with big people I know at the networks and get you onto writing a good daytime soap, that's where the real money is."

"I don't want to be on a daytime soap."

"You will, you will, maybe made-for-TV movies."

"They're terrible."

"Not when I can get you what I can get you, chik-chik."

Now Skinner's look was roguish and to Seaton's embarrassment he felt Skinner's hand on his knee under the table.

"You could just lie back and let me do the work. We get on well, we understand each other, we always have, and as to *that* side of things, any little sexual favors I'd bestow on you would be thrown in for free."

Skinner laughed and massaged Seaton's knee. Seaton drew his leg away swiftly. A red tide was forcing its way upward through his thorax. A second passed and then it broke, all over the table.

"Sick," Seaton roared, "is what you are."

Waiters turned.

Unable for a moment to go on, Seaton paused, then said, "I can't remember ever being so shocked at anyone in my life. And on top of what you've just done to another human being, you suggest this kind of professional *marriage* to me. You have to spoil, don't you, there's something in you compels you to spoil everything you touch and damage what's precious to other people. All my life I've hung on to one important compensation for what I am. I've just loved and not expected love back because I wanted just to love and that's saved me and made up for what people call the sin of it. You pervert it, Skinner, you pervert it. That girl Patience loved you the way I'm talking about, not asking for anything back, and you threw it away and now you want to pervert *our* relationship. Don't you know that I loved you? Well, that's over. Andre, would you bring *me* the check, please."

Skinner sat silent, hunched up, he seemed to be hollowed with a tacit admission and no comeback, his face was immensely drawn with the loss of something precious, not Seaton, part of himself. He sighed and reached out for the little wicker basket on the table.

"Oh, well," Skinner said, "they have good breadsticks here."

Oh, look, there's God

THE NOTE in Gin's secretarial small handwriting just said "We'll be staying at the Briarly on East Fifty-fourth Street." Who was we?

Mrs. Wycomb? The anonymous mother? Had Gin lost her senses and married? They had not seen each other since 1948 and here it was almost exactly nineteen years later. Would she still be wearing her hair in two little buns over her ears and those spinsterish sensible oxford shoes? As if to conceal her passionate soul she disguised herself as a spinster.

Watch out for *her*, Mrs. Wycomb had said that day in the wind.

Now Gin was a sharp wind herself on the phone, cutting through the artificial.

"Seaton, is it?"

"Gin, how are you? What are you doing here?"

"We're here until we go up to Vermont for a course we've come to take."

Who was we?

"Who's we?"

"I'm with my son."

Her son, how extraordinary, then she *had* married.

"And how are *you*, Seaton? Rich and famous, are you? Rolling in money from your success?"

"Well, not really *rolling*."

Then a pause before sharply, "I read the book," and that was all there was going to be, no further word of praise. A date was made for dinner next Thursday. "How lovely to hear from you," he said to the dial tone.

The success, though, was real. Unexpected as rain in the Sahara.

One long, wet Labor Day weekend, staying with Dorothy Wormsley in her Easthampton house, he had idled away an afternoon scribbling notes on her expensive cream Tiffany notepaper for an idea he had had in the shower, just toying with a notion that three weeks later had become *The Crying of Poor Mouth*. As usual with him he was more at ease working with elves or fish or ghosts than with human beings, freed from the naturalism of what people expected to read about people; the work extended itself into a parable that was endearing and only as true as any myth needed to be. In his little story Poor Mouth was a Sioux Indian boy, not yet ready for war, who was killed at Little Big Horn when a cavalry horse bearing one of Custer's men fell on him before he had been able to fire a shot. But no one cried for him among his people and his little ghost wandered the empty world of Indian boys who have died inauspiciously in battle and to no avail until the Great Spirit of the Lake said to him, "Go and search for one other unfortunate creature for whom no one has shed a tear and if you can find it in your heart to weep for him or her, perhaps you will be redeemed and allowed to enter into oneness with your forefathers." So Poor Mouth traveled on the long road which has no destination but met no one who needed tears until one day he at last came upon a miserable woman under a tree rocking back and forth in her woe and chanting strange lamentations to herself. He leaned over her and asked her who she was and why she was lamenting and she said, "I was Benedict Arnold's second wife and out of all people in history I am the least known or remembered and I am a person for whom there is not the slightest pity on earth. Could you imagine anyone weeping a tear for Benedict Arnold's second wife?"

"Well, I will weep for you just because you are so pitiful," Poor Mouth said and so he wept for Mrs. Arnold and put an end to her lamentations and he himself was redeemed for having a horse fall on him before he ever fired a shot and he was united as one with his forefathers.

"This nonsense," said Matty Sawyer, his agent, "almost had me in tears." No one, Matty said, is going to publish this, but if we can find the right person to do tiny exquisite illustrations, somebody like Prunella Press in South Carolina might do a five-hundred-copy run that might sell fifteen.

Winifred Justine Rokesbury's tiny illustrations were so intriguing in their pathos, especially in her interpretation of Mrs. Arnold under a willow tree (which later also weeps for her), that it may have encouraged Prunella Press to bring out the little thirty-four-page book in a larger printing than usual, and owing to some cosmic confluence of fate and accident popular Liz Closter of the *Daily Post* was given a copy for a Christmas gift and said in her column, "This is adorable trash and I urge you to read it," repeated it on her weekly television appearance on NBC, although she failed to mention the author's name but gave a rousing plug to Winifred Justine and at the same time notified eight and a half million viewers that the Duchess of Windsor had ordered forty copies for friends and Marlene Dietrich had phoned Liz personally to send copies for pals in Paris. Within three weeks the Prunella Press people were working in overtime shifts to get out more books; never in their seventy-year history had they had such a success, perhaps due, as a less enthusiastic reviewer noted, to the book's brevity, one being able to read it in the half hour often needed to await the arrival of room service.

Seaton, his pals said, some enviously, was made, and Poor Mouth would take his place alongside Winnie-the-Pooh.

Ironically what he considered to be his great work, a six-hundred-page historical fiction about Ivan the Terrible, still lay unpublished and perhaps, as Matty said, rightly so.

On Thursday evening he asked at the desk of the Briarly for (not knowing her married name) a Miss Spaulding? The lobby of the Briarly was as inhospitable as a crypt with stone floors and bare gray walls boasting flameless iron flambeaux. She must have been registered under her maiden name for he was immediately directed to number 14G. There she was, not changed, dressed in discouraging brown, her old-fashioned buns over her ears, no makeup. No fuss, they might just have seen each other last Thursday.

"Gin."

"Well, Seaton, you've put on some weight in this land of plenty. Never seen such dementia over food."

The suite had been misdirected into looking like an apartment with overstuffed chairs and sofa in a mole color and woodcuts on the wall.

"What will you have to drink?" She herself had the minutest white vermouth, a doll's drink. They sat opposite each other and edged around mutual discovery until he said boldly, "So you married."

"What gave you that idea?"

"You said that your son is with you."

"My son *is* with me."

She smiled, deprecating his assumption. "Oh, no, never. But you must understand I had him the year before we met, he's twenty now."

Another of her mysteries, like Mrs. Wycomb.

"He's been kept with trustworthy friends far away on a sheep station until I reclaimed him a couple of years ago. Nobody ever knew, not even his father. His father was a distinguished man. You'd know his name at once if I told you, once a colleague of my father's and about the same age as my father and with his own family. There was never any intention of us breaking up his marriage and anyway what passed between us was only for one night and we never saw each other again. When I knew that I was pregnant I also knew at once to whom to go. They took care of everything. I was for seven months a young widow, Mrs.

Dalton they told people, and I was accepted; they are eighty miles from the nearest one-horse town, which helps. I was driven even further to Cooloolabah Plains, where he was born and where not a soul knew me or my friends. It was the simplest arrangement: they had had no children; he was to be left with them until he was eighteen. Two years ago he came back to me."

All of this was narrated with oceanic calm.

"And—has he accepted *you?*"

"Without question."

He remembered her eyes now, little black dots, blacker than ever at the suggestion of a son's disloyalty. A darker look came over her face.

She began hastily now to explain about her son, Tony was his name; about his having a religious bent, although in essence it was in opposition to formularized religion—it was antiritual, a crusade to get God out of religion "for God's sake," she said without a scintilla of humor because Seaton had almost laughed at the epigraph. Nevertheless the son was in earnest; he was, to the n'th degree, spiritual by nature, secular in intent. Gin's eyes flickered now with the light of him. He was, she said sincerely, the purest soul she had ever encountered; she was, if not a disciple, a votary carrying his lamp, she was redolent with the inspiration he had implanted in her.

Yet where was he?

The uncomfortable thought had begun that she might be a little mad. Hadn't she exterminated a mother whose dereliction she found unpardonable? Had her killed in a horseback accident while all the time she was getting the afternoon tea in the next room? Wasn't it possible that due to some latent atavistic need she could conjure up a son, an immaculate conception?

If she were mad, she would fall into that Sunday school-teacher category of people who tend the sick and visit the old, never saying boo to a goose until one day they take a carbine rifle and shoot eighteen people to death in a supermarket. He was recalling how she had told him years ago with that intent and deadly look how, if she only had the chance, she would kill

Hitler. Now she was going on about her boy, Tony, and his unworldliness and how nothing material in the world touched him.

"He has never been touched," she was saying but whether or not she meant this as a precaution was not clear. "He is undefiled." Her eyes were lit with the pride of him, she gloated.

"What it comes down to, Seaton, is a purity of the spirit, he's the pure in heart. He also happens to be beautiful."

"I see."

"Do you?"

Now she was frowning, her eyes black again, dotted at him.

"I want you to understand something. If ever I found out anyone had tried in any way to corrupt him, they would have to deal with *me*. Do you understand?"

Really, it was insulting to have her ascribing motives when he and the boy had not even met, if the boy even existed.

"Gin, I'm not a pederast."

"Just so you know where we stand."

And it would be like her to invent an apocryphal child who was angelic, inviolate. They were in New York, she was now explaining, because Tony had been enrolled in a course in something called higher metaphysics at St. Phillip's Academy ("more of a nonsectarian priory," she said) in Saint Johnsbury, Vermont, where he would be incarcerated for three months. She would find a little house nearby, she would wait. The people at St. Phillip's had been impressed with a paper Tony had written on the underlying nature of the miracles.

She was entranced or mad or both.

Nobody appeared. Were they going to sit here all evening discussing this amorphous boy?

"I see that you need another drink," Gin said and at that moment there was the sound of a key in the door.

"And here he is," she cried out, jumping up to meet him. Tony didn't look especially sanctified, merely wet from walking some blocks in the rain without a coat and apparently unaware of it. He was ash blond and his skin so white he might have been

cloistered from daylight for some time. He gave Seaton a warm
dry hand without much enthusiasm, the handshake of a prince
regent.

"Hello."

He refused a drink, sat, occasionally smiling at the background musing his mother made; she deferred to him, offered
him a choice of subjects, none of which he took up. His deep blue
eyes rested on his mother most of the time as though he were
waiting for her to signal to him what to do or where to go next.
He might have been very slightly retarded; he laced his knuckles
and cracked them, he waited.

Once, to entreat his attention it seemed, Gin laid a hand on
his knee and he turned and looked at her with doglike intent, a
gaze so concentrated that it might have been a laser beam and,
seemingly conquered by it, she left her hand on his knee while
she went on talking and it made significance of the two of them
as though she had drawn an invisible line around them, making
them an island; she spread her fingers on his knee, annexing him.
So this was her ultimate triumph of obsession, all her thin spinsterish life she had had obsessions with transparencies like dignity
and honor, now she had him, the saint (whether or not he was,
was beside her point; she had created him as an untouchable),
replete; it was no wonder that she warned people against touching him; it would be the same as, God forbid, corrupting her.
Would Seaton, she was asking, descending from some ethereal
bastion, care to take "pot luck" with them, there was quite a
decent little no-nonsense restaurant in the hotel.

Few people were dining in the noiseless gray-carpeted dining room, which seemed more hushed than a library, but as they
were ushered to ugly Jacobean chairs, Tony Spaulding paused
and said in a most casual aside, "There's somebody seriously ill
in this room," to which Gin made no reply except to nod as
though he made these spectral declarations all the time. They had
been seated and handed unwieldy leatherbound menus when all
of a sudden a distraught woman darted across the room followed
by two waiters carrying a gray-faced man laid back on a chair and

whereupon the maitre d' bent over their table explaining apologetically that the gentleman had suffered a mild heart attack, to please not be concerned. Tony replied that he would have the sirloin steak with the lyonnaise potatoes and that he liked it rare.

"He has this gift," Gin said in an undertone to Seaton. "He sometimes can see ahead."

Whatever metaphysical attributes the boy had, no spiritual intensity exhausted him; he ate like a starved hound, putting away a large steak and following it with a slab of blueberry pie and ice cream. Not a word out of him while Seaton and Gin struggled with veal croquettes without enthusiasm but once (all in a flash it happened), when Gin had dropped her napkin and bent to retrieve it, freed for a second from her superintendence, the boy turned to Seaton with a dazzling smile. It was the smile of heaven but it was tinged with a knowingness of flesh; it titillated in a shameless way, so much that the wine glass in Seaton's hand trembled and spilled red across the virgin white cloth—so upset was his equilibrium that he avoided looking at Tony for the rest of the meal.

Outside Gin and her son stood arm in arm watching while Seaton, thankfully freed, got into a taxi. It had been an unsettling reunion with Gin and all the way home in the dark that boy's smile was burned into the retina of his vision. Once home, he mixed a strong double scotch in the hopes of erasing it but it stayed.

It remained on and off the following week. Then Gin telephoned, asking Seaton to come to tea. She had arranged an "ersatz" Australian afternoon tea with electric kettle and "what looked like crumpets but were little English muffins."

Gin cut into a nut loaf and smiled. Afternoon sun poured tranquility over her; she seemed, for her, unusually amiable. She passed plates around. The saintly son seemed lost in dark thoughts; head in hands, he stayed remote from conversation. He stirred his tea in silence.

Gin had begun what apparently was to be a fond reminiscence. Again she smiled.

She said, "My father's will stipulated that I go to a girls' finishing school near Armidale when I turned eighteen. I found most of the girls inane and haughty and I was lonely until this dear, to me, person came to my rescue. My English teacher, Miss St. Clare. She was a lamp unto my feet; she introduced me to Conrad and *Heart of Darkness*. I had never been able to talk to anyone before and the floodgates opened. Often she had me to tea in her study, sometimes to listen to music. I would have done anything for her, she was beyond reproach, and then one evening as I was crossing through the cloister, I saw two figures, two lovers, kissing in the shadows in a way that, well, two women shouldn't. They were so physically absorbed that they didn't hear my gasp. It was Miss St. Clare and a girl named Louise, a flatulent white-faced girl of utterly no distinction. In a second, everything came cruelly apart. Later that evening I slipped a note under Louise's door saying to meet me the following evening at the little stone fountain, that I had something to tell her. She came, that stupid girl, all in white, as though to profess her purity, and I said, 'Sit down by me, Louise,' and she sat down beside me on the edge of the little fish pond and immediately I pushed her backward into it and she put up a struggle but I held her down, there were goldfish and weeds in her hair and every time she would come up gasping I pushed her down again and gradually she stopped struggling and I was holding this dead weight when I was seized from behind. It was Miss St. Clare, beating me over the head and then pushing me away while she lifted Louise out of the pond and, applying some kind of first aid, kneading and pummeling her until Louise began to wheeze and cough and then she vomited green slime all over the two of them and Miss St. Clare was holding her up. Miss St. Clare said to me, 'I will report this to the headmistress and have you expelled.' Of course I knew she never would, she knew I would reveal all the appalling details of the affair with Louise and so I simply walked away and then I turned back and said to them, 'Perverts.' "

Gin was smiling now as though there was no irregularity in drowning a girl in a fish pond and, smiling, pleasantly recalling the fish in the girl's hair, she turned to the despondent saint. "Darling," she said, "if I butter you a slice will you try this delicious nutbread? No? Then can I tempt you with a little puff pastry?"

"No," Tony said and passed a hand across his face as if to erase the picture of her reminiscence, then he cast a look at Seaton that might have been a whispered admission of his solitude. Or something to do with love.

"I quite like this Orange Pekoe," Gin said, "it's acerbic."

Then on the following Sunday when, half-dressed in sweater and old pants and making feeble notes about what he might say if called upon to speak at the Public Library dinner to honor him and his *Poor Mouth* along with truly celebrated writers, Seaton's downstairs buzzer rasped suddenly and like everything else in this old brownstone converted to small apartments, the intercom's reply to his asking who was there resembled gargling. A voice said that it was "only balding." Who?

He buzzed the release to the front door and peered over the stairway to see the young figure, brown tweed jacket, no hat, hair flying, taking the stairs two at a time.

Tony Spaulding, laughing, panting. You see, mother had Seaton's address but he was not in the phone book so—

"Wondered what you might be up to."

"Well, come in."

"Look, I have a U-Drive Pontiac and I wondered if you weren't busy if I could take you down to a place I know in Bucks County, near Erwinna, a damn nice old inn. Would you be interested?"

Ridiculous, but Seaton was trembling.

"Where's your mother?"

"Gone up to Boston until tomorrow to see an art show, some Goyas on loan from the Prado. Would you be interested?"

"I'm not even shaved."

"I'll wait."

Whatever talent it was, it was hypnotizing. On one hand sensibility ordained caution, on the other demons rose winking and tempting. Seaton sat down in the pretense of making up his mind. It was the personification of ambivalence in the boy that made it hard, impossible, to refuse him. Perhaps, the devils muttered, Gin would never know and even if she did, wasn't the boy twenty and his own person no matter what succubus she made out of any man who so much as reached for his hand in passing.

"Should I pack an overnight case?"

"You won't need much."

Tony Spaulding was tossing the car keys up and down and grinning. The decision had been made and Seaton said, "If you'll just let me shave and put on some decent pants."

He went into the bathroom. There was a feeling of preordination about it, he was telling himself, it was meant to be. Nevertheless he had to reach for the styptic pencil to stem the little flow of blood beneath his ear where he had nervously nicked himself, his hands were shaking so.

Bag in hand, he said to Tony, who was reading *The New Yorker* with what seemed faint disapproval, that he was ready. For what?

Outside, mumbling, was one of New York's ever-present crazies, clutching a soiled paper bag to herself and glaring, pleading to be accused of some vile thing, filth had so ingrained itself into her that one could scarcely tell where dirty flesh ended and rags began; she was like an old broken bird of prey, the hair, once lustrous, was coir matting. Motherfuckers, she screeched to anyone passing, don't you look at me, Jew killers, she hissed. But Tony paused and gazed down at her while she seemed to be about to aim spit on him. "Quiet down now," the boy said with an infinite tenderness and reached out a hand toward the sooty face as the woman shrank away from him but, strangely, she had stopped screaming, her dark tormented eyes were wide with either terror or some faint recognition of love. She was quiet, she turned away, and they went on toward where Tony had parked the hired car.

He drove like someone possessed; they whipped through the Holland Tunnel as if they were being pursued and on through New Jersey to Pennsylvania where, farms appearing, he seemed to relax and then, turning down a final red dirt road toward a valley where the large brick shape of a once-splendid house was resting after all its years in a grove of white birches, the late October Indian summer sun having come out suddenly from behind black thunderclouds and cast a beam across the valley, the boy spoke for the first time since they had left New York.

"Oh look," Tony said, "there's God."

Or Joe Jones, he might have said, it was so commonplace to him, his strength to believe was so commanding that he had been long ago able to perceive Deity in air and water, perhaps in fire, in ice. Whatever power he had, to foretell heart attacks and quiet the insane, came from this total acceptance of his faith, unquestionably sincere. So Seaton was quiet, like the mad woman, and deferred to him.

Mrs. Van Hoörsen welcomed them; she obviously had great affection for Tony Spaulding. She led them upstairs to a large friendly room with two generous beds and a view of the hills around them. Dinner was from six on, she said, they were having a lamb stew this evening. She withdrew reverently, closing the door as if on a chapel.

Without a by-your-leave or any excuse, Tony immediately lay down on one of the beds and was instantly asleep with the tranquil breathing of a tired child. Seaton lay on his bed and gazed at the ceiling as the light faded and now, regarding the situation with a degree of calm, he found, surprisingly, no need for regret, no alarm, and strangely enough no want. Just acceptance. It was new, a new thing, this serenity, and later when Tony got up and silently went into the bathroom, closing the door, and was gone a long while, he realized that this probably was Tony's hour for meditation, sunset, and the idea of it, instead of alienating him from Tony, seemed to draw him closer, it spilled over onto him like light.

They dined, mostly in silence, in an almost empty dining

room, no ugly suspicion obtruded that the elderly couple across the communal table might be casting silent aspersions on this provocative union of middle-aged man and youth, but Tony, seeming as always prepared, faced them boldly with a bare-faced honesty and his natural purity beaming through; any curiosity they may have had deliquesced. How nice they were, this man and boy, both Australians, a country they had always wanted to visit. The old couple smiled on them, passed the corn muffins.

"But we have to get going early in the morning," Tony said upstairs, "I must get home before mother," and it was the first time that Seaton had noticed the clenched mouth, the brownish look when she was mentioned, and Gin stood between them with sword in hand. But quickly she was put out of sight with the light as they were left in the dark about the purport of her guardianship and as if some intangible halter had been loosened, the boy was instantly in Seaton's bed and all doubts were then resolved, their touching with what seemed foreknowledge of each other might have reached back a thousand years and come again to life in this moment of finding the same sweet mouth that one had known before on some other plane. Nothing else existed in their harmony together, no word needed to be said, no heartbeat commented on; to have said "I love you" would have been presumptuous, like not wholly accepting a yellow beam of light as God; there was no need for the redundant words of love, but afterward for Seaton, only redemption and the sense of being purified as if he had been churned in boiling surf.

Awakening in the early morning, exaltation was still with him. So often the morning awakenings were with repugnance and hideous reminders of the previous night's contortions—last night's love had withered into a wretched courtesy, the caricature of witnessing two lovers anxious to be rid of one another—whereas waking now he turned to see the boy asleep without a glimmer of regret, only the quiet exaltation. Instead of polite vacuum there was a song and the song continued into the new day although nothing was said between them beyond each asking the other, Was this comb yours or mine?

And gourmands, they ate hugely, consuming Mrs. Van Hoörsen's small pancakes as manna; Seaton devoured eight and Tony twelve.

The song continued quietly. Finally something had to be said lest it burst the heart. "I'm happier than I've ever been in my life."

"I *know*," Tony said.

Naturally he would, part of his gift. One thing more, Seaton said, apologizing for this excess of joy. "They're giving me some plaque or other tonight at the New York Public Library and I'm to bring anyone I like. Funnily, I hadn't decided on anyone. Could I have been imagining you?"

"No doubt."

"Would you come?"

There was distinctly a hesitation.

"Gin could hardly trouble herself about you, about us, in a well-lighted room with five hundred people."

"It hasn't anything to do with her," Tony said. "I was just communing. Yes, I would like to be with you."

When Seaton got out of the car on Eighty-second Street, Tony drove off quickly without a farewell of any kind.

But the song lasted all day and into the evening. When Tony arrived he seemed paler than usual but not otherwise changed. They shook hands like slight acquaintances and he refused a drink and Seaton, nervous, had two scotches while they waited for the limousine the Library was sending. But after a long silence he said, "I have to tell you one thing and then I will never mention this again. Up to now, there has always been something missing and it was to do with the heart, with gladness if you like. There never was real joy. Until now, until you."

Excuse him, he said, tears starting up, there was something in his eye. It would be too ornate to say it was the dazzle of heaven that was in his eye and fortunately at that moment the downstairs buzzer gargled.

"That will be the car."

When they got out of the limousine at the Library the first

thing that Seaton noticed was that Gin was standing halfway up the steps under a streetlight. "Did you know she was coming?" he asked Tony. There was something disconcerting about her standing there. "She can't be invited inside, it's a sit-down dinner."

"Hello, Gin," Seaton said. "What a surprise." He made a movement, as he always did, to kiss her, but she took a quick step backward and said, "There'll be no more of your harmful love, Seaton." He saw then that what she was taking out of her large handbag was a gun. He also saw that she had misapprehended his entire life for this moment of truth, and in the sudden flash of whiteness that precedes the atomic convulsion he saw that he had been tricked, chosen at random, heartlessly, by the saintly boy to be the boy's instrument of freedom from his mother, that the boy had planned, left hints of his escapade, knowing she would be demented enough to accomplish this in the name of his purity, thereby ridding himself of her forever or for a lengthy time. All this Seaton saw in the blinding light, unable to turn around because of the terror that the boy might be smiling, so absolving the crazy woman. He continued on up the steps until the explosion cracked into him and in the seconds left him he saw that he almost understood his life and his reason for being and in trying to hold on to it so that he could touch infinity, he stretched out one hand just before he fell sideways into nothing.